The Iron Couch

a novel

Daniel Ross Madsen

THE IRON COUCH
Copyright © 2017 by Daniel Ross Madsen

COVER ART
Copyright © 2017 by Daniel Ross Madsen

SEEING THROUGH A GLASS
Copyright © 2017 by Daniel Ross Madsen

Lyrics excerpted from MOONLIT NIGHT
Copyright © 1980 by Daniel Ross Madsen

All rights reserved. Published in the United States of America by Daniel Ross Madsen. No part of this book may be used or reproduced in any manner whatsoever without written permission except in the case of brief quotations embodied in critical articles and reviews.

This book is a work of fiction. The characters, incidents, places, and dialogue are drawn from the author's imagination and are not to be construed as real. Any resemblance to actual events or persons, living or dead, is entirely coincidental or used fictitiously.

Paper back ISBN 978-0-9990478-1-1
e-book ISBN 978-0-9990478-0-4

ACKNOWLEDGEMENTS

Writing this novel has been largely a solitary undertaking. Hours became weeks and months with the company only of the characters in my head while I attempted to breathe life into them, get to know them, give them voice. Luckily, there have also been human interactions along the way for which I will always remain grateful. In no particular order, I would like to express my heartfelt thanks to the following people:

To women's lit author, Bonnie D. Tharp, thanks for reading an early draft of another novel under a different title, now discarded. That novel proved my manuscript was no exception to Hemingway's adage about first drafts. Thanks for your recommendations. To Ginny Todd, academia's loss was my gain. Thanks for the patient hours and numerous suggestions made when you read another manuscript, also now discarded. Your lessons, however, have been retained. To thriller writer Philip Donlay, thanks for answering aviation questions at a critical layover. And, thanks to Kent Stedman for introducing me to Phil.

Special thanks go to someone who is behind the scenes of every English language writer and, arguably, every writer who makes a living at it: Edmund Spenser for his work more than four hundred years ago helping to develop modern English. Writers everywhere should remember that mere decades after the invention of the Gutenberg press, Spenser worked closely with his publisher, William Ponsonby, paving the way so that writers could start making a living by selling their published works to mass audiences, thus freeing them from reliance on the sometimes unreliable patronage of the royals and nobles while giving writers greater freedom of expression. To writers, I ask that the next time you receive a royalty check for your work, take a moment and think of the root of the word "royalty," then look up and say, "Thanks, Edmund."

To you, the reader, thank you for buying this and inviting my characters into your lives for a brief time. Writing is about you more than the writer. Without readers who pay to read, literature as we know it today would not exist, and writers like me could not afford to tell the stories that roam the halls of our imaginations looking for a way out. I hope you read, think about, and above all else, enjoy this book. If you like it, the greatest compliment you could pay me is to tell someone. That is the only way I, or any other writer, can grow an audience and hope to write more.

Now, the most important acknowledgement of all, to my wife Maxine, who cherished every word I wrote, even those flushed down with the first drafts. She is a tireless—even eager—first reader and effective copy editor who catches those words and punctuation marks orphaned by deletions and insertions and draws my attention to passages that need help. You are my heart and soul. Without your support in every sense of the word, this book would not have been possible. I love you now and beyond forever.

The Iron Couch

DEDICATION

To all who have paid a price for their singularity.

Chapter One

I WANT TO GO HOME, back to my old life, and be normal again—if "normal again" is still possible—but, standing in the way is figuring out what I'm doing in suicide watch. The obvious assumption is that I tried to commit suicide—or someone thought I did. However, I have no such recollection. Perhaps, then, someone thought I might be in danger of attempting suicide. I don't know what would make them think that. Whatever, I just want out of here, and Margaret, my psychiatrist, keeps telling me that until my memories come back and I've dealt with the events that scared them off to begin with, I'll be staying in this place a while longer. At least with any luck I'll get a regular room soon.

This place, by the way, is Mount Liberty Residence, and I had only heard bare mention of it until I came here in April. Or so I think it was April. It was in the spring, anyway—facts, which I've always thought I had a comfortable grasp on, some even say a steel grip, have been a little fuzzy for me lately. It's the middle of June now, and in a few days the summer solstice will usher in the longest day of the year announcing that summer is full on.

Liberty, as the other residents call it for short, is in the foothills south of Glaser Falls. People around here call these hills mountains, but the peaks barely rise above forty-five hundred feet. Off in the distance, though, are some peaks tall enough to remain snow-hooded all winter long and have ski lodges. I've never been skiing because, frankly, I don't like the idea of fighting gravity down slippery trails and the probability I would fall and break some bones—or something worse. Plus, skiing is usually a family or couples activity, and both rule me out.

Liberty is set well off of a secondary county road, and you could easily drive by it if you weren't looking for it. The property is tree-lined, as are most places in these parts when you get out of town. At the start of a long gravel driveway is a motorized iron gate. Inside the gate, a low understated sign, gun metal gray with white block letters, set on top of a rough cut granite slab, probably quarried from these same hills, marks the entrance. The slab is about half a pickup length long, one-half pickup length wide, and about one step up. That's my guess from my hazy recollection from the day I was brought here. I don't remember anything else about that day.

I know the road, though. As it ascends following the path of the river gorge, it curves sharply inward, leaving Mount Liberty Residence between the road and the canyon. Further on, the road continues alongside a cliff and intersects a two-lane highway that follows the curves, switchbacks, and meanderings of the Glaser River canyon before looping into itself at the summit and going back into town.

I once wondered if the road followed the contour of the river or if the river followed the contour of the hill the road was on. Really, though, that's an unimportant chicken-or-egg question, but because of my curious nature, I had to ask. My geologist buddy Michael Emory told me that definitely the Glaser River had patiently cut its way through the rock over millions and millions of years. Therefore, the road follows the river. He'd explained to me there had been creeping collisions and uplifting of layers of rock, still going on at a snail's pace deep in the earth's crust, and that's why the exposed layers pointed upward at an angle.

I haven't heard from Michael in a while. I don't remember if I let him know that I had moved in here. When I get a new phone, I'll have to send him a text.

Mount Liberty Residence is a residence in the sense that people live here. At the present time, occupancy is one hundred forty two, not counting me because I will be out of here soon. In truth, it's a mental hospital, a different kind I'm told. The emphasis here is that the resident—patient—is as much a part of his or her own treatment team as the psychiatrists and staff are. Whether or not that works I don't know; I'm not a psychiatrist, nor did I ever want to be one. I'm a professor of computer engineering and physics and a researcher in artificial intelligence at Finial University, a private science and technology institute. And, that is exactly where I'd prefer to be right now.

At first, I had a hard time calling this place by its nickname because I'm a stickler for exactness. You might say I'm obsessed with accuracy and detail, which is good for an academic. It's also pretty common for people like me with Asperger's Syndrome.

I've come to learn my neighbors at Liberty, among other diagnoses, are schizophrenics, those tormented souls who see and hear things that aren't really there, and people with dissociative disorder who don't really feel much emotionally and do irrational things like cutting themselves with whatever sharp objects they can get their hands on or burning themselves or doing other destructive things to themselves. And, they are often suicidal. My theory is they do those things so that they can feel something, anything.

I haven't met any of the other residents yet (because I'm not allowed to for the time being,) although sometimes late at night when I can't sleep, I hear the grating shrieks of a tortured woman. "Satan," she once cried out, "I know your voice and I say 'No!'" I wonder what torture she called "Satan." I don't have a radio or a television in my room, so when the poor soul cries out, I turn on the media player in my head and search for music for the calming effect of something like Smetana's *The Moldau* with its rippling, swirling flute duet quickly joined by clarinets, smoothing out when the stringed instruments come in like calm deep currents flowing placidly—no, happily— downstream with an assured strength like the mighty Czech river the piece is named after, or, to drown out her pleas for help, Wagner's *Ride of the Valkyries*, imagining, at high volume, the agitated, galloping strings overtaken by trumpets and French Horns, the horsemen in my mind coming to the poor woman's defense (or mine,) or the monotone, rat-a-tat beat of Desiigner's *Panda* to lull me to a stupor so that I can ignore, say, the details of the erotic dreams she sometimes seems compelled to shout. (I hope they're dreams.) That's my version of plugging my ears and chanting *la la la la*.

I do this until I run out of the parts I know, then replay them from the beginning in a loop stuck in my head until I notice her shrieks have stopped, or more commonly, until the music dissolves into a jumbled, disjointed mess and I fall asleep.

When morning sunlight creeps in through the long narrow slits in the wall up at ceiling level, she no longer cries.

Each morning, Margaret sends an orderly to escort me to her office for therapy. It's a big office with an ante-room, a big desk, big windows that look out onto the big hills across the canyon, big wood book shelves with lots of books, and off to the side, a big double door that goes into an even bigger room used for group and individual therapy — all in stark contrast to my tiny academic office at Finial University. In the room is a couch, a genuine psychiatrist's couch, such as I always thought was a myth.

The therapies they use here include the usual suspects of Freudian psychoanalysis — free association, dream interpretation, and all of that — Humanistic therapy, Gestalt therapy, drug therapies, group therapy, individual therapy. But, Liberty was founded by Margaret, as she told me, on her theory that traditional therapies alone aren't always enough and are sometimes too structured. So, she added hypnosis, meditation, and psychic readings to her list of available therapies.

On Margaret's bookshelf is a worn out copy of the *Diagnostic and Statistical Manual* with pages dog-eared and stained with circles of coffee. If you were to look in it — which I occasionally do while waiting for Margaret because I'm also a bit of a fanatic about reference manuals (and she's never said I couldn't) — many of the disorders listed there, Margaret said, can be found here at Liberty. That's how I know there are schizophrenics and sociopaths and the like residing here.

As for me, I know the reason I'm here is because I woke up one morning with gaping holes in my memory and freaked out about it. Even though I said it was in April when I came here, it could have been earlier, it could have been later. With a smorgasbord of therapies available, though, recovering my memory ought to be a slam dunk, even though nothing has worked so far. Nonetheless, any minute now my memory could come streaming back like a flash flood. Then I'm gone, out of here. Margaret said so.

Chapter Two

THE COUCH IN THE THERAPY ROOM, upholstered in gray, red, and white plaid, is more comfortable than I thought it would be; the gently sloping side supports my head and shoulders as I lie stretched out. There is no side panel at my feet.

Margaret has hypnotized me. This is the first time I've ever been under hypnosis, and it's like nothing I've ever experienced. My body and limbs float as if on air, levitated, unfelt. My mind seems wide awake, yet peacefully distant from where I lay down a short while ago. Absent is the continuous flow of anxiety that has lurked just beneath the surface most of my life, always ready to leap out, which I have learned to restrain by practice and sheer will alone and by intense focus on my work—my real work of research.

Up until now, Margaret has used traditional therapies to try to unlock my mind. She usually asks neutral, open-ended questions intended to draw something out of me, questions beginning with "Tell me about," or "What does that mean to you," or "How do you feel about." I'm sure she knows I recognize them for what they are. Nonetheless I try to help her because I understand helping her is also helping me. The answers just haven't come. If hypnosis is such a good therapy, I don't know why Margaret has waited so long to try it. Maybe I'd be home by now if she had tried earlier.

She starts today by asking what's been on my mind. What has been plaguing me is the fact that I am not tenured and will lose my job if I don't get back to work soon. There are students who need me—the bright stars in a galaxy of the ordinary who merely go through the motions just to get passing credit. They're about my age, too. I was just lucky enough to graduate early and get two doctorates and a good teaching job three years ago by the time I was twenty-two. Those bright stars need me to guide them, and, truth be told, I need them. They inspire me.

And, my research—my life's work—will be lost if I lose my assistant, Hannah Tuttle, and the university's resources. I couldn't take it if that happened.

But, those aren't the words coming out of my mouth. "It was an accident," I say, unsure of where that came from.

"What was an accident?"

"Falling into the ocean." An eternity of silence crowds its way in.

"How did the accident happen, Simon?"

I hear only her voice, distant, disembodied. The lights are dimmed. She is seated to my side and almost behind me, and I can't see her. Does she think I'm like one of her dissociative patients who intentionally harm themselves?

We continue with these and similar questions to which there are no answers forthcoming until I say, "I've already told you everything I remember."

And Margaret says, "Very well. I think that's enough for today. When I count backwards from ten, you will wake up."

She brings me out of hypnosis. I'm very tired, as if I have been through a struggle, not at all refreshed as she said I would be. It's quiet while she taps in some notes on a tablet, barely inside my peripheral vision. From here on my back looking past my feet, I see the wall of arched Mediterranean-style windows that look out as clearly as if there were no glass into an uncluttered distance. I hear the shushing of the mid-morning wind outside, lulling me to sleep. I am tired; the tormented woman down the hall from me kept me awake last night with her screams and dreams.

Margaret continues keyboarding, then looks up. "We have made good progress, Simon. I'll see you again tomorrow."

"When will I be getting out of here?" Still reclining, I crane my neck to look at her. She manages a rare smile.

"Soon, with good progress." She picks up her cane and stands. "Same time tomorrow."

With that, we leave the therapy room together. She turns left, in the direction of her office, her cane creaking a little under her slight weight, while Josh, an orderly with huge biceps, escorts me straight ahead toward my room. For a moment I feel good. I may get my wish to go home; I'm tired of this place. But, the happy feeling fades as I enter my room, the Cotton Ball I call it. Josh stands silently, stoically, in green scrubs by the open door and watches as I strip down to my boxers and put on the hospital gown I laid on the bed before leaving an hour ago. I suppose they had me change to street clothes so that I would feel normal, or perhaps so that I didn't stand out while walking through the halls. I'll have to ask sometime. Josh mumbles a thank you in a high tenor voice that belies his massive size, then closes the door behind him and walks away with the real clothes I had been wearing.

I don't remember signing anything that handed over all my rights; but, apparently I did. My memory is photographic when it's working right—which of course it isn't right now—and that's partly why amnesia is driving me nuts. The only reason I can see the papers now is because Margaret produced them a few days ago when I asked her, "How can I be held against my will?" to prove I had voluntarily committed myself. But, I'd written on the admission form, right there on the first line of the first page beneath my name, Simon Hensley, my address, and insurance company, the reason I came here was I had, or have, amnesia. I said nothing about wanting to kill myself. So, why suicide watch? At times, I think about asking then it slips my mind.

The biggest black hole in my memory is the period between New Year's Day and the day I checked in here. At some time, I must have said or done something to make Margaret believe I'm a danger to myself. I just don't remember what I could have done. For now I'm forced to trust her.

I've learned Margaret is Swiss by birth, a psychoanalyst by profession, and a psychic healer by accident, although I'm not so sure about the psychic healer part or how that would supposedly happen by accident. By nature, I'm a skeptic; by training, a man of science. And paranormal stuff like ESP, psychic readings, séances, near death experiences, etc. don't ring true. Except for sometimes.

How it was that I came to Liberty instead of another mental hospital is unknown to me. When I asked Margaret how I got here, all she said was I had been brought by a young woman, but didn't tell me who the young woman was or if she even knew her identity, and I keep forgetting to ask. I wonder if the young woman could have been Hannah. Nevertheless, here I am, struggling to remember what I probably should just forget.

That's the purpose of dissociative, or psychogenic, amnesia. It's a coping mechanism, a disruption of memory stemming not from disease or injury but, rather from stressful or traumatic events the mind wants to repress. Dissociative amnesia picks and chooses what you remember. And, that's why I can remember only parts of the recent past. And so I wonder, if what happened to cause my amnesia was so traumatic my brain wants to forget it, why should I try so hard to remember? Margaret said I can move on with my life only when I can face whatever it is I have forgotten. Therefore, here I stay for now, officially a resident of Mount Liberty Residence.

Chapter Three

MY ROOM IN THE SUICIDE WING is no luxury suite, nor is it very residential. It's a dinky four paces by five. That doesn't give a man very much room to get up and move, to pace while he thinks, as I often do when there's something on my mind. At home, I sometimes run for miles while I think things over. Here, I feel as if I have been confined inside a big, fluffy cotton ball. So, after a few days of enduring my stay here, I named it that: the "Cotton Ball." The walls are as soft as the white featherbed, conspicuously absent of coil springs, loosely laid on the floor in the corner. I sleep on it and not in it because there are no sheets, and sit on it, too, because there are no chairs. Everything is white: ceiling and floor, walls, toilet and sink—white, white, white—everything except a smoke-colored fish-eye camera that glares at me night and day from the ceiling in the far corner. I call it the Cyclops. I hate the Cyclops. Sometimes it seems to taunt me as if it's smarter than me, knows something I don't. The only thing that affords me any privacy at all is a single partial wall about three feet high placed next to the toilet.

The only clothing I have is one pair of boxers and one pullover paper gown—both of them white—and a single pair of white terry cloth slippers with rubber grips in the soles. That is the sum total of the belongings I'm allowed.

Every day I get a shower and a fresh set of white disposable clothes. The only thing in this wing that has color is the soap, green Irish Spring. I have no belt, no shoes, no razor. My toothbrush and hairbrush have to be left on the counter next to the sink in the men's showers where they are collected by an aide each day after I am finished using them.

At first, I sometimes shouted and cursed at the Cyclops and gave it the finger. When I wasn't shouting, I slept and slept and slept. I dreamed horrible, ugly, insane dreams I couldn't remember upon waking. I only remember night terrors, waking in a sweat, shouting. Eventually, I settled down. Maybe the Klonopin Margaret prescribed helps to settle me; maybe I simply needed time to adjust. Either way, I take the medication dutifully every day, wishing I could stop taking it, thinking there is no drug to solve my problem.

This morning after my dose of Klonopin, Margaret had those real clothes delivered to me: a red polo shirt with a little green alligator where a pocket should be, a pair of beltless khaki colored pants, sharply creased, and a pair of cordovan loafers with some of those ridiculous tassels on them I've always thought look pretentious on my fellow professors who sometimes wear them with their tweed jackets. Jeans and sneakers are just fine with me. I've got a new pair of black high-top Chuck Taylor All Stars, but, they're locked up where I can't get to them so that I can't do any harm to myself with the shoestrings. Not that I would want to.

Margaret has summoned me unexpectedly to the therapy room connected to her office in the south wing where there is little or no foot traffic in the hallway to distract us. An orderly, usually Josh, always comes and gets me, and we follow a red stripe on the floor down this hallway and that, right turn here, left turn there, curving around mostly unstaffed nurses' stations and onward until we come to a set of double doors where the line stops and the orderly knows the rest of the way. Past the doors the floor is carpeted.

The room is about the size of a large living room, longer than it is wide, and can easily seat eight or ten people comfortably yet intimately. Here is where Margaret holds group therapy sessions, from which she has excluded me, and Gestalt psychodrama—where people role play to act out their problems—from which I have excluded myself. I told her if I wanted to act, I would have gone to acting school. She said that was okay anyway, she didn't think Gestalt therapy was right for me.

After three weeks of seeing little color besides white, I drink in—no, I gulp—the laurel green walls painted in subtle faux designs with streaks of dark green and swooshes of dark brown. Flecks of deep red randomly dot small patches here and there, accenting the short-pile carpet, also dark red about the color of spilled wine. The carpet is easily marked with the impressions of my footsteps and Margaret's, hers in the pattern of step-step-dot, the dot being where she had put her cane as she limped across the room.

I asked Margaret once why she chose dark red for the carpet. She looked at me quizzically for a moment, smiled, then replied it was because she thought *bright* red would be "too much."

My eyes are drawn to the wall of windows and, beyond them, the tree-covered granite hills just across the gorge behind us, fir and spruce trees and old pine trees towering over maples and oaks, in full leaf. With the sunshine streaming in, I imagine a warm Mediterranean breeze gently stirring the air and a feeling of contentment as if I were in the Greek islands where philosophy, mathematics, astronomy, the arts, and western civilization share their beginnings.

"I had some extra time today, Simon, so we are going to try hypnosis again." Margaret had come in while I was looking out the window. Her voice shocks me back into the moment. Margaret is old enough to be my mother. She told me a while back she came to the United States over twenty-five years ago after practicing a few years in Europe because, in her words, there is *so* much pathology here in America. I always supposed the same could be said about Europe. Nonetheless, she's here now. Her once black hair, now laced with silver-gray, hangs down and curves slightly inward, almost touching her jawline, which slopes toward a narrow chin. As always, she is wearing a dark colored, jacketed pantsuit that gives her an air of austerity and sobriety, which is exactly what I want in someone who's messing with my mind.

"Hypnosis is a very powerful tool for recovering memories," she says, the same as she said before when we came up with zip. "Now I want you to choose a place to sit or lie down wherever you will be most comfortable for a while." I go for the couch, as I did last time, kick off my shoes, put my feet up on a length of folded sheet at the foot of the couch, and nestle in with my arms folded across my abdomen. "I want you to remember everything we talk about during this session." That's a stretch given my condition. "Now, place a finger, any finger you want, lightly upon your forehead."

The room is completely silent and I hear only Margaret's voice. The lights have been turned down and my eyes are closed. Within the context of psychotherapy, Margaret's Swiss-German accent, guttural enunciation, and hypo-nasality seem perfectly suited and make me feel as if I were stretched out on the famous upholstered couch of Dr. Sigmund Freud himself.

"Now focus your attention on the spot where your finger is," she tells me in a low tone, but not as soft as one would use to lull a child to sleep. "Focus all of your attention there and think of nothing else." I do as she says. "Feel the warmth where your finger touches your forehead. Concentrate on the warmth. Let your attention linger there feeling all the warmth. Do you feel it?" I nod. "Now, keep your attention there. That spot will feel warmer and warmer with every passing second." As before, it does. "Now it begins to spread and you can feel warmth all across your forehead." She's right again. "Let the warmth spread. It's soothing."

The warmth spreads across my forehead and flows down my cheeks. When she instructs me to, I remove my finger and the warmth stays and continues to flow across me, as if I were submerging in a hot bath, across my eyelids, across my cheeks, and circling my ears. My muscles become so relaxed, my arms and legs so tired, so heavy I can no longer lift them when she tells me to try.

She tells me to imagine I am standing at the top of a stairway. The stairway appears. Then she calmly urges me to begin to walk down those stairs, taking my time. There are ten of them, she says, and she will count them for me as I go down: One, two; and as I descend my legs feel so tired and so heavy. She tells me, with each step I get more tired: three, four; each step is more difficult and my legs become heavier, and I become more tired. She says, when she gets to ten, I will be in a deep, deep sleep and will hear nothing but her voice.

She continues to the count of ten and her promise is fulfilled; her voice sounds as if it were inside my head and I am alone.

Margaret calls me by name and tells me I am now standing in front of a door at the bottom of the steps and behind the door are memories now shut off to me. She directs me to open the door.

I see the door, and I open it.

"Now look around and tell me what you see."

What I saw behind the door was dark water, black sky. I was alone, piloting a chartered fishing boat on the open seas headed for land. It was the last night of spring break, and I was due back at work teaching classes the following morning. I think—yes I'm sure—I had chartered the boat earlier that day and gave the boat's captain some money for what was supposed to be a half-day deep sea fishing excursion. After that, I don't remember anything until the motor murmured, sputtered, and then stalled, cold dead. The needle on the gas gauge indicated there was at least a quarter tank of gas. The lens on the gauge was cracked so I tapped it several times. The needle didn't budge.

The boat was about ten paces long and had outrigger poles protruding haphazardly in front and back from which fishing lines could be dropped and clear the hull; but I don't remember fishing. There were long hinged boxes lining the sides for stowing rods and reels, and movable depth finders and fish finders. But I don't recall using any of them. Those boxes also doubled as seats for passengers; the cushions doubled as flotation devices. Overhead was a small upper deck with a second helm. Undoubtedly, the boat was perfect for deep sea fishing. But, I don't fish. I don't even eat fish. I find the texture of their flesh to be unpalatable and their smell to be repulsive. I don't know why I was there.

From the upper deck I made my way to the back of the boat to see what I could do to revive the dead vessel with no tools and no mechanical skills. The seas were rough and rocked the boat, but I had finally found my sea legs and climbed down the ladder and made it without any problems to the stern where the motor housing was located.

The smell of gasoline got very strong as I approached the stern, and before I knew it, I was standing in a puddle of the flammable liquid pooled at the base of the engine compartment. Despite that, I raised the lid, an upside down U made of rusty hinged sheet metal that looked like a homemade affair. It fit loosely and jiggled a little as I lifted it to have a peek inside. Even in the dim light provided by only the stars and a partial moon, I saw glistening fuel had leaked all over the twin engines from a weather-checked fuel line, and with a certain amount of alarm registering in my head figured the engines must have stalled merely because of a fuel pressure issue or because of the air-to-fuel ratio. Either way, I thought taping the fuel line would do the job long enough to get me back to shore. I simply needed to find some tape for a temporary fix, then I could be on my way. When I lowered the flimsy lid to go looking for tape, the lid shifted, scraped the metal frame of the housing, and sent out a small spark. Because I was standing in gasoline, seeing the spark scared me, and I lurched, dropping the lid the rest of the way, which sent a bigger spark. When I saw yellow and orange flames explode in front of my face and felt searing heat shoot up my leg as my pants caught on fire, I lurched again and stumbled and ended up in the ocean.

At that point in this morning's hypnosis session, my thoughts began to drift. Margaret ended the session and I returned to the Cotton Ball, where I am now, still thinking about those recovered memories.

    I lie down. The feather bed is remarkably soft for being situated on the floor. Even though it's shortly after ten o'clock in the morning, I fall asleep and dream.

Chapter Four

THE FOLLOWING MORNING, nine o'clock sharp, I'm again in Margaret's therapy room, feet on the couch, dressed in street clothes. This time, I'm rather anxious to tell her about my dream yesterday. I'm positive it was a recovered memory.

I dreamed that after falling overboard, I thrashed around looking for a way to get back aboard the boat and extinguish the fire in the burning engine compartment until I began to sink. "I can't swim," I tell her, "at least not in the typical sense and not for very long." Motor skills and muscular coordination tend to be somewhat lacking in some people like me with Asperger's; my only athletic ability lies in pitching a wicked fastball, if I may say so myself, which ability was hard won with applied physics and hour after hour of practice. I was urged on by Geoff Gibson who had taken me to my first baseball game when I was a child. But, I just never got very good at swimming. If I were to stand a chance of surviving, I would have to overcome the certain panic I get from not having something solid beneath my feet to stand on. I had to let my feet dangle below me, because I can tread water only if I am in almost six feet of water stretched out to nearly my full height, as if I am standing upright, leaning slightly forward, doing a sort of breast stroke.

Similarly, to float I must be in almost six feet of water leaning backward.

The ladder at the stern was too close to the fire for me to safely climb aboard, and there was no other way to get back on. So to stay afloat I pushed off the hull with both legs as hard as I could and backstroked away from it, drawing my arms up along my sides and pushing back toward my waist without ever taking my arms out of the water. I don't know what kind of stroke that's called or if it has a name, but it's the only way I can swim. That's just the way it is. It's slow, it's not pretty, but it works. To complicate matters further, I have to stroke gently or I sink. So there I was pulling long, even strokes underwater as fast as I could, as slowly as I had to, trying to get away from a burning boat I figured could explode any second.

And it did. It's amazing how little gasoline is needed to cause an explosion and light up the night sky, especially out there beyond the reach of streetlamps and beach torches. Flaming material flew overhead in short little arcs like Fourth of July fireworks and seconds later splashed down, tiny floating fires that burned out one at a time. The boat was still in one piece, but fire blazed near the engine compartment, therefore I abandoned any designs to board again.

The explosion, though small, was apparently enough to tear a hole in the hull sufficiently large to take on copious amounts of water. I had scarcely managed to escape to a safe distance when the ocean swallowed the boat and the night went black and quiet.

My head barely stuck out of the cold water which lapped around my ears, and every so often I got a mouthful of the briny stuff and had to spit it out. I began to shiver, not knowing if the shivering was from the cold or from fear. After a while, I felt a wave of warmth and then really became afraid that hypothermia was setting in, my body temperature was no longer being regulated, and my arms and legs would become useless numb appendages, dead weight that would pull me down. A perverted sense of relief came over me when the water felt cold again and it became apparent the warmth had come from a passing current. Nonetheless, fear quickly returned. Even though hypothermia hadn't set in yet, I felt it was certain to if I didn't get out of the water soon.

As I lay on my back, buoyed some by the density of the salt water, looking toward the heavens I did a bit of primitive dead reckoning and watched the constellation Virgo move from right to left as the night went on. I was headed south and should eventually wash ashore on one of the islands that lay to the south or southeast if I could stay afloat long enough; that is, unless some current or undertow swept me past land and out to sea forever.

I told Margaret about the dream. But, now, I begin to remember more. Before I fell overboard, I had something in my hands.

"What was it?" Margaret asks.

"A box—No. A laptop." I swivel around and sit on the couch facing Margaret.

"What were you doing on a fishing boat with a laptop?" Her voice is monotone; her fingers tap away on her tablet.

A feeling hit me like a gut punch. "It was my machine. My invention."

She looks up at me, her face marked with a frown. "Where is it now?"

"Gone. Lost." My muscles feel shaky, my hands quiver. The inside of my nose stings. My vision blurs, and I hope Margaret doesn't notice I'm tearing up.

She doesn't take her eyes off me. "Simon, what were you doing out on the ocean?"

That's a good question. The nearest ocean is a thousand miles or more away. "I don't know."

"Where were the captain, the crew, tourists?" Still monotone.

"I don't remember any captain, crew, or tourists."

"Tell me why you were alone at sea after dark?"

I shrug, palms up. "I can't."

Chapter Five

BACK IN THE COTTON BALL a few hours after the morning's session with Margaret, I remember more. I remember interminably floating, inexorably thinking.

I've heard it said when you face sudden death, your life flashes before you. If that's true for everybody I don't know. As for me, while I had endless hours to stare at the dark sky, I thought about my life thus far in lingering detail, asking myself what I would do differently if I could live my life over—the usual questions I suppose many people ponder when imminently faced with their mortality. Had I lived my life right? For an immeasurably small fraction of a second, I thought about it then answered myself I believed I had. Immediately, though, I doubted the answer and pled into the open air for mercy on my soul and forgiveness for transgressions I didn't even think I had committed.

Until now, guilt hadn't been an operative attribute in me, but I had been introduced to the concept when my mother had become a Roman Catholic at Geoff's urging following my father's death. As I already knew, Geoff wasn't an observant Catholic, but he had persuaded my mother to give church a try to help with her grief. And off to catechism class we had gone.

I stopped going to church long ago because it had become apparent to me many natural things are too often ascribed to the supernatural; I claimed no particular religious affiliation. But, something about the training had stuck, because as I backstroked in the dark water, I saw Sister Xavier in my mind's eye wearing her black and white habit in front of the catechism class at St. Francis de Sales Roman Catholic Church, moving stiffly to avoid brushing against the dusty blackboard behind her, a crucifix above it, reciting Pope Gregory's list of the Seven Capital Sins, the ones that unless absolved before death threaten you with eternal *damnation*. She always seemed to emphasize the word as if she enjoyed having license to say it. Sister Xavier had required us to memorize them, but they had long lain forgotten in my mental archive. At the moment, though, with a little aid from my photographic memory, I brought them into focus on the blackboard beside her: pride, greed, envy, wrath, lust, gluttony, and sloth. I had known some people who in my estimation could have run the gamut of sins. As for me, though, I had always kept to myself and had never done anything I thought could have been lumped into any of those categories. After grappling with my conscience for a while, I decided I was grappling over nothing. There was no priest around to absolve me, so I absolved myself.

But the absolution felt hollow and incomplete. Something was still amiss. The ocean sloshed around me, and I was overwhelmed with doubt and fear. "Mercy!" I begged into the dark air. "I don't want to die! I have work to do!" The stars stared back at me, silent and motionless.

When the first streak of light parted the sea from the sky, I was still backstroking. It must have been eight or nine hours that I had been floating. I was chilled to the bone; my arms ached; my legs felt like stumps; but I was alive.

The day's warmth was a welcome relief, but since the sky was the only thing I had to look at, the sun glared in my eyes and I had to close them. It was then I realized how drowsy I had become. I must have drifted off to sleep momentarily until I took in a mouthful of water and began to choke. I thrashed to get my head completely above water, then heard a voice that at first I thought was a waking dream. It said over and over again, "Look to your right." I finally recognized the voice. It was my dad's. My father had died when I was seven. I looked where he directed me. There, a few yards away was a debris field, rising and falling with each churning wave, but in a syncopated way compared to me, so that as the wave I was riding rose, I could sometimes see the debris; sometimes I couldn't. "Go to it," he told me. I had a bearing on its general direction so I turned, twisted, pushed, and pulled until I was on a course to intercept it.

I backstroked through a drifting, disperse oily sheen and had to be extra careful not to get a mouthful of the foul stuff. A few yards further, I looked backward over my shoulder as well as I could and aimed for a large flat object, hoping it was one of the flotation cushions from the boat. I grabbed ahold of it and found it to be a thick board, possibly part of a crate from another shipwreck, slick with a bourgeoning growth of algae. It wasn't one of the cushions, but it would do. My arms were sapped of strength, and the slippery algae made it difficult to climb on top. The board was long and wide enough for me to stretch out completely. Finally, I rested.

I had read humans can live three minutes without air, three days without water, and thirty days without food. One time, I had also read the incredible survival story of an earthquake victim in Armenia who had lived thirty days without food and water buried beneath rubble before being rescued. That I rode the waves on my slimy board through thirteen cycles of day and night, dark and light was almost as astounding — to me anyway.

When I eventually washed ashore, I must have been unconscious. For when I woke up, I had been turned over flat on my back and was lying in the sand next to the board that had saved me. What I saw next was brilliant sunlight forming an aureole around an angelic face leaning over me. Her mouth had been on mine. She pulled back, lips still parted. Her breath was sweet, and it filled my lungs. A deeply tanned face, eyes with prismatic concentric rings of blue and green, like the mystic fire topaz in the pendant my father had given my mother, came into focus. Her hair was pulled back out of the way. She smiled. I turned and coughed up saltwater and climbed to my feet, looked around to thank my rescuer, but she was gone. I knew I was still on earth, alive. Mercy, indeed.

The morning after that flood of memories came to me I call for Margaret to tell her about them, still in my gown and slippers.

"Congratulations," she says, smiling while she leans on her cane in the doorway of the Cotton Ball. Perhaps she smiles more than I think. "You've had a major breakthrough. And, you've told me something I need to know."

"What? That I finally remembered something?"

"That you want to live. I don't think we need to keep such a close eye on you anymore."

I don't remember ever not wanting to live, but I don't argue. "Good. Do I get to go home?"

"Patience, Simon. Not yet. But, I think you will like your new accommodations better than your current one." She uses her cell phone to call for Josh to bring me street clothes and to show me to my new room. I'm disappointed at not getting to go home, but this is a step in the right direction.

"Could I have my own clothes . . . and my Chucks?"

"Of course. I'll tell Josh to bring them to you." She smiles again, and then taps the handle of her cane playfully against the door frame. "We're getting somewhere, Simon." She turns and makes her way down the hall.

When Josh brings my clothes, he steps out this time while I change.

Good-bye, Cotton Ball.

Chapter Six

MY NEW ROOM ON THE SECOND FLOOR of the southwest wing is palatial compared to the Cotton Ball and has a large window overlooking the grounds. I pull back sheer curtains and open Venetian blinds, seeing the full expanse of the property for the first time. The place is huge. With some quick mental comparisons with farms I had seen before, I guessed there must have been at least one hundred sixty acres here. There are a lot of people outside milling about. To the left, a cluster of three men are talking about something, one animatedly waving his hands. On a bench, a lone woman is reading. Under a shade tree, another lone woman sits silently in the lotus position, hands in her lap, with the thumbs and index fingers of each hand pressed together as if they were pinching something unseen. Others stroll along the far hedgerows on the sides, tiny as ants, and the fence line along the back.

Through a gap in the trees at the back of the grounds that must be at least a hundred yards away, I can see the granite cliffs on the other side of the gorge that skirts the south end of town. Jagged pink and yellowish gray layers of rock sharply incline until they run into the sky, fractured here and there like an eggshell or the thick ancient oil painting of a classical master. On top sits an old growth forest that has never been harvested as far as I know.

I cross the room from one end to the other. It's five paces by six, barely enough room. That's a habit I seem to have: measuring a new area in paces; when I run, I sometimes measure in pairs of strides. For instance, I may mark the distance from a lamp pole to a corner as thirty pairs of strides or the distance from one object to another as so many pairs of strides. It's just a way to tick off short distances for no apparent reason.

This room has a real bed with a curved headboard, a foot board, and a brocade bedspread neatly tucked in place. I stare at the bed, then poke it a little timidly to make sure it's not a water bed. The last thing I want now is the feeling of floating. There are also a closet, chest of drawers, and a private bathroom with a private shower. Above all, there is no Cyclops glaring at me.

I go back to the window and look out, my thoughts turning now to my research, artificial intelligence. I've been avoiding thinking about it for a while.

I once read the United Nations Population Division has estimated the human population of the earth in the year 2150 could reach as high as almost twenty five billion, more than three times the current population of seven billion. If humans don't manage resources wisely and efficiently, there could be utter disaster trying to feed, house, and clothe that many people. And, that is where my research comes in. New technology is needed that will provide fast and accurate results for things that require vast amounts of data input with many different variables, running massively parallel operations in order to provide realistic solutions for real everyday problems: accurate weather modeling to mitigate human-caused climate change; sustainable energy sources; food production; medical research and development; robotics; bionics; transportation, etc.

I was working on the solution with more than a little bit of help from Hannah who coded my algorithms into something usable by a computer.

Perhaps I got the inspiration to solve the world's problems using science that even Einstein called "spooky stuff" from my father, who, like me, had Asperger's Syndrome and was a professor at Finial University. Except, his field was biology. His particular interest was studying the quantum effects of sunlight on photosynthesis. Spooky stuff I didn't get into.

Dad built a greenhouse addition onto the back of our house before I was even old enough to remember and made it his personal laboratory. From the looks of it, though, you would have thought he was a botanist. Plants were everywhere, all kinds of them: potted plants, hanging plants, green plants, flowering plants, vines and ivy, cacti, alpine plants, rain forest plants, and many others. And, as he said with a wry smile, they were not your garden variety of plants, either. Many he had grown from seeds imported from exotic places like Brazil, Southeast Asia, and Siberia. To the untrained eye, it looked like jungle pandemonium. Nothing could have been further from the truth. He had carefully placed each plant where light could be strictly controlled. Rain forest plants had been given dense shade. Plant lights with programmed timers hung over Tundra plants to supplement nature so that they could receive light up to twenty hours per day, eight months per year, and for four months per year were given as little as four hours of light per day. Along the wall adjacent to the house, which still had the original painted lap siding, he had a work bench lined with scientific equipment, microscopes, stereoscopes, and others. There were tall, three-legged stools I would climb up on to watch him as he worked.

I remember the first time he set me on his knee, inviting me to peer into his tiny world of plant cells with the green chlorophyll and rectangular membrane walls surrounding the nucleus and mitochondria inside. I marveled at seeing those things under intense magnification, looming large, yet invisible to the naked eye. And, I enjoyed the closeness and what was to be too little time with my father.

I have since taken over the greenhouse as my home laboratory. There are no longer any plants hanging around, just a lot of computer parts and connections, cables running where plants used to hang. The bench is still there, though, and the stools. I haven't been there in a while. I miss it.

Chapter Seven

THE STAIRS HERE AT LIBERTY are just outside my room to the right, eight concrete steps, a landing with a one hundred eighty degree turn, then eight more steps. The metallic sound of the door opening echoes in the stairwell. I walk outside for the first time since coming here, stopping on the terrace to take in a deep breath of fresh outside air. Then, I go down three more steps and out onto the commons. It feels good to walk. The sunshine feels good on my face; the sunburn I got at sea has long since healed, and my skin has stopped peeling. I walk to the other end of the building. When I turn around, I see a young woman who looks like Hannah coming my way. I turn sharply in her direction, suddenly feeling lighter, more cheerful than I have felt for a long time. My face lifts, a smile at the ready, and I start walking toward her. Appropriate or not, I'm going to hug her and hold on. It's been so long since I saw anybody I know.

    A dozen or so yards away, she must see me smiling. But, she looks away. Someone else is waving to her and calling her over. She smiles and waves back. It isn't Hannah. I stop in my tracks and watch as she veers off.

    I should have known it wouldn't be her. I guess I had just hoped — well, never mind. Hannah may be aloof, but that doesn't have to translate into disinterest, does it? Although she did make it perfectly clear there was no room for anything but an arm's-length, working relationship. Simply put, I don't really know what I feel for her. Nevertheless, she crosses my mind a lot. She's the best programmer I've ever met, and I've taught some good ones. She doesn't talk much, not even to herself like many other programmers when they're working out code or debugging a program as though it were a rebellious adolescent. Hannah's not pretty in the classic sense. Her nose is a bit long and sharp, her eyes round and wide apart. Her ears are a skosh large. In her case, the sum of the parts is greater than their total; there's just something about her. Maybe it's pheromones. Maybe it's the way she looks in skintight running outfits when she leaves the lab ready for a good stress-relieving run at the end of a long programming day. I can't say what it is.

Now, I feel a bit silly simply standing here, watching the woman walk away. I head back to my room.

Chapter Eight

THE FOLLOWING MORNING, nine o'clock sharp, I'm back with Margaret, this time in her office and not the therapy room. I had planned on perching myself comfortably on the couch and telling her about the Hannah look-alike. Before I can get to it, she says to me, "Simon, our appointment today will be very short."
"No hypnosis?"
"Not today. And not by me anymore."
"By whom?"
She gives me one of those pregnant pauses usually intended to either intensify or to stall. "Yourself."
"Me? Self-hypnosis?"
"Yes. We have made such good progress with your hypnosis, I want you to try it by yourself." She eyes me. "Oh, you won't find this in the *DSM* or anywhere else." She must suspect I've been reading some. "This is therapy custom tailored for you. You're a special case."
"Hypnotize myself?"
She pushes her chair back from her desk, crosses her legs, lifting her bad one by hand and laying it on top of the other, then shifts her weight in the chair. "Remember each time I have put you under hypnosis, I told you that you would remember everything? I meant

everything. Just repeat those same steps." She nods. "You can do it for yourself."

Great. I get to take myself down dark stairways and open doors to my unconscious. Then an idea comes to me. "If I can do that here, why can't I do it at home?"

"Because the second part is I want you mingle, get to know some new people without me around."

Meeting people isn't my thing. It's unnatural to me. It means looking them in the eye and small talk and smiling whether or not I feel like it. Most people will be bored to tears talking about the things on my mind: quantum physics, quantum computers, quantum bits. I, on the other hand, am bored to tears when they want to talk about the weather or sports—other than baseball, of course—or other trivial matters. "Mingle?"

"You can do it," she said. But, it's one thing for me to greet a new class each semester, fresh young faces eager to learn—or at least eager to get credit for the course. I have a prepared presentation, and if I feel funny looking at them, I can look over their heads at the back wall and they won't know the difference. "Make some friends." It's another thing to strike up a conversation with a stranger.

"I've got friends."

"Good. Tell me some of their names."

"Michael Emory. I've known him since college. And Geoff Gibson. He was my dad's friend and that makes him my friend, too." I couldn't think of anyone else.

"Where is Michael, Simon?" Her tone is suddenly void of expression. She looks straight at me.

"He's been working on a geological site somewhere. . ." I struggle to recall. It's been a while since I talked to him. "Somewhere in the desert, I think."

"I'm sure Michael's a good friend, but I think you need more than one friend — and Dr. Gibson. Trust me on this, Simon." She gives me a look, one of those knowing looks as a wise mother gives her child. "I have an intuitive feeling."

"Is that a psychic healer thing?" I ask, being perfectly sincere.

She uncrosses her legs with help again from her hands, and in a body language kind of way, pulls her chair up to the desk, signaling we're through for the day.

"Think of this as a type of free association," she says. "You'll be free to roam around associating with people, relating to the events of their lives and, hopefully, the events of yours. No one will be keeping tabs on you. But, I want you to check in with me once in a while or whenever you feel the need to. Just try it. Okay?"

Chapter Nine

A FEW DAYS LATER, I've had very little luck making new acquaintances. Margaret's constant urging aside, I've about given up; it just isn't easy for me. But, I'll try again. There is a small group of residents who seem to spend all of their time in the television lounge. A large television is mounted on the wall above a fake stone fireplace. A couch and six cushioned upholstered chairs are arranged in a sort of semi-circle in front of it, filled with mesmerized people. I stop in the doorway and watch a few minutes of the show that's on. Instead of going in, I turn around and head to the dining room to be by myself where it's quiet.

Across the room, set casually on the counter, is a box of saltine crackers. The sight of it bothers me in a way I can't explain. I get up from the table, bring the box back, stand it on end in front of me, and stare at it until something comes to me.

A few minutes later, I leave the dining room and go outside for a late afternoon walk on Liberty's grounds down a path of freshly laid, reddish pink cedar chips that fill the air with their aroma. The grounds have been cleared of brush for a distance of about one hundred seventy five pairs of my strides away from the back of the building and are grassy with some flower beds bearing red and yellow mid-spring blooms along the foundation of the building and the fence line. On the far side, the grounds end at a tree line that's one hundred ninety-eight pairs of strides long. Each pair of my strides averages eighty inches in length. I have measured my individual strides and use pairs to reduce inaccuracies from variances in each step. Therefore, by my rough calculations, I confirm my guess that Liberty is located on a one-quarter of a mile square piece of land.

Beyond the clearing is a tree line; beyond it lies a thicket of brush. In one spot, the tree line parts almost imperceptibly. I didn't notice it the first three times I walked by. It looks as if it could be the opening of a path not recently taken, so I follow it into the thicket, winding around in serpentine fashion. My hunch is right. The unnoticed path leads to a clearing where there is an old wrought iron bench that looks out over the gorge that lies far below its feet, separated only by a wrought iron fence about five feet high with spear point tips on the end of each baluster. It's the same kind of fence that is at the back of Liberty's grounds. Here is a lovely place for quiet reflection, and I claim this little glade as my own space.

Some of last year's brown oak leaves crumble beneath my fingers when I brush them off the iron bench to clear a place to sit. The bench isn't bad at all. The back reclines a little, and vertical iron slats curve outwardly, welded to a cylindrical bar forming a loose curl at the top that isn't too bad to sit on with my feet perched on the seat. I can see farther this way. When the breeze settles, I hear the water rushing in the gorge below. When the wind picks up, I hear only the pine needles scraping the air and the deciduous trees' leaves flapping. Now and then a bird whistles, another chortles, and I wonder what reason they have for such cheerfulness.

I begin to remember something.

I remember the metal tower I made from scratch that held six quad core processing units that was to be the prototype of my portable quantum computer. It was about the size and shape of a box of saltine crackers set on end, a simple frame, open on two sides, made from thin perforated metal that looked as though it had been constructed from a child's Erector Set. The green colored printed circuit boards with the processors and chipsets were fastened into the sides of the tower. They were linked via USB cable to an inexpensive laptop which was already programmed with the algorithm Hannah had coded, thus making a total of seven processors that were supposed to run massively parallel. It was a classical computer that was supposed to synthesize multiple functions running simultaneously inside a quantum computer. If I was right.

Early in the morning on New Year's Day while others were sleeping off parties of the night before or were waiting for bowl games to start, I was in the computer science lab at Finial U. For me it was time for the first practical test of my new system. After eleven years of theorizing, designing, and planning, I finally had a full set of instructions Hannah had helped write and finely tune: a learning algorithm that constructed a model of the world around it and could reprogram itself, with intuitive error correction in response to new input. In essence, it was an algorithm that could perceive, learn, grow—and dare I say it, use judgment?—just like its biological inspiration, the human brain. I had concocted some problems to challenge it and was only moments away from finding out if a machine could be made to think like a human. I knew it could; I just had to prove it. If successful, this would be one of the most important moments in human history and would immortalize me among the great names of technology: Bill Gates, Steve Jobs, and (I hoped) Simon Hensley.

Seconds after I gave the execute command, the laptop monitor brightened and a series of commands flashed across the screen in white letters faster and faster until it blurred into a solid white block, and I thought I had done it. Suddenly, the circuit boards sizzled and crackled, and sparks sprayed my arms and face with hot pinpricks. Smoke burned my eyes. Vapors from molten wiring swarmed inside my nostrils like stinging bees, the air tasted like chemicals. The smoke alarm shrieked; I choked and coughed.

I pushed my stool away from the counter, unplugged the power supply, then jumped back to collect my thoughts. The sparks stopped immediately, but the fumes still choked me. I went over to the windows and opened them, letting in a swoosh of fresh, cold air. Moments later, the alarm silenced itself.

When the tower cooled down, I pulled a Phillips screwdriver out of a tool box, ripped the processing units and chipsets out of the tower, scooped up the burnt-out power supply, and dumped them all into the recycle bin, a gray plastic barrel, landing with a thump. The only thing I kept was the tower frame.

I was about to leave when I remembered the laptop. The screen was black now, but earlier the blue screen of death had glared at me through the smoke. I picked it up and sniffed the vents on the bottom side. Just as I thought, it smelled burnt. It, too, went into the recycle bin.

I turned off the lights in the computer science lab and stepped through the door into my adjoining office, stopping to look at the printout on the opposite wall — the schematic for a revolution in computers. I felt as if I had finally perfected the architecture, but it was all a complete waste of time because of one small problem: I didn't have the right material for a processor, one that could achieve the effects necessary to imitate human thinking. There weren't any silicon chips that fit the bill. According to my theory, what I really needed was a crystalline lattice that would allow tunneling effects to create microscopic pathways through which information could find shortcuts to its destination, thus working faster, running multiple solutions at a time. It was all theoretically possible, but my algorithm was years ahead of materials science.

What that all meant was I really couldn't tell what I'd created. It may not even have been enough to earn me an honorable mention in future science fiction novels. It may not even be worth scoffing.

I took in a deep breath of smoke-tainted air and blew it out. I must have been the only person in the science building that day, and that was definitely a good thing after setting off the fire alarm.

I looked again at the diagram — both a marvel of science and a work of art, if I may say so myself, definitely worthy of Da Vinci. But so useless. I pulled it down from the magnetic whiteboard and crammed it into my pack, wadded. Two steps later, I was in the darkened hallway, backpack filled with journals and designs slung over my shoulder and walked home, feeling as dark and cold as if the snow-laden winter clouds overhead had fallen on top of me. The frigid air stung my ears, thickened my lips and cheeks.

I wondered if—no, I feared I would end up like one of my idols, Charles Babbage, and his exquisite invention the Analytical Engine, the world's very first computer. His plan was complete with a printer designed to produce inked hard copy of the engine's calculations—in the 1840s. Now days, Babbage is often depicted as a caricature mad genius in steampunk alternate history novels where events that really happened don't, and things that didn't happen do. His Analytical Engine performs all sorts of feats, such as solving crimes in a Sherlock Holmes fashion. Or miniature versions are implanted into the heads of robots. That's all nice and interesting fantasy, but the truth is more stark.

When Babbage died in 1871, his most famous invention had lain unfinished for over twenty years— abandoned, I now noted, for the lack of materials. Before there were silicon chips, before there were transistors, before there were vacuum tubes there was nothing to power the world's first computer except a locomotive-size steam engine and a two-and-a-half ton tower of precision made brass gears that would theoretically spin and crank out solutions to problems, controlled by a stepwise sequence of operations—an algorithm—written by Babbage's assistant, the world's first computer programmer, Ada Lovelace. But, instead of grinding out calculations, the project ground to a halt because Babbage had lost his funding and had a falling out with the engineer who manufactured the necessary parts that couldn't be produced by just anybody.

Likewise, my saltine-cracker-box sized tower of precision microchips sizzled and burned up—in my analysis—because of the lack of materials.

Babbage was eventually vindicated long after his death when in 2002 a working model of his calculating engine was completed in England. He had been right all along. He just hadn't lived long enough to see it work.

Neither do I have a hundred and sixty years to wait.

Chapter Ten

LATER ON NEW YEAR'S DAY, I sent an email to Hannah, who had returned home to Minnesota to be with her family for the holidays, and asked her to take one more look at the code to see if she could determine why the program produced nothing but sparks and noxious vapors and asked if she could report her conclusion when classes resumed in about three weeks.

Hannah replied she had been snow-bound for several days and eagerly took on the task. She was both remarkable and reliable, possessing the exquisite mind of a mathematician who viewed the abstract with a unique intuition that seemed to defy her male counterparts who vastly outnumbered her.

Three semesters before, it was a stroke of luck she had transferred from another university at the same time I was a bit stymied. When I had shown Hannah what she would be working on, she had taken only a few minutes to look it over and uttered a single word, "Intuition." When I asked her what she meant, she looked up from the printouts and told me, "If you want to create artificial intelligence, true intelligence that emulates human thinking, you can't have just logic. You've got to include intuition. How many people do you know who use only logic?"

Hannah apparently figured out how to program a machine to use intuition. She wasn't the only brilliant graduate math student at Finial U, but it turned out she was far and away the most intuitive—in my opinion. I told her once her mind was an elegant balance of left brain logic and analytical functions with right brain intuition and artistic functions in perfect synchronicity. "Synchronicity" was perhaps a Freudian slip; what I meant to say was her left brain and right brain seemed to function in perfect *synchronization*. But, what a meaningful coincidence that at a particular point, Hannah would come along with her unique qualities and would design intuition into the program. Perhaps it was synchronicity.

Patterns in her work started showing up when she would return portions of the code to me for review. I saw instructions that more or less said, "if the results of this operation *don't seem right*, try this." I tried to imagine how a machine could determine how anything should seem, but I went with it. Such instructions, I thought, might have been what it took to infuse the code with intuition and might lead to creative solutions and to emergent behavior from the machine, that is, getting results, oftentimes better than you would normally anticipate, as when three tenors form a group and sound better than they do as soloists.

Though Hannah was among the most promising math students Finial University had seen in a while, I learned later, her transfer was less about Finial's good reputation and more about preserving her own. It seems that at her old school, a tenured professor kept hitting on her, which she had regarded at first as annoying. But, all of that attention had become flattering. By her own description, she was overweight and frumpy at the time, a condition I can assure you has been corrected if it ever needed to be, and she had been too deeply involved in her work to indulge in having much fun. She stopped short of saying their relationship went further than not-so-innocent flirtations, but I speculate they must have. Word had gotten around at her old school, and Hannah had become extremely embarrassed and feeling her privacy was being violated by what people were saying, whether or not the things they said were true, so she transferred that year to Finial U.

Hannah didn't tell me her history all at once. It took some time for her to relax a little and talk about herself. When she did, she was quick to tell me any relationship she had with faculty would be purely academic. But, I later realized, she stopped short of putting any such limitation on relationships after her graduate work was finished.

That would give me time to think. I am not one who is particularly smooth or glib when talking to the opposite sex. I once asked an attractive young woman if she would go to dinner and an off-Broadway play with me. "Yes," she had said without hesitation. "You would?" was my response. As soon as those words hobbled out of my mouth, I felt as if I had surrendered most of my IQ points. We went out anyway, but she had little to say when I explained the difference between bits and bytes and other assorted technical terms. I soon ran out of anything to talk about. We never went out again.

So, when Hannah left open certain possibilities after our work was finished, I felt a sense of relief.

After working with her for a while, she reminded me on occasion the sole part of my design that actually seemed to work, in theory anyway, was the program she had spent many months perfecting and tweaking from the algorithm I had given her to work with. "Are you bantering with me?" I asked her after one such occasion. I didn't know if women banter with men, if she was being playful, or if she was asserting what was to her a self-evident truth and declaring she should hold a rightful place in history like Ada Lovelace. That is, if my invention were to become viable — and valuable. Hannah gave me a tight-lipped smile instead of an answer as she left my office, hips swaying, and returned to her desk.

Hannah's desk faced a wall in the computer lab where she sat almost sideways to look at her monitor, her back at an angle to the rows of computer stations behind her. Her desk was usually stacked with papers and notebooks in an organized disarray. On the wall above her desk in a simple wood frame hung a collage of reproductions of daguerreotype photos of Ada Lovelace. Ada was well photographed for the 1840s, probably because she was also a Countess. The photos showed clearly, in addition to being smart, she was pretty. Her skin was smooth and clear; dark, silky hair with not a single one out of place framed her heart-shaped, cherubic face. She wore high-waist, bell-shaped floor-length dresses with puffy sleeves, the most fashionable attire of her time.

I suppose Ada was a fitting model for Hannah, but it is also true Ada died young at the age of thirty seven.

On the surface, Hannah appeared to be much less formal than Ada and preferred to wear jeans most days when she wasn't in her running outfits. She sometimes wore expensive designer jeans with glittery fleur-de-lis designs on the back pockets. One time I chided her that she was apparently paid too much as an assistant. I was just bantering—testing the waters, perhaps—but she shot back she had bought them at a Goodwill store for eight dollars. Whether or not that's true, I'll take her word for it. Feeling duly chastised, I shut up. But the glitter did draw attention to her well-formed glutes, and she had to know it. The only jeans I ever saw her in fit as tightly as a second skin.

I thought it odd at first, but Hannah would sometimes refer to herself as "Ada." Again, I wasn't sure how playful she was being, but she might electronically sign the latest iteration of code with "A.L." to signify she was finished with it. Or if she needed something, she might say, "Professor, to perfect your *Quantum* Analytical Engine, Ada needs. . . " and then her request would follow. I didn't really see the levity in it and would have preferred she ask outright for whatever she needed. But, I got used to it and eventually became rather fond of it, although it would have been a bit much if she had referred to herself as "the Countess."

While waiting for Hannah's report during the three weeks following the New Year's fiasco, when I wasn't sleeping, I spent most of my time in near-total isolation at my technician's bench in the greenhouse lab at home working through the code, one more time, then again, then again, and dissecting the hardware designs as well, debugging and looking for flaws.

Heavy gray clouds, dark as dirty mop water, never lifted. Not for a single day. Even in the greenhouse during the day I had to use a lamp. Neither did my spirits lift. I felt somnambulant, lethargic, worthless, dimwitted, inadequate. Consuming generous amounts of caffeine was the only thing that kept me out of bed. If I had gone to a medical doctor, I'm sure he or she would have prescribed something for depression. But, I didn't go.

With two days to go before I expected to receive Hannah's report, I had been through the entire program again, line by line, and found nothing wrong. Everything checked out perfectly. My conclusion was simple. Materials science wasn't ready for a room temperature, portable quantum computer. Like Babbage, I was ahead of my time.

Outside the window in back, the old oak tree, bare at the top with persistent, dead brown leaves hanging on below, swayed in the wind partially lit by the moon. I shut down the computer, turned off the lights in the greenhouse, ambled exhausted to the bedroom, and crawled in bed.

After a few hours of tossing and turning and burying my head so deep under my pillow that I eventually had to emerge for air, my cell phone rang. It was Michael.

It wasn't like Michael to call. He usually texted or just stopped by when he was in town. Even though Michael is the only person in the world I feel comfortable calling a friend, I wasn't in the mood to speak to him just then. His habitual cheerfulness didn't match my mood.

I took the call anyway. I could tell Michael had been drinking. He talked faster, and his Texas accent, usually tame, was more pronounced. But, it wasn't terribly surprising he'd been drinking. Michael was a life-of-the-party kind of guy, always ready for a good time, quick with a smile, and quicker yet to tell a joke. I'm no good at telling jokes, so I don't even try, which seems to make people think I am more serious than I really am.

I had known Michael since my undergrad days at Finial U. Even though I was almost ten years younger than him, and everybody else, he had always included me in conversations and activities. Before I had got to know him, the others had always shied away from me, I supposed because I was some kind of oddity, that adolescent kid who kept setting the grading curve. That didn't seem to matter to Michael. And, when Michael found out I had pitched in youth baseball, he'd asked me to show him a pitch or two. I showed him all I knew, and he got pretty good at it, too, especially with the fastball. After that, we would often play catch, sometimes "burnout" between classes.

As far as I knew, everybody on campus at least knew who Michael was, and when he'd enter a room, there'd always be somebody calling out his name to get him to come over. It was because of his gregarious nature we had become buddies. But, we had become friends because of his serious side I'd always thought he'd kept carefully hidden to protect his thin party-boy veneer, the source of his popularity. How sad a truth it seems the more serious you are, the less popular you remain. Lucky for me, though, I supposed he felt comfortable talking to me because it was obvious I was serious about science.

We had often talked of his plans to use the science of geology to keep energy gluttons from sacrificing the environment. Some of his ideas were kooky, some seemed solid. And I told him of my plans to enhance the world with a new generation of computer technology. Perhaps, we'd dreamed, our plans could someday work together.

We'd lost touch a while back for no better reason than busy schedules, and when my head cleared the fog of sleep, I realized I didn't know where he'd been.

"Somewhere in the middle of the Mojave desert in Nevada," he said.

Michael was a crusader for green energy of all kinds: solar, wind, but especially enhanced geothermal systems. One time he had even spent a night in jail because of a demonstration he had participated in, protesting a proposed nuclear power plant. *Nookular*, he would pronounce it after a few drinks of anything. Over time, I had chided him into the correct pronunciation—when he was sober, anyway.

Ever since I had known him, his environmental views had put him at odds with his family who owned a prosperous oil company in Texas. A few years ago after receiving his doctorate in geology, Michael had started his own company, Deep Source Energy, on a shoestring to explore geothermal energy to power the electric grid as a viable alternative to hydrocarbons or nuclear energy. That was one of his best ideas. When Michael had refused to join the family oil company, his dad had gone ballistic and threatened to disown him.

Michael seldom talked money or business with me, just ideas, so I had never known how well he was doing.

"What happened? Big oil and big bucks get to you?" I knew of the large mineral deposits out there and couldn't imagine what else might have lured him.

"Oh heck no."

"Then... what?"

"I'll tell you all about it when I'm in town. I'll be there day after tomorrow and we can get together. I got something to show you."

"What?"

"Can't talk. Too many ears."

"In the desert?"

"Electronic ears."

Whenever Michael came to town, he stayed at my place in the spare bedroom upstairs that used to be mine when my parents were still alive. He had called to make sure he still had lodging. Of course he did; I welcomed his company.

Chapter Eleven

MICHAEL WASN'T JUST THE FIRST FRIEND I MADE IN SCHOOL. To this day he is my only friend, if you don't count Geoff Gibson, who is more like family. Making friends isn't hard. It's meeting new people who aren't students that's hard, deciding what to talk about, what's trivial, what's meaningful, what we have in common, if anything. Since the usual sequence is to meet people before becoming friends, it's easier for me to simply keep to myself and my work and be thought of as a loner, when in truth, I crave companionship as much as anybody else.

Being here at Liberty has shown me what true isolation is. How I miss the hustle and bustle of the crowded corridors of Finial U, the collage of voices blending into an unorchestrated mixed chorus, the laughter, the way the halls clear, doors close, the bell rings, the scuffle of feet and books as people take their seats. At my lectern, I know what to say. I talk easily to people, who under other circumstances would be my peers, until the bell rings again, the room empties, the hallway fills, and I go alone to my life's work, my research.

Chapter Twelve

ALMOST THREE WEEKS AFTER the New Year's disaster in the lab, nineteen days to be precise, a new semester was about to start, and I had to go back to work, ready or not. The first day of classes was Tuesday, therefore everyone should have had an extra day for air travel to get back to town, Hannah and Michael included. By evening, I hadn't seen a sign of either one of them, and, I must say, I was looking forward to seeing both of them. My winter break had run its course.

The evening had gotten late and I was still in my office after having perused the code for the latest of the innumerable times. My office was the second door to the right from the outside door at this end of the hall. As I was about to leave, I saw through the windows across the hall that it was dark outside. I closed my door and started to lock up when I heard Hannah's voice.

"Dr. Hensley." She was dressed for a run and looked better than a professor should take notice of. She handed me a notebook and a flash drive containing her notes and an executable copy of the program. "It looks good to me. I couldn't find anything wrong. The *program* for your quantum analytical engine seems to be flawless." She smiled.

"Thank you, *Ada*." Okay. I could play along. Maybe it would help. I smiled back and let my hand linger as I took the flash drive from her warm hand. "Seriously, though. . . why do you think it doesn't work?" She withdrew her hand.

"If I had to render an *un*scientific opinion—"

"Yes. That's what I'm asking for. Intuition."

"Well, we, that is you, programmed it to interact with its environment and apply its new-found knowledge in new, and I might add intuitive, ways." There was a gleam in her eyes. "We succeeded."

"That's it? We succeeded?"

"However—" I knew something was coming. "It's a victim of its own success. It's doing everything you asked it to do. The problem is, I think, there is too much going on in all the massive parallel processing for the current generation of processors we're trying to use. They can't handle it. Not the seven processors you linked together or even seven hundred processors could handle it. In a phrase, it's going bonkers."

Going bonkers is the last thing you want a computer to do. But, I wasn't totally surprised. That tends to happen with quantum computers, which are largely theoretical; there are only a small number of prototypes in existence. My first year physics students already knew what I had told my freshman computer classes every semester. The term "quantum" simply means something came in a bundle, or a quantity: A turkey breast sandwich on country white bread with mustard, lettuce, tomato, and pickle was a bundle; their or their parents' cable or satellite television subscriptions came in a bundle. Usually at about that point someone would say, "I get it," to which I always say, "Not so fast." And then I explain further at the atomic level freaky weird things begin to happen in those bundles which is why atoms can be infamously split causing nuclear reactions either in power plants or bombs. And along come some new counterintuitive rules that tell us matter can exist in more than one state at a time. And then there is quantum tunneling which means certain waves can tunnel right through something you would normally expect to stop them. After explaining that, though, I told them the quantum stuff was beyond the scope of this course and they didn't have to worry about it. That always brought a sigh of relief.

Classic computers like the ones in most homes and offices in the developed world run one process at a time for a single problem and arrive at a single absolute answer. Unlike them, quantum computers run multiple processes in massive parallel for a single problem and arrive at a number of solutions, assigning each one with a probability of being the correct answer. That is the fuzzy logic almost everybody had heard of.

The problem with quantum computers is they are massive in size and massively expensive; and they tend to interact with their environments causing failure called "decoherence" where the multiple solutions collapse into a single solution like a classic computer. To avoid decoherence, quantum computers must be kept isolated at temperatures as low as -300° F/-184° C.

It was those points my research had focused on. I wanted to design a computer that would intentionally interact with its environment in order to learn and adapt to its environment, yet be portable and not require temperatures that make the south pole look like a tropical resort.

I had known all along I was attempting the near-impossible. But once upon a time, human flight was thought to be impossible. Still, at times like this, the thought of Don Quixote and tilting at windmills came to mind.

"There's one other thing," Hannah said. She had been able to test snippets of the code on her classic computer for debugging purposes, as I had. The problem always seemed to come when I tried to run the entire program all at once in massive parallel. "I detected emergent behavior in the algorithm. Every time I ran a test, it would do something surprising. For instance, one time, I made a mistake in an input, and it had corrected it by the fourth iteration and had rewritten the code."

"Self-correcting." I nodded my approval. Maybe I wasn't tilting vainly.

"It was fascinating to watch it take over, but at the same time wicked spooky. Gave me goosebumps."

"It's just a machine. It'll do what it's told." I had written the program to follow an initial set of instructions, run multiple parallel approximate solutions for any problem, and narrow the probabilities. Probabilities are never zero. Therefore, a large number of solutions are always possible. Hannah had added intuition to the program. So, surprises shouldn't be surprising. All of that taken together, the program apparently had rewritten its own code based upon its findings and kept executing the instructions and writing new code until it was satisfied, almost as if it no longer needed a programmer. "There's no ghost in the machine. But, the biggest problem is I'm dead in the water, or my research must now turn to physical materials that can—" At that moment, the heavy metal doors at the end of the hall clattered and cold air rushed in ahead of Michael. His bass-baritone voice echoed when he called out my name from down the hall.

We shook hands, and Michael gave me an A-frame man hug with a couple of sharp swats on the left shoulder blade. I returned the swats followed by a firm grip on his trapezius muscle. I've never been real comfortable with guys hugging each other, although I understand it's now a social norm and a guy can seem out of touch if he refuses one. We turned to face Hannah, our arms now over each other's shoulders like a couple of drunken army buddies.

"Dr. Emory, this is Hannah Tuttle—"

"Michael," he said, breaking loose and stepping forward. When they shook hands, Michael held on longer than a normal handshake, and it seemed as if he couldn't take his eyes off of her. Michael was what I supposed you would call ruggedly handsome, although that was hard for me to judge. He was not quite as tall as I am, and I didn't think he had the athletic build I had, chiseled in my early years by youth baseball and kept fit by my exercise regimen. Still, he wasn't in *bad* shape. And, he had a square chin with one of those indentations in the middle that never gets shaved right. His hair was sandy brown, curly, and shaggy—as normal—and stuck out from under a black cowboy hat cocked low over his forehead. His nose had a small hump from being broken in a fight years ago, defending, he had said, the honor of his home state of Texas in some smoky, out-of-town wayside grill. I had always thought it was really a bar.

"Dr. Emory is in town for a visit," I told Hannah. "He's been doing some geological work out in the desert."

Hannah smiled pleasantly and pulled her hand back from his. "Nice to meet you, Dr. Emory."

"You look like you're ready to go out for a run," Michael said.

"Every night. Do you run?"

"Never away."

I thought I saw the corner of Hannah's mouth twitch a little, but she never let go of her smile. "Well, I've got to go. . . got to run," she said, her smile now broadening with apparent amusement at her own pun. Michael tipped his hat like a true gentleman. She turned and walked away briskly.

Michael watched her intently. In that tight black outfit, her buttocks flexed, her hips swung. She stopped at the door and put on the puffy, blue down-filled coat with two white stripes around the upper arms.

"Y'all got anything going on?" Michael's eyes were glued to Hannah until she had passed through the doors.

"Yeah. She tweaks my algorithms."

"She tweaks my algorithms, too."

"I don't think we mean the same thing." At that moment, a torrent of undeserved jealousy ran through me such as I had never before experienced. Hannah had made the boundaries very clear. Still, I had looked ahead to a time when she was no longer my assistant, when it might be more appropriate to explore the possibility of a personal relationship. "She's the dictionary definition of standoffish."

"I know the kind," Michael said and smiled while still watching her. "Adds to the mystique."

I turned and started to step into my office, something the science department had found a way to miniaturize, but Michael stopped me. "I've got a taxi waiting for me," he said. "I went by your house but you weren't there, so I came here to let you know I'm in town. I've got a couple of stops to make before calling it a night. So, I'll meet you at your place when I'm done, if that's okay?"

I walked with him to the waiting taxi. Michael offered to have the taxi drop me off at home, but I declined, because they were going a different direction and I preferred to walk, anyway. As I headed toward home, off to the right some distance away, I thought I saw Hannah silhouetted in the lamplight at the corner of the parking lot. She was standing still on the sidewalk by the curb, facing a large oak tree, not running in place as I had seen her do before while she was waiting to cross a street. Her head was bobbing, animated. I moved closer for a better look and confirmed from the stripes on her coat sleeves it was Hannah. She said something, but I was too far away to hear. I stepped closer. From the shadow of the tree a silhouetted figure stepped forward. It appeared to be a man wearing a dark colored business suit. Thinking she might be in trouble, I started to run towards her but stopped when I heard him say something in a raised pitch I couldn't understand and then my name. ". . . Hensley. . ." There was something else I couldn't hear, then clearly a demand, "What's his secret?"

"I told you, there *is* no secret. There's nothing. *Nothing*. Now go away and leave me alone," was

Hannah's reply. Then she took off at a full sprint in the direction of the dorm. They apparently hadn't heard or seen me because neither one looked my way. I slipped behind a tree and watched her leave, keeping an eye on the silhouette who also watched her until she turned a corner and ran out of sight.

I thought about confronting this nosey stranger, but their exchange rattled and puzzled me, it all seemed to be over, so I decided not to. The research I had been conducting was my own and not the university's, done on my own time—yes, of course, with university equipment and with Hannah's help for the last several months. But, I had kept my work quiet, and Hannah had been held to confidentiality. I trusted her. Who would know about my work? It wasn't hard to figure out who might want my algorithm and design. The answer was simple: a lot of people—if they knew about them.

It took the full walk home and the activity of the last minute hustling to get the house ready for Michael's visit before I was again calm and collected.

Later that night, sometime after eleven, I was in the greenhouse and heard a car pull into the driveway. Headlights swept across the side of my neighbor's house, then glared off the glass in the greenhouse. When I went up front to check it out, Michael was thumping the front door with his knee and almost fell into me when I opened the door. Under each arm was a twelve-bottle box of Blue Moon Belgian-style Wheat Ale.

"You know where the fridge is." I pointed over my shoulder with a thumb. Michael went past me, and

I stepped outside and went to the taxi that sat idling in the driveway.

The driver had the yellow trunk lid open and simply stood over Michael's bags, a Pullman and a roller carry-on, looking at them. In the corner of the driver's mouth was a freshly lit cigarette with a small glowing tip. This was probably one of the few times during his shift when he could sneak in a smoke, and he didn't seem eager to hurry it along, even though the meter was running. "I'll get those," I said and hoisted them onto the driveway. Michael had packed lightly. When I asked the driver what the fare was, he peeked in the window to check the meter and gave me the figure. I recoiled a little then handed him five twenties and a ten, almost all the money I had on me, and told him to keep the change, figuring I'd settle up with Michael later.

"Your friend is a hoot," the driver said, pocketing the money. "Talkative guy. Whew!" The cigarette pinched in his lips bounced up and down as he spoke.

"Always has been." Especially when he'd been drinking. But he could also be quiet as a Trappist monk when he was in a contemplative mood.

Back inside, Michael had put one box of Blue Moon in the refrigerator and left the other on the counter. When I came in, he had two bottles out and handed one to me. I exchanged it for a Frappuccino.

Unlike my friend, I didn't drink. Not at all. I was a teetotaler and had been since shortly after Michael and I became buddies. I was so young when I started college, I had earned my first PhD before I was even of drinking age. But as undergraduates, Michael had introduced me to bingeing—not that I regretted it, although I probably should have. Even so, it didn't take long for me to realize drinking was expensive, made me lose control—and I must have control, at least over my faculties—say stupid things, and made me sick the next day. It may not affect others that way, but that's the way it was for me.

Michael plopped on the couch that was set perpendicular to the unlit fireplace and framed a small conversation pit, stretched out his booted feet in front of him, and took a swig of beer. I took one of the two wingback chairs facing the couch, took off my shoes, and stretched out my sock feet. The furniture was old but comfortable and had been left to me with the house when my mother died.

"So, what have you been doing in the land of cholla and caliche?" I asked.

Michael held the bottle with his thumb and forefinger curled around the longneck in true cowboy form, took another swig and said, "I landed me a big deal this time, Simon. *Big* deal. Not like last time when I lost my shirt." I didn't know he had lost his shirt. I knew Michael had tried business ventures before and wondered where he'd gotten the seed money, but then thought it must have come from the same family oil money he'd always claimed to hold in contempt. "Joint venture with the U. S. Government. Lots of money, enough to get me out of debt and then some." Swig. "And the checks never bounce, although Uncle Sam is usually slow to pay."

I sensed a "but" coming. "The problem is. . .?"

"Red tape, regulations, compliance inspections, record retention, reports, bureaucrats, politicians. They *spy* on everything we do." He took a long pull, swallowed hard, and exhaled contentedly. "Plus, after those solar companies and the others that the government put money in went belly up, I really have to woo the congressional representatives who could pull the plug on our funding at any time. Kissing ass really isn't my thing." He swilled the last of the beer, raising the bottle straight up for the last few drops, and went to the refrigerator to retrieve another. "Need another one of those iced coffee things—crappuccino—while I'm in here?" he called out from the kitchen.

"Nah. I'm good."

Michael's passion always had been enhanced geothermal heat, which he was convinced could save the world from the effects of carbon emissions. Enhanced geothermal systems, he'd explained many times, tap into the trapped heat that comes from the natural, safe radioactive decay of granite deep in the earth's crust. Water circulates from the surface through the hot dry layers of granite far below and comes back to the surface as steam to run generators that produce as much electricity as nuclear, coal-, and oil-fired power plants. Whole cities and regions can be supplied with abundant clean electricity that way. The problem was with the drilling. "Five or six kilometers deep," Michael had once told me. "Twenty to thirty thousand feet. That's as deep as Mt. McKinley and Mt Everest are high."

Boring into the earth so deeply was expensive and time-consuming with conventional drilling rigs. That was where Michael's company came in. Instead of using drill bits, he used a jet burner pointed at the ground that blasted its way through solid rock. The process is actually old technology, he'd told me once, rather confused as to why it wasn't used more. It was called 'spallation' because it throws back bits and pieces of rubble called 'spall,' similar to pointing a garden hose with a pressure nozzle at the ground, making a hole, and getting splattered. Once they're built and operational, enhanced geothermal systems create cheap energy. Until then, they're expensive to drill.

That was where the deep pockets of the government came in, he told me before going to the kitchen. "We're out there night and day," Michael said after returning from the refrigerator, fresh bottle of beer in his hand, "punching hole after hole trying to find the fastest and most cost effective way to do it. We never run any pipe; we don't have any generators. We're just focused on the spallation part." Michael added his contract required a certain amount of secrecy for politically sensitive reasons and that was why he hadn't let me know his whereabouts before now.

"I like it out there, Simon." He seemed to switch gears a little.

"The desert you mean?"

"Yeah. Out there night doesn't fall. It drops. Like a thick, heavy black blanket coming down on you all at once. Sometimes when the rigs are shut down and the lights are off you can see all the stars. All of 'em. More'n you'd ever see here in the light polluted skies of the city." He leaned his head back and finished off another Blue Moon. "You know, there are over five thousand stars and celestial objects visible in the northern hemisphere to the naked eye." It sounded like *nekked ah* now. "A thousand visible at any one time as the earth turns. But I swear, Simon, it seems like a million out there." Michael set the empty bottle on the floor next to the couch. "And, I've seen 'em a lot. All those wonderful stars and nobody to share them with except a bunch of roughnecks, and sometimes not even them." The drawback of Michael's gregarious nature was it seemed he needed to have a lot of people around him. "And to think, to someone out there on one of those dots of light looking back at us, we're just another dot of light. I wonder if they know we're here." But, there was his contemplative side and the desert seemed well suited for it.

"Sometimes," Michael said, "I send the crew into the nearest town a couple of hours away for a few days' furlough, and I stay behind to do some of my personal work. If I have time, I go on into town and meet up with them. If I have time. Work comes first." His head started drooping, then it jerked up again. "It gets a little lonely out there." He stretched and looked around as if there were something to see.

"How do you back up your files out there? Do you have a network and a backup server?"

"It's the desert, and we're mobile. We can't get that fancy. Company files are uploaded through a satellite link to a backup site somewhere in the cloud. My personal stuff—there are ways to back up something other than on a server. Flash drives, CDs. It's hard to hack into a flash drive in my pocket or a CD in my suitcase. Or, how about this: even old fashioned paper backup."

"Paper? Such heresy! And I thought you were a friend of the environment." My mock surprise was lost on him. His eyes were almost shut.

Michael's head drooped a little, then perked up. "That assistant of yours?"

"Hannah."

"Is she attached?"

"You mean, is she seeing anyone? Not that I know of."

"Would it be a problem. . . I mean. . . if while I'm here. . . Would it be a problem if I asked her out for a nice steak dinner?"

I was caught off-guard, but I had no claim. "That's up to her."

"I don't want to cause any problems with her being your assistant and all and you being her teacher. But, if it's okay, and if I have time. . . I might. . . I might see. . . " His head drooped again, and his breathing became steady.

I went to my bedroom and pulled a blanket out of the cedar chest at the foot of the bed and draped the blanket over Michael. Then I took the empty bottles to the trash and went to bed.

In the morning, the blanket was folded neatly on the couch. Upstairs, the bathroom smelled of a men's scented soap or deodorant. Towels were neatly hung on the rack. A clean cereal bowl was in the drainer by the sink in the kitchen. The refrigerator had been restocked with twelve bottles of Blue Moon. Empty beer bottles and other trash had been taken out to the cart beside the greenhouse door. But, Michael was nowhere to be found.

Chapter Thirteen

MY VISITS WITH MARGARET are shorter these days and unstructured. If I want to talk to her, I drop in, if she's there. This morning, I wind through the hallways to her office, no longer needing to follow the narrow red line painted on the floor, to tell her what I remembered about my machine and Hannah and Michael and all.

"So, do I get to go home now?" I ask.

"I think you will benefit from staying with us a while longer, Simon."

"My memory's getting better."

"It's a gradual process." She looks down at her tablet for a moment. "Have you heard from your friends Michael and Hannah?"

When she says their names, a pang hits me in the stomach, a feeling I can't explain. Adrenalin, maybe; dread; fear. "They don't know where I am. And, my cell phone was in my pocket when I fell into the ocean. I need to go home so that I can contact them. Besides, what does that have to do — "

"Simon, you're progressing very well. Continue, and you can go home soon."

That's that. She's not going to release me, so I give her a quiet nod as I lift myself off the couch, then leave and go to my safe place, the thicket.

I've been coming to the thicket sometimes as often as two or three times a day to sit on the bench and look across the gorge. No offense to Margaret, but I find more therapy here than I think would be possible anywhere else on earth, even on the legendary couch of Sigmund Freud himself.

The gentle slope of the clearing is at such an angle that by sitting on the back of the bench with my feet on the seat, I can see over the fence, unobstructed. Below is the Glaser river, which now seems to be a microcosm of life in that its placid flow is inevitably and periodically disrupted by boulders jutting out and churning the waters into manic fits. I know the river is down there, and on a still day can hear it, but even from this vantage point, I can't see it. Across the gorge stand the tree-topped granite cliffs I love to stare at. An old mining road, seldom travelled any more, cuts a swath through the trees. I can't see it either, but I know it's there.

Sometimes when something is on my mind besides quantum bits and stuff like that, I pass time by jotting down a few thoughts here and there in meager words, such as I can employ. Today, I give up straining my eyes trying to detect signs of the old mining road I used to drive up, open the notebook I brought with me, and scratch out a few lines for no one else to read but me:

SEEING THROUGH A GLASS
Just past my windshield lies an open road.
Come, go a ways with me; we won't go far.
We'll go somewhere and lighten up our load.
What joy to know exactly where we are.

The Iron Couch

******

After a long while of patient silence, the sun starts to set; the thicket darkens; the spring air cools down and infuses me with a slight chill. I stand to return to my room and happen by chance to look down. There, in untrimmed grass lying next to the leg of the bench, is a pencil. I pick it up. It's the eraserless kind, not the thick beginner's type or the stubby type often found on the back of a church pew, but a full length pencil that looks new. One end has been sharpened and shows wear; the other end is elegantly capped with a shiny painted metal tip. Something about it seems vaguely familiar, but I can't figure out what. I look around for other telltale signs of intrusion upon my special place of solitude, then put the pencil in my pocket and head back to my room. There, I lie down and stare at the ceiling. Unaided, memories come cascading.

Chapter Fourteen

MICHAEL HADN'T BEEN AROUND the house while I was home since the night of his arrival, although there were signs he had come and gone: the now familiar scent of his brand of soap in the upstairs bathroom, clean dishes in the kitchen, plenty of beer in the refrigerator. I wondered if he had been spending his time with Hannah. Lately, I had caught only glimpses of her on campus. In truth, since Hannah's work was complete I had few reasons to run into her. Even so, the thought that she might be avoiding me upset me, so I put it out of my mind.

It was February and a blast of arctic air had set in dropping temperatures to the low teens with overnight lows in single digits. On the fourth day of Michael's stay, he finally showed up in the afternoon.

"You still got baseball gloves, Simon?"

"Yeah, in my closet."

"Go get 'em and let's play some catch."

"Are you nuts? Haven't you noticed it's cold outside?" But, after enough goading and questions about my manly endurance, I gave in, thinking now *I* must be nuts. We went to the back yard, which was narrow and deep, and I stood under the half-naked oak tree throwing back toward the house so that any stray balls colliding with the greenhouse would be on me and not on Michael. Altruism aside, I also thought I was the better aim.

Cold or not, I must admit it felt great to wind up and let loose a good, solid pitch. I recalled how we used to play burnout between classes, so I loosened up my arm and put a little pepper on the ball. The smacking sound when the ball hit Michael's leather was music to my ears. I felt pent up frustration being released, frustration about the machine's failures, about Hannah. Michael returned some fireballs of his own, right on target. I had taught him well. I thought about Hannah and how Michael had flirted with her. I threw harder, and the ball popped loudly in Michael's mitt. He shot back harder. On it went, salvo after salvo. The more I thought about him and Hannah being together, the harder I threw.

Then, Michael turned to the side and paused for a second or two. He wound up, corkscrewed his torso, raised his leading leg, and drew his pitching arm back like a catapult. I felt retribution for my fastballs was coming. Without the thick pad of a catcher's glove, this was going to hurt if the ball didn't land perfectly in the pocket. But, I stood my ground, eyes focused on the ball. His form was perfect; he let loose, seemingly with everything he had.

The ball hit my mitt like a paper wad. I looked around on the ground thinking it must have been deflected. Michael stood grinning at me with his gloved hand resting on his hip. I looked in my glove. There lay a translucent globe smaller than a ping pong ball.

"What's this?" I asked.

"Let's go inside and I'll tell you all about it. It's cold out here. Who's idea was it to play catch on a day like this anyway?"

When we were inside and warm, I repeated, "What is this?" I held it up between my thumb and forefinger.

"The short answer is it's a xenocryst."

"What's the long answer?"

"It's a crystal that was already perfectly formed when it came into contact with molten rock that hardened around it. An example would be a diamond found in volcanic lava. This one was embedded in granite as it cooled and hardened millions and millions of years ago. From some known factors, such as the depth in the earth's crust where it was located, its apparent state when it was deposited, and approximations of travelling through space, I calculated that this little gem is exactly. . . a lot older than Earth and had to have been ejected fully formed from some long lost star system and travelled a real long time to get here."

"If it came from an ancient star, wouldn't you then expect it to be a heavy metal like gold or silver, or something?"

"You'd think. But, I said 'star system,' not star. What if it came from a planet that got caught up in some massive star's supernova and got swept clear out into deep space along with the other debris?" He looked at me as if for approval or acceptance. All I could do was shrug my shoulders. "Anyway, that's my theory. I'm a geologist and not an astronomer, and I've never known of anything like it. This crystal is virtually indestructible, so I couldn't do any carbon 14 tests on it to date it more accurately. Look here. It's hard as the hub of Hell." He threw it against the hardwood floor with what seemed to be as much force as he could muster. It hardly bounced, not as you might expect of something so lightweight. And it left no mark on the floor. "Harder than diamond," he said after picking it up and examining it for scars. "See. Perfectly unblemished."

I took it and inspected it closely. He was right. "Where'd you get it?"

"In the spall pile, out in the land of cholla and caliche, as you put it. It got blasted loose. Stuck out like a fly in a bowl of Cheerios. And when I checked it out under a microscope, I saw its internal structure was made of lattice. You almost never see crystal lattices that form spheres. I've never seen or heard of anything like it, so I've been studying it. That's where I've been the last three days." I felt relieved he hadn't been with Hannah and foolish at the same time for being jealous when I had no right to begin with. "A buddy of mine from grad school works in one of the most sophisticated geology labs this side of the continental divide. He let me do all kinds of tests on this thing." Michael paused, rubbing his chin. "And, it's low mass. That's why I had to wind up as if I was going to bowl you over just to get it to you." He laughed, and that made me smile. "Thirsty, Simon? I'll get you a crappuccino from the fridge."

"Sounds good," I told him.

When he returned and sat down again, Michael leaned forward with his fingers curled around a Blue Moon, supporting his forearms on his thighs. He hesitated a moment and looked straight at me. "Simon, we've known each other a long time, and I've got to know I can trust you not to say a thing about this to anybody. *Anybody.*" Michael had known me long enough and well enough to know staring directly at my eyes was a strong move. I knew he meant it. "Not until I tell you it's okay."

"What's so confidential about a rock?"

Michael's gaze left my face and locked onto the crystal I was by then nervously rolling in my hand. "I've run some x-ray spectroscopy, checked it under a tunneling electron microscope and did a bunch of other tests. This is a completely unknown crystalline structure. There isn't anything like it cataloged anywhere." He looked again straight into my eyes. "I've discovered something brand new."

"You sure of that?"

He was so sure he was already calling the new mineral "Emorite" after himself. He went on to say, "And, this crystal is absolutely, flawlessly pure." He pulled out some images he had taken with an electron microscope. The lattice-type structure was omnidirectional. "It has two configurations according to the math I did. One is inherently unstable, the other inherently stable—"

"So, it's in two states at the same time?"

"Now we're getting to the good part."

Michael explained that inside this material electrons bonded naturally into the kind of pairs needed to become a superconductor, just the material I needed for my computer design. The last step. The finishing touch. The world's first room temperature superconductor was in my hand. My fingers quivered. He said the crystal seemed to always be absorbing and reflecting minute levels of energy from its environment, and that was why it was warm to the touch.

"Are there more of these?" There had to be more, even if only a few. As good a friend as Michael was, he wouldn't give me his only sample.

Instead of answering me, Michael looked at the time on his cell phone and said the Emorite was mine to keep and that made us partners, and we could do legal paperwork someday if "the thing" worked. He leaned in and reiterated, "I need you to keep this confidential. The potential is huge. Beyond imagination."

We clinked our bottles, raising a toast to his discovery, our hopes for what it might mean for my research, and something else: our plans to save the world had just begun.

Chapter Fifteen

THE TIME CAME for Michael to go back to the job site, and after I returned from dropping him off at the airport on Saturday night, I began to wonder whether or not I should even be in possession of an unknown mineral that came from government property and could technically be stolen, although Michael had explained the xenocryst was refuse. His contract with the government gave him the duty to dispose of refuse responsibly and was silent about mineral rights. His interpretation: the xenocryst was his to keep.

My worries, nonetheless, didn't stop me from running to the greenhouse to do some tests of my own. My home lab was basic but sufficient for many purposes. At the end of the work bench where I still had the old microscopes and stereoscopes my dad had used in his biology research stood a small Faraday-shielded booth, which was in reality an inexpensive metal wardrobe I had modified to protect the equipment in case my house was struck by lightning. Inside it I kept oscilloscopes, their distant cousins signal analyzers, various antenna analyzers, and other meters.

After hours of testing, no equipment I had even came close to being able to analyze the xenocryst. I grabbed my coat, started up my Jeep, and made way to

Finial's lab, which was imminently better supplied than mine.

I worked through the night testing the Emorite, subjecting it to every scope Finial had and every test I could think of, including some I invented. One test of particular interest showed the crystal was emitting duplex signals at very low energy levels. It appeared to be transmitting and receiving simultaneously. If there were ever a Nobel Prize awarded for geology, Michael should be its first recipient.

A couple of texts to Hannah at about seven o'clock in the morning, and she agreed to substitute teach my classes for the day. She said it would cost me. I offered a steak dinner in payment, but got no reply. I raced home.

In the greenhouse, I fashioned a cradle for the xenocryst out of spare circuit boards, exchanging and soldering microchips here and there. The hard part was making a concave seat for the xenocryst to be mounted with tungsten wires contacting the edges of the superconducting layers. The resulting cradle was smaller than a deck of cards. It had a nylon strap stretched over the top of the xenocryst, firmly holding it in place, and a USB plug connecting it to the laptop. In appearance I had a prototype.

Chapter Sixteen

IT HAS BEEN A FEW DAYS NOW since my last memories came back. I've been hanging around Liberty, not doing much, and haven't been back to the iron bench. After finding the pencil the last time I was there, I've been hesitant to go back. Nevertheless, today I relent, seeing little harm in someone else having discovered that little glade, too, and not wanting to lose such a special place.

After a mediocre lunch of a rubbery hamburger on a dry bun with lettuce, mustard, and ketchup, potato chips that left my fingers greasy, and a cup of plain applesauce for dessert, I leave as quickly as I can for the thicket. No one ever seems to notice where I go; no one follows; no one asks. That suits me fine.

Here, curiosity gets the better of me, and I explore for other entrances to the clearing where the pencil's owner may have entered. In the dappled shade, upon close examination, I see signs the native grasses and weeds have been disturbed some time recently. Their natural pattern has been mashed flat in places and in other places bent against the grain, both with a stride shorter than mine.

I follow the trail into another thicket that leads away from Liberty, marking my path by piling pinecones, pine needles, or fallen twigs, to where the trail ends between some aspens at the back of a large lot. The total distance I've traveled from the bench is about the length of a football field, I guess. Just ahead lies a huge white outbuilding or barn.

Once again, curiosity gets the better of me, for I am not normally one to trespass or to snoop. But, finding the temptation irresistible, I go to the barn and walk around it looking in windows that have chunks of putty falling off of window panes fouled by birds. Inside is an old Airstream travel trailer with flat tires, its chrome exterior reflecting sunlight from over my shoulder back into my face.

From another window, I see crates and boxes large enough for a person to crawl into, covered first by tarps then by a thick layer of dust. A side door is unlocked, so I go in and all the way to the back. The dust on the floor is so thick it's almost as if the barn has a dirt floor. Footprints from my Chucks leave a trail.

The objects that drew me to the back are three flat-tired trailers, partly covered with a canvas tarp that doesn't completely cover the rusty iron bars underneath. The trailers look like animal cages, each large enough to hold a big cat, like a lion or tiger. Next to the cages sits a sprawling wooden construction. I peel back the heavy tarp and find a concession stand with the word, "Popcorn" painted on the side in faded red letters.

Not far away is an object whose shape is recognizable. I have to turn sideways and squeeze between crates to get over to it and confirm my guess it's an electric organ. Compulsively, I set my fingers on the keyboard. To my surprise, the thing is plugged in and blares out. I nearly jump out of my shoes, but then I settle down and impulsively play all I can remember of Bach's *Toccata and Fugue in D minor*, the first three measures. As a kid, I could play the whole piece. I quickly decide to leave before I'm caught.

The following day, I go back to the clearing, unsure of whom or what I will find there. I am not one who likes to meet new people very often and have always felt awkward being introduced to someone. During introductions, the polite thing to do is to look people in the eyes; and that's not something I like to do. It's an Asperger's thing. I don't mean any discourtesy to strangers or acquaintances, and I don't know how others feel; but as for me, looking directly at someone seems to invite too much attention to myself. And if the other person looks in my eyes, I feel as though they are seeing me naked.

Usually when I go to the clearing, I take a book or an e-reader from Liberty's skimpy library to while away my time on the iron bench. Today, I brought neither; I simply want to sit here and think, or perhaps zone out.

After a while, there's a slight rustle behind me, then footfalls quietly pad their way closer, slowly, hesitantly. I feel someone staring at the back of my head. I turn sideways to see. There a young woman, about my age, stands quietly a few yards away. We regard each other in utter silence. For a moment, she looks at me with an expectant look as though she knows me and I should know her. But, I've never seen her before.

Her hair is dark, almost touches her shoulders, and is swept back by a pair of glasses perched on top of her head, while at the same time she is wearing sunglasses. Her long-sleeve Henley shirt is untucked and unbuttoned partway, exposing a v-shape of fair skin just below her throat. When she reaches up with both hands to switch the sunglasses for the clear ones, her shirt rides up above her blue jeans, revealing a tight navel and flab-free midriff. Thick hair falls down around her face.

Eventually she says, "Hello," then brushes her hair behind her ears with her fingertips.

"Oh, hi," I say, a bit clumsily, befuddled about why I'm so strangely and immediately attracted to her.

"I hope I'm not disturbing anything." She slides the fingertips of her right hand into her pocket while she clasps the shoulder strap of her bag with the left hand.

"No. I'm just enjoying the view."

"It's a great place to think." She steps forward to the bench, sets the bag down, and pulls out a notebook. "Or write."

I pivot and hop off the bench.

"Do you have some place you have to go?" she asks.

"No . . . I . . . don't want to intrude." I don't want to leave, either.

"We can share the view. It's big enough." Her tone is soft, yet it says the issue is settled. "And so is the bench." She points toward it and sits down. I follow her lead. "My name's Andrea Siannas."

"Simon . . . Hensley."

"How do you do, Simon Hensley?" She smiles sweetly and holds out her hand.

Her grip is firm, yet light. Her hand is soft and warm, and I don't want to let go. Her nails are decorated with appliques. I turn her hand upward and use the designs as an excuse to hold her hand a bit longer, her palm in mine, no longer gripping, just lightly touching. "Those are pretty designs. Do they mean anything?" She doesn't pull back. I look up at her.

"Just geometric figures. Like the ones I see when I close my eyes at night before I go to sleep." She moves a little and the notebook on her lap falls to the ground, spilling an eraserless pencil into the grass at her feet. She waits a moment before bending to pick it and the notebook up.

"You don't see pencils without erasers very often," I say.

"It's a trick I play on myself. If I can't erase, it forces me to write better."

"What are you writing?" Then I thought for a moment my asking might be intruding, so I added, "If I may ask, that is."

"It's the memoirs of a girl growing up traveling with carnies—the people who work in carnivals. The carnival is owned by her parents. . . my parents. It's about the places she goes, the things she does, people she meets. Nothing anybody else will be interested in. It's just something I want to do."

I'm intrigued and talk her into telling me about her story. As she does, I feel my spirit lighten, freshen, as if a bottle inside me that has held something stale is uncorked and the staleness seeps out, replaced by wisps of clean air.

Andrea Siannas, I learn, owns a defunct carnival she inherited from her parents. Both are gone now. She grew up travelling the back roads of America, home schooled by her mother, while they worked state and county fairs, roadside circuses, and any place they could get a permit from Mexico into Canada, from the Atlantic to the Pacific, and even across the Atlantic. Their traveling show took entertainment to the folks who lived in small towns and backwater places too small and too far away from large cities to attract the big name circuses. Her father drove the truck that hauled the Airstream they called home before they bought the big house that sits to the northeast of Liberty. Her mother drove a box truck that carried her organ, some magic equipment, and other items. Along with three other trucks and an eighteen wheeler packed to its roof with bleachers, folding chairs, big top canvas tent, they caravanned down Interstate highways, state highways, and county roads taking with them animals and cages, concession stands, and everything they needed to put on a small time show.

Everyone had multiple duties. Their eighteen-wheeler was driven by the husband and wife team of trapeze artists. Clowns were jugglers and cooks.

Andrea, like me, was an only child, and together with her parents, they had also spent three years touring Europe where she became fluent in French and Italian. She can name and describe over one hundred twenty varieties of French cheese.

Her father, always dressed in a neatly pressed tuxedo and top hat, was the ringmaster, emcee, animal trainer, stage magician, or whatever role he needed to play. Her mother, Alexis, played the organ, loudly and with frequent, strategically placed arpeggios for theatrical effects, such as when Andrea's father would get a lion to jump through a burning hoop.

Her mother was also the magician's beautiful assistant, overdone with makeup, bright red cheeks, dark eye shadow, heavy eyeliner to highlight her features for the crowd to see, dressed in a tight, low-cut red leotard with short silvery fringe along the collar, and with long legs dipped in fishnet hose, also for the crowd to see. As the magician's assistant, she was often cut in half, levitated, made to disappear, or shape-shifted.

Shape shifting was Andrea's first job. She was too young to remember much, but her parents had always told her she had been a quiet baby and hadn't uttered a single word before the age of three. She had seldom even cried. Her enterprising father had found a way to put Andrea's quiet demeanor to good use. He designed and built a box about the size of a small coat closet and painted it flat black. Alexis would step inside and the door would be closed behind her. After a magical incantation, the door was opened and — voila — there was tiny Andrea dressed the same as her mother, sitting quietly on a stool. Of course, then a few more magical words were spoken to restore the adult Alexis, while Andrea was whisked off stage and left in the care of a carnival worker until the show was over.

When she eventually began to talk, Andrea was talkative, like a little professor. Again, her enterprising father found a good way to put her eloquence to use. But, she tells me, finding out what that was will have to wait.

We have stayed here side by side on the bench until the sun's last glimmer has left the granite cliffs and threatens to leave us alone in the dark woods. The air stills. Crickets chirp. In the distance, cicadas pipe their calls.

I have never known anybody as easy to talk to as Andrea, so warm, so calming. I feel as a wanderer must feel when he's been away so long he has forgotten home but has finally found the place where he belongs. I don't want to leave. But, eventually I have to. Margaret put very few rules on me, and one of them was to be back each day before sunset so that no one would have to go out looking for me in the dark. There is no choice.

On the way back to my room, my feet feel lighter — literally, physically lighter. I pick up the pace. I need to hurry. The sun is already down. I go faster, then a little faster. I take off running. I haven't run in months and breathing is labored. I feel a rush of energy, excitement. I keep on running, not wanting to stop, past the back door of Liberty to the far hedge row, turn right and go a hundred feet or so and turn right again along the fence line that skirts the gorge all the way to the thicket, then along the thicket, then to the back corner of the building and around again. My head feels clearer than it has in ages. I don't know if that's from the rush of oxygen to my lungs or the rush of blood to my head. Or the feeling I got from Andrea. I keep running, running, around the back lot, probably two, maybe three miles in total until I come again to the back steps and plop on them, huffing, soaking up the warmth stored in the concrete. I look up at the trees silhouetted against stars already lit up. I'm late. What the hell.

I've got to get out of here.

Inside, I avoid contact with anyone else, and nobody says anything to me about being late. There is still activity in the commons as I rush by. Some people are playing cards or putting together puzzles. Some are reading. The TV group, two women and a man, who always hog the television argue over what to watch. A singing talent show? A cooking contest? Or Alaskan families in the wild? I go straight to my room, turn off the lights, lie on my bed, and begin the descent down the long dark stairwell Margaret has taken me down before. I count ten steps, then ten more. I relax, lose my sense of location. There it is. Ahead of me. The same door. The one that has so far opened into nothing. And I try to open it.

The following morning, I wake up still in my clothes, still on my bed. It's early, dark. Before breakfast, I put my sneakers back on, change into a T-shirt, and head out the back door as quietly as I can. At the bottom of the concrete steps, I bend forward, gently at first then sharply to stretch my hamstrings and then my Achilles tendons, using the steps to elevate each foot before setting out to run around the perimeter. My leg muscles reach and pull, propelling me forward, waking my body up, sharpening my senses to the cool morning air, the carefree calls of birds, the feeling of openness. I run a few laps, then stop at the back fence, look down at the rock ledge as light begins to creep into the gorge below. Chipmunks scurry away with nuts, chattering as a family would talk over the breakfast table. Then I set out running again. With every step comes a glimpse of a memory until one is in full view.

I remember how Hannah used to run. There was a graceful athletic spring in her step—not a labored plodding, pushing off of each foot like many runners often seen on the street. She fairly glided effortlessly for miles. One day while I was running, I ran into her at the corner of Elm and Fulton. She was running in place, waiting for a light to turn green, and also looking as if her lower half had been dipped in Spandex. We exchanged greetings, and I ran with her the rest of her course. There didn't seem to be any breach of our covenant of professionalism, therefore a time or two more I coincidentally ran into her at the same corner. She never said I could run with her, never said I couldn't. But, the silent runs were awkward, and I soon stopped going there.

Chapter Seventeen

IT'S TWO-THIRTY A.M., dark, quiet. I'm looking out my window at the yellow-gray sky. I remember more.

On the black slate countertop in my greenhouse lab, the untested prototype sat before me, the Emorite crystal snapped solidly in place. There was nothing left to do but to install the program, give it problems to solve, and see if it would work. Despite my desperation to know what the xenocryst could do, if anything, I hesitated, reluctant to face another failure. I put off testing it for another day and carefully packed the machine into a book bag, took it to my room, and went to bed.

From that time on, I determined to keep the prototype with me at all times to keep it secure and to keep it handy.

Late on the Saturday night after Michael had left, I was grading student papers in my office next to the computer lab with copious amounts of caffeine doing little to overcome my torpor. The prototype lay inside its pack on the floor at my feet. After reading the umpteenth paper, I stood to stretch my legs and twist my torso, coaxing out a few pops, then sat down again and picked up another paper, tried to read it through bleary eyes and found myself tapping a pencil on the side of my Frappuccino bottle. Unable to concentrate, I kept glancing at the backpack, and finally put the paper down. I pulled the unit out, set it on the desk in front of me, and simply stared at it for a while.

Eventually, I pulled a flash drive containing the program from my pocket and inserted it into a USB port. My fingers tapped away at the keyboard, but at the last second, I recalled the New Year's Day fiasco. As a precaution, I moved into the computer lab where there was a fire extinguisher which I removed from its mounting on the wall next to the door and placed it on the tabletop next to me.

I turned on a single lamp over the workbench so as not to attract too much attention if anybody else were on campus. My finger hovered over the keyboard, hesitant to make the final keystroke before executing the program. Then, I did it.

Nothing. Goose egg. No program. No sparks. No smoke. The screen went black.

Dismayed but less than surprised, I sat back in my chair trying to count the number of failures to add this one to. Before I was up to New Year's Day, the screen flickered and flashed the message, *Formatting hard disk drive. Wait . . .*

"What!?" I shot to my feet and bent over the unit in a stare down with the screen. "You can't do that. I didn't write that into the program." Maybe Hannah had. But why would she? Formatting wipes out everything on the disk: the operating system and all data, possibly including the algorithm I had just installed. A burst of fear hit me. The flash drive might be wiped clean, too, so I jerked it out of the USB port. It was hot, and so was the laptop. Puzzled, all I could do was watch and wait. After several minutes, the screen flashed the message, *Formatting complete*, and went black.

I reread the notes in my office, jotted down some things, and scribbled through several equations until the muscles around my eyes felt as if they were going into spasms. When I finally shoved my notes into a pile at the back of the desk, it was after two a.m. The unit had cooled down. I put it in the backpack and left it for dead on the floor in my office. With this added to the list of failures, big and small, I lost count.

For the next several days, I went about my business as usual, trying to keep the machine and the string of failures off my mind. I didn't see Hannah all week, and if I had, there would have been little to talk about. And, to keep my promise to Michael, I couldn't say anything about the xenocryst. Thinking about the machine gave me a sick feeling in the pit of my stomach and the thought perhaps I would have to give up in defeat.

But, that wasn't like me.

Each day after work, I retreated to my greenhouse lab, read and reread my notes and lines of code, carefully drew out the diagrams over and over, reworked formulas night after night until I got downright angry—at myself, at the machine, at the thought of being defeated. "No!" I pounded my fist on the workbench. "I will not quit! Even if it kills me!" No one heard me, but it felt good to yell it anyway.

The following Saturday night about nine o'clock, I grabbed a coat, shoved my hands into my pockets, and walked from my home lab back to my office, where I had earlier abandoned the machine, to take it home to work on it. When I went by the stone pillars at the entrance on School Street, I spotted a number of cars parked under a lamppost in the visitor section. Until the last year or so, it had been highly unusual for visitors to be on campus so late; but recently I had been seeing them on Friday and Saturday nights. Otherwise, the campus was vacant and the buildings were darkened.

Warm air soothed my face from the chilly walk as I stepped into the science building. The jingling of keys echoed in the dimly lit hallway when I unlocked my office. Undisturbed on the floor lay the black backpack, invisible until the lights were turned on. I pulled the unit out and to my astonishment, the screen was on and a glowing green cursor blinked in the upper left hand corner. I supposed the unit must have been on the whole time, even though I distinctly remembered shutting down the power button. Encouraged it had not blown up or started a fire, I began to type some commands, expecting to get a log of the computer's activities over the last week.

After I had typed the first two letters, the keyboard froze. Then the screen said, *Intrusion blocked*. I slapped my hand on the desk at the thought of being blocked out of my own creation. *Access denied*.

I could tell by the blinking cursor and the faint purplish glow at the center of the translucent crystal that background operations were being performed. While I watched, streams of characters scrolled up the screen too fast to read. If I was right about the machine's architecture and capabilities, it could be running through several hundred parallel iterations per second, each one building on the previous one to arrive at an accurate solution to whatever problem it was solving.

I put the crystal under a polarizing trinocular transmission microscope and zoomed in close to peer deeply into the crystal while it was doing whatever it was doing. The purple glow turned out to actually be two opposing spirals, a blue one that appeared to spiral inward toward the center and a red one that appeared to spiral outward from the center. They superimposed and from a short distance appeared as a single purple helix.

But something else happened, too. As I moved to one side of the unit, the xenocryst grew brighter. When I moved to the other side, it dimmed. I repeated the motion several times and concluded the crystal must have been picking up a signal that my body interfered with when I got in the way.

I picked up the unit, aimed it in the direction of the signal, stepped outside my office door, and proceeded down the dark hallway. At the end of the hall just before a right turn into an intersecting hall was an alcove with vending machines. The multi-colored lights and the whirring refrigerator motors from the soda machine were the only signs of activity.

The unique factor Hannah and I had programmed into this machine was, I hoped, the ability for it to interact with and learn from its environment without needing to be isolated, thus making it portable and useful everywhere. I feared as I walked toward the snack machines that the unit's birth of brilliance would be to learn the list of snack items and beverages or how to make change.

My fear was allayed when I walked past the alcove without incident. The signal grew stronger, and I picked up my pace until many steps later I was at the door of a meeting room at the far end of the science building. By then, the purple spiral inside the crystal was flickering wildly. I quietly set the unit on a table in the hall and opened the door just enough to slip in. The meeting room was dimly lit, like a theater, and large enough to seat several hundred people. A dozen or so dots of candle light were scattered around. My eyes took several minutes to adjust to the dim grayscale. Patchouli incense had been pulled toward the door when I opened it, and I peered through the vapors. The whining timbre of pan flutes accompanied by wind chimes and slow arpeggios from acoustic guitar played through the overhead speakers followed later by the hollow sounds of Gregorian Chant. The bizarre atmosphere immediately struck me. I had stepped into a foreign land, a place I didn't belong, a place I didn't want to stay. But, I didn't leave.

    I took a seat by the door and watched while I got my bearings in this strange world. Dispersed around the room were a couple of dozen people broken up into groups of five or six seated either in semi-circles of upholstered arm chairs or at round tables. A good bit of distance separated each cluster from another.

    Across the room, I made out the silhouette of Dr. Geoff Gibson, the head of Finial's psychology department, a man I had known for most of my life and who at crucial times had been an important friend. I didn't think he saw me. Geoff was about the age my father would have been. It was well known around Finial that Geoff had been a Catholic priest in London at one time, but was no longer an observant Catholic. Many faculty speculated Geoff had been defrocked for improper behavior. Some conjectured he'd had an affair with a woman parishioner, or perhaps more than one. But because he was unmarried and never talked of being in any relationship, some speculated he may have been gay.

While I peered across the meeting room, I recalled that it was hard to tell what was truly on Geoff's mind, and this event was simply another example.

I couldn't hear what people around the room were saying, but I saw some of them had their eyes closed; others' eyes were wide open; some eyes were glassy as though they were filled with tears. A few people smiled; a few laughed.

If this were some kind of group therapy Geoff was conducting, then I was violating professional confidentiality by being there. But I knew Geoff was a teacher and a researcher and didn't believe he had private patients, so I stayed longer.

With my eyes fully adapted to the darkness, I ventured further into the room as stealthily as I could, a voyeur who didn't want to participate or be detected, and found a seat in a dark corner.

The room wasn't loud with the clamor you might expect from a gathering of people this large, not like a party. But, the tones weren't hushed either. People seemed to pay close attention when others talked.

At a table nearby, a woman who looked like the center of attention talked to a man whose eyes never left her. I presumed she was the host of the group. He nodded in apparent agreement with her and gave short replies I couldn't hear.

After about half an hour, Geoff stood and announced it was time for a short break. Groups broke up and people began to mingle. Some made a beeline for the restrooms, some headed for the snack bar. The lights came up a little, the room filled with talking and laughter. The atmosphere, now party-like, mercifully drowned out the music. A small group, including the woman I had seen talking to the man nearby, seemed to spontaneously huddle around Geoff. I stayed in the shadows as best as I could.

After about fifteen minutes, everybody began shuffling around, reforming into different groups. I took advantage of the commotion to duck out, hoping to remain unnoticed. But when I stood to leave, the woman host caught my eye. We made eye contact for a fleeting moment, but neither of us said anything. I nodded politely and slipped out the door as quietly as I'd slipped in, picking up the machine from the table where I'd left it.

Oddly, when I got back to my office, I set the unit on the desk and shut it down, but the crystal continued to shine bright purple for a long time — fifteen minutes, maybe thirty, before it began to flicker a little. I sat staring into the machine's eye, wondering what it was doing and watched it slowly fade to a glimmer.

Chapter Eighteen

THE FOLLOWING MONDAY AFTERNOON, an unexpected visitor arrived at my office door in the science building. It was Geoff Gibson. Though Geoff's office and mine were in the same building, we didn't ordinarily see a lot of each other anymore, mostly because of differing schedules, which seem to be the modern hindrance of close relationships. Geoff stepped all the way into my office and sat down on the visitor's chair. After delivering a preamble that he was calling on me because we hadn't had a chance to sit down and talk, really talk, in a while and what a fine man I had grown up to be, how proud my dad would be, he got around to asking the question I supposed was really on his mind.

"So, what did you think?" he said.

Geoff was a friend, but not the same kind of friend as Michael. Michael and I were the kind of friends with whom we could share our dreams, aspirations, plans for the future. Geoff was a friend-of-the-family. After my father died, Geoff had looked in on me a few times while my mother and I were still grieving, took me to some baseball games, and even got me on the baseball team where I learned to pitch. I had always regretted my dad never got to watch me play. I had even used Geoff as a reference when I applied for my teaching job at Finial.

"About what?" I asked.

I couldn't remember many times when Geoff and I had "really talked" except a few years ago when he'd confided in me the real reason he had left the priesthood was he could no longer support as divine or supernatural many things he took to be nothing more than natural. He could no longer serve the sacrament in good conscience because his opinions, his core beliefs no longer permitted him to. He'd told me he was aware of what others said about him behind his back, and it didn't matter. I took that conversation then — although it was a one-off — as a rite of passage, as Geoff accepting me fully into adulthood with a man-to-man talk and not just asking how my pitching arm was or how things were going in school.

"I saw you Saturday night in the meeting room," he said.

I had just taken a sip from a fresh, cold bottle of Frappuccino. I put the lid back on the bottle and set it down. I turned to look at him, paused, then asked him, "What was going on?"

"What it looked like. Séances."

I leaned back in my chair.

"It's my research," he said.

"Séances?"

"Paranormal phenomena. I've been studying them on the sly for a long time. Since before you were born."

Now I had to wonder if paranormal events were the sorts of things he thought of as perfectly natural, the reasons for which he had left the priesthood. He claimed he didn't care what others thought about him, yet he had kept his paranormal research quiet. As for me, I had always thought paranormal occurrences were nothing more than mere coincidence, hoax, or worse yet, outright fraud.

I reached for my cold drink and slowly twisted off the lid and took another sip.

"Tell me what you saw at the meeting, Simon."

I reached for a pencil and traced the letters in the condensation on the label of the cold bottle with the eraser. I suspected this was another one-off man-to-man. "I saw tricksters taking advantage of the gullible. Maybe some were even vulnerable and desperate."

"That's what I thought you would say. It was real, all real."

"If it's so real, why have you hidden it all this time?"

"I can't afford to be labeled a kook along with everything else some people think about me until I have more proof."

"But now you risk holding those sessions on campus? And you don't want to be labeled a kook?"

"The scientific method says to construct a hypothesis and subject it to testing. I've been doing that. Now I have reams of data going back nearly thirty years. I am so close to demonstrating we are all connected to something much larger than ourselves and that connection will explain that paranormal phenomena are actually quite normal—in a weird sort of way. A few more pieces of the puzzle and I'll have a plausible theory."

A few more pieces of the puzzle and all he would have was a puzzle.

"It wasn't mere coincidence," he said, "that you stumbled upon my research. It was a *meaningful* coincidence, perfectly timed." He didn't say how it got timed that way; I didn't ask. After a few moments, he got up, closed the office door, and leaned against it, talking quietly. "Let me tell you the full story of why I left the priesthood."

I had been tinkering with my machine trying to figure out why the purple spiral sometimes glowed brighter and spun faster than at other times, to no avail at the moment, when Geoff had arrived. I slid the unit aside.

"I wasn't long out of seminary at St. Mary's College, Oscott in the U.K.," Geoff said, "and my request to be sent north, perhaps to Northumberland or to Scotland was pending. Inexplicably, I was assigned to a diocese in the south of England at Eastbourne in East Sussex instead. Early on, I was invited to high tea—dinner—at the home of some of the most prominent parishioners. Their daughter, Fiona, who was just graduated from university, was also there. Fiona was dazzling with her hair pulled up, her long slender neck, the way her red pouty lips touched the rim of the teacup; her glistening blue eyes had a hint of mischief. I could barely look at her. I knew better." Geoff stopped as if he were pulling himself back from some place unseen to me but vivid to him. "Now, I know you think you know where this is going, Simon," he said as he returned to the chair, "but bear with me. There may be a surprise or two."

He continued, "I returned to their home on several occasions and also spoke with Fiona at church, although I never took her confession. I couldn't deny I had growing feelings for her, and she must have felt it. One day in the fall, she showed me the garden behind their house: roses still in bloom, bright yellow chrysanthemums; and when she turned to point at some ivy, brilliant red climbing up the gray stone back wall of the house, she brushed lightly against my arm and lingered there for a moment before stepping back, but remained close. I smelled her sweet, powdery perfume.

"My feelings were all jumbled up, a maelstrom of tortured thoughts of guilt swirling around a visceral excitement I'd never felt before. Seminary hadn't prepared me for anything like that. Later that year just before Christmas, Fiona came into the confessional. I knew immediately from the perfume it was her. She didn't speak; she slipped me a Christmas card with a handwritten note that simply said, 'Father, forgive me. I'm in love with you.' Then she left. I continued regular pastoral visits to her family's home. I met with her parents—and her; we drank tea or wine or brandy, talked, and laughed. By the spring I had decided I could no longer continue on feeling the way I did. I rang her up and told her I'd like to talk with her. When I arrived at her house, she suggested we go for a walk where we could talk in private. I agreed and she drove us to the Birling Gap and the Seven Sisters. You must seem them sometime, Simon. They are beautiful white chalk cliffs on the coastline near East Sussex overlooking the English Channel with miles-long walking paths. We walked slowly, keeping pace with each other. We talked little. I was shy, and didn't know how to bring up the subject I wanted to talk about. She walked close to me, her hand sometimes brushing against mine. We stopped near the edge of the cliff and watched the ocean waves rolling in, one after another. Dark clouds were coming in and the breeze took on a sudden chill. I knew I had better say my piece before the storm came in. I took both of her hands and felt their warmth in mine. When I touched her, a feeling passed through me that I couldn't explain. I finally got the words to come out. I knew she was the one who had given me the Christmas card. Her cheeks turned red; her lip quivered slightly. She squeezed my hands. I felt the same, I told her. I knew it wasn't proper, but I couldn't help it. I had fallen madly in love with her, and if she would have me, I would leave the clergy. We'd find some way to support ourselves, although I doubted there was much demand for an out-of-work priest. I'd have to figure out something else.

"She threw her arms around my neck and pulled me in tightly for a kiss that seemed to last forever. When we broke apart, we looked at each other and laughed out loud. I yelled, 'I love you' so loudly that another couple on the path stopped and gawked at us. Fiona grabbed me again and swung us both around and around as if we were dancers on top of a music box. A stormy wind had come up and we were too close to the edge. I tried to pull back. When she stopped whirling, she lost her balance and tumbled over the cliff.

"I was devastated and angry, *furious*—at myself and at God. For years. Why had he allowed her to die? Was it to keep me in the clergy? Why was I so important that it was necessary to take her life like that?"

When Geoff stopped for a breath, I said, "That's a moving story, but what does it have to do with séances?" He raised a forefinger as if to appeal for my patience or silence.

"I had done nothing to betray my vows," he said, "so I continued in my duties carrying a bitter load of anger for two years. Late in the evenings, and only then, I drank so that I could sleep. At first it was wine, then brandy, then Scotch. The realization came to me one day I had to get as far away from England as I could, to an English-speaking parish. I requested to be transferred to Australia. But, of course, there has to be an opening, and there wasn't. Before long, a parish in the States had an opening and I took it.

"A year or so later, a woman came to confessional asking for forgiveness for a venial sin. She said she was a psychic medium and spoke regularly with the dead. As a practicing Catholic, she was aware of the church's stance that it is up to God and Him alone to whom the dead are permitted to speak, but she couldn't help it. She had been receiving those communications ever since she'd had a head injury.

"Instead of giving her penance, I asked her to tell me more. She said, 'I feel you have suffered a great loss, Father. . . a death, someone dear.' 'Yes,' I told her. She said, 'A spirit is with you now. I can see its aura, a feminine presence, not maternal. No, it's definitely not your mother. A young woman. She fell. She fell to her death. I'm getting a name: Fyodor, Fedora. It's not quite coming through.' 'Fiona,' I said. 'Fiona. Yes. That's it. She's smiling and wants you to know she has never left your side and she never will.' Then, she looked right at me and asked, 'Are you feeling guilty, Father?' 'I have for years,' I told her. 'Fiona said it wasn't your fault.'

Geoff paused as if he were searching for words or thoughts; or maybe he was truncating them, I couldn't tell. He went on, "I told the woman as far as I was concerned she needed no forgiveness or penance if what she demonstrated to me was an example of her so-called venial sin."

I summarized it for Geoff. "And that's how you got started with the paranormal."

"We had many more conversations outside of confessional, and she taught me how to communicate with Fiona for myself." Geoff looked at me as if he expected me to scoff, then he went on. "And I have talked to Fiona every day of my life since then. There has never been anyone else for me."

Why was Geoff telling me these things now, after hiding his activities for so long? I decided to let it be. Without further explanation, Geoff stood to leave, but when he got to the door, he turned around. "Won't you come again Friday night?"

There it was. The real reason for his visit. To draw me in like a convert. Did he have some need to proselytize? Was the priest in him coming out? Did he think he truly had something worth sharing? Why should I go back? His story was a sad, lovely one, but I was a man of science, rational, fact-driven. I didn't even believe in an afterlife and couldn't even explain why life existed except as a cosmic accident. As far as I was concerned, it — life, existence, consciousness — all started here and ended here. Human consciousness was merely a product of our brains, just as a computer's output was a product of its processor. There were no souls, no spirits to carry on after our bodies die. There was no other place to go, no judgment. I had come to believe those things years ago after I had left the church myself. Maybe Geoff wanted my approval as a man of science, not as a friend. I had better things to do than to witness parlor tricks.

But, what would it hurt? What was science without curiosity?

"Okay. I'll be there."

"Eight-thirty," Geoff said, then left.

Chapter Nineteen

FRIDAY NIGHT, EIGHT-THIRTY SHARP, I walked into the meeting room. Here and there were round tables with folding chairs and put together conversation pits made up of upholstered easy chairs arranged in small circles. Geoff was nowhere to be found. I had wanted to catch up with him after the meeting. Maybe not tonight.

The room was dark, illuminated only by candles at the center of each grouping, dim emergency lights spaced out along the baseboards, and the red and white "Exit" signs above the doors. One other light, a single overhead fixture shined down on a counter at the back of the room where refreshments had been placed: cookies, fruit, and cans of soda. I checked out the refreshments, but they had already been picked over.

The room was more empty than full, perhaps with fifty or sixty people in attendance; most had already taken their seats, a few still milling around or making a last trip to the restroom. The upholstered chairs were already taken. The only available seats were at the tables.

Nobody paid any attention to me as I sauntered around the room taking it all in: the confluence of the ancient, candles and incense, with the modern, cell phones and tablets invisibly tethered to Facebook, Instagram, Twitter, via the Internet.

As if on cue, people took their seats while I remained standing over by the wall. A woman, apparently one of the hosts, saw me and motioned me over to her table, telling me they had room for one more. I nodded at her.

"Welcome," she said to us all. "I'm Victoria." She appeared to be in her late-fifties to mid-sixties, dressed like an aging hippie in a sleeveless floral sundress and had long, flowing wavy hair, artfully unkempt, streaked with gray. She lit a cone of incense while she spoke and fanned the billow of smoke until it became a wispy blue-gray filament, drifting across the candle's flame, leaving behind its pungent aroma. "Remain open-minded and you are in for a treat tonight. I hope you will have a special experience this evening."

Open-minded. Special experience. I had come prepared for this. In the last week, I had read three books about Harry Houdini, and one written by him, *A Magician Among the Spirits*. Just in case I needed them, I had brought those books with me packed inside the book bag with the machine, which I had set on the floor beside my chair. I had begun to keep it with me all the time. It was too valuable not to; it contained a lifetime of research and design.

With Houdini's help, I was armed and ready for a special experience of my own.

When Victoria was ready to start she said, "I never discuss my religious affiliation, but I invite each of you to take a moment, and in your own way, ask a blessing for us tonight that only good and positive things will come through." She closed her eyes with her hands resting in her lap, palms up and instructed us to do likewise. I was the only one at our table with eyes wide open.

Following the moment of blessing, she gave us a small exercise to practice. She instructed us to cup our hands over our mouths and breathe lightly into them for a minute or two while she did the same. I went along with it, thinking it was a bunch of bull. Then, Victoria pointed to a woman and asked her to turn her palms toward Victoria while the rest of us continued to breathe into our hands.

Victoria turned her palms toward the woman. "Do you feel a flow of energy between us?"

"I'm not sure," the woman said.

"Do you feel something different when I move my hands closer to yours?"

"Like a tingling? Yes. I feel something." Victoria moved closer to her. "It's stronger now." When Victoria backed off, the woman said, "It's fainter now." She claimed she still felt the tingle even after Victoria moved away several feet.

One by one, Victoria went around the table demonstrating this exercise, something Houdini hadn't mentioned. When she nodded at me, I waved her off. After she was finished with the others, she turned again to me and asked if I wanted to try it. In truth, I did want to, just to see what would happen. With our palms facing each other, to my surprise, my fingers tingled slightly as they would do before going numb. It was a subtle feeling, but grew stronger when she moved closer, fainter when she moved away.

Victoria told us she had just demonstrated an unseen energy, the life force, she called it, a cosmic energy that connects us and all the elements of the universe. To me, the so-called life force was nothing more than a demonstration of the power of suggestion, which, I admit, must have been stronger than I had realized. She said if we were tuned in and could feel the force, we could also learn to tune in to other energies that would open up things to us that are natural, not spooky and mysterious. "Does anyone have any questions?" she asked.

For a long moment, no one seemed eager to speak, including me, and I had loads of questions better left for later. Victoria fanned the red tip of the incense with a legal pad she had pulled out of her bag. She appeared to be about to speak when one woman broke the silence. "I think you should know I'm a skeptic. I accepted the invitation to come only because I've always been curious about spiritualists."

A skeptic, yet like me, she said she had felt the tingling in her hands.

Victoria smiled. "Actually, I'm not a spiritualist, I'm a Socialist."

Oh brother, a comedienne.

Victoria leaned in and lowered her voice. "But, don't let that get around. Not everybody here welcomes Socialists." She looked in the direction of a man with white hair.

"I just thought with you being a medium and all—"

Victoria sat up straight and grinned. "Thank you, darling, but I haven't been a medium for years." The woman sat back and became quiet with a puzzled look. Victoria tugged at her plus-size waistline. "But, even when I was a medium, I wasn't a medium. Oh, I was psychic then, I just wasn't a psychic medium."

Not even a good comedienne, but it was an easy room and everyone except for me seemed to be eating it up.

"I prefer just to think of myself as a normal person who has psychic powers — as we all do, really. I like to think I am spiritual but not a spiritualist."

"I don't get it," the woman said. Neither did I.

Victoria leaned forward, softened her voice. "From my life experiences and the experiences of others I've known, I've learned we can nourish our spirits by learning from other spirits outside this mundane plane we live in. In the spirit world. Just the same as we learn from and help each other here. But," she waved her fingers as if she were shooing away a fly, "the spiritualists of old were mostly fakes and sideshow performers."

"How do you know that?" an older man asked.

Houdini had proved that; but I didn't say anything. Coming from her, though, the statement seemed as if she were standing in a crowded fog saying the next person was hazy.

"Just read Houdini's books and how he duplicated the old-time spiritualists' parlor tricks. In the nineteenth century, spiritualist séances were an entertaining fad for the bored affluent that bled over into the early twentieth century. I don't even like to be associated with the term."

So, she had read Houdini, too. That could explain why I hadn't seen any trumpets or moving tables, or heard any bells ringing. She, too, had come prepared.

"If what you're doing here tonight is true today, why couldn't it have been true back then?" the man asked.

"Of course, it was. But the honest psychics kept it quiet and didn't make a big show of it. Would you, if you knew someone as famous as Houdini was out to 'expose' you?"

"Again, how do you know that?"

"From my grandmother." She smiled big.

"Psychics run in families?"

"Perhaps some more than others. But, actually, psychics run in the human family."

"How is it you can communicate with the dead?" another man asked.

"The same way you can," she said. "It's part gift, part practice. Everyone can do it. Spirits are actually desperate to communicate with us. As you may learn in future sessions, if you're lucky, some spirits' sole job is to communicate with us. You just have to learn to listen to a higher vibration, like dogs can hear whistles we can't."

Now I wasn't ready to say there was any truth to all of this nonsense, but the germ of a thought hit me. I scooted my bag with my foot until I could unobtrusively put it on my lap. "This 'higher vibration'" I asked, "could it be an ultra-high frequency? Like a wavelength an antenna could pick up?"

The machine had been programmed to learn from its environment and not go nuts. The xenocryst had demonstrated the potential superconducting properties necessary to achieve that. And the purple spiral inside the crystal had spun like a whirling dervish at the first séance, indicating to me something serious was going on inside. Looking back on it, the unit had led me to the séance. I sneaked a peek inside the bag before she could answer. The purple dervish was at it again.

"Far out question," she said. "I don't know enough about science to answer that. As far as I know, only people can do it. But, I've known some psychics who insist their pets are psychic, too. . . I'll stay agnostic on that one."

After that little demonstration, Victoria moved things along. "Has anyone had experience talking to spirits?"

"I think so," one man said. "I had a friend who died many years ago, and another psychic gave me a message from him. I'm just wondering if it was true."

"Let me ask you, do you believe in life after death?"

"I don't know." He shifted nervously. "I suppose in some way."

"That's okay. You don't have to believe in anything for it to be true." She paused for a moment, looked upward. The group fell silent. "Your friend. . . you were very close, like brothers, but he wasn't your blood brother, at least not in this life. I see the two of you with a third person."

At that moment, I recalled Houdini had told how he had gleaned information about prominent people in the small town of Garnett, Kansas by walking through the town cemetery and deducing from the largest or most ornate monuments who the prominent families were. Then he talked to town busybodies and learned more about the prominent people before giving a public reading that night. He dropped real names, real facts; doing so made him look clairvoyant. Maybe Victoria had learned something about this man, talked to someone who knew him, before we began. Or worse, maybe he was a plant.

"I hear a song," Victoria said. "Don't know what this means. 'Roll, roll, roll.' Is it rock 'n ' roll? I can't tell. But, I can almost hear the two of you singing it."

I inched away from the table and slid the bag down my shins and opened it just enough to lift the cover of the machine and still hide the purple glow, attempting to do so without being detected. Words streamed by, like closed captioning. *Roll, roll, roll. Roll your window down. Let the breeze blow away your frown.* Strangely, the words scrolled across the machine's screen, first sending a chill down my spine and causing my thinking to stall out, then upon a moment's recovery, leading me to think that psychic thought waves could possibly be high frequency transmissions being picked up by the crystal and displayed on the screen. Immediately, I dismissed the idea.

"I can see the three of you listening to the radio. . . in a car maybe? Is this sounding familiar?"

"Yes. It's dead on," the man said.

The only rational explanation was Victoria and the man must have been colluding.

"I get that you three were singing, all silly-like." She smiled and tapped her cheek with a forefinger. Was the tapping a signal to someone or a nervous habit? I turned my head to follow her gaze and saw only the "Exit" sign. "Roll your window down. Something about a frown. I'm not sure what that means."

"I do," the man said. "It was a top forty song playing on the radio back then. We actually hated it, so we made fun of it by singing it . . . well. . . with goofy voices." He smiled and shrugged his shoulders, looking a little embarrassed. "I know it sounds dumb. But, we had fun with it." He looked around. "I guess you had to be there."

"The third person was a woman," Victoria said. "I sense you were very close to her, too."

"Still am. We got married later. She's the only other person who knows anything about that evening and the way my friend and I used to mock that song. It just wouldn't make sense to anybody else. You know, a private joke."

There was a plausible explanation. Maybe Victoria knew his wife. But, if they were not colluding, Victoria had made a lucky guess. Yet, it was hard to dismiss that I had clearly read "girlfriend" and "wife" on the machine's screen as the man spoke the words. It didn't appear to be a speech-to-text translation, as I had momentarily conjectured may have been the case.

"Your friend came to you this evening to confirm for you there is life after death. You can accept that with confidence. He is very happy there and will greet you when your time comes to pass over."

So far, there had been no spooky atmospherics, no smoke and mirrors, no static, no voices straining to be heard from beyond, no ghostly apparitions walking among us, glum and sullen, peaceful and saintly, or desperately pantomiming a message.

In Houdini's day, spirit voices were purportedly heard through so-called spirit trumpets. But Houdini exposed them as voices of living people calling from offstage, not the "great beyond." Bells rung by spirits eager to prove their presence were, in truth, bells rung by nimble toes slipped out of altered shoes and surreptitiously slipped back in again.

We can do better tricks than that now. At the prep academy I went to, on the last day before graduation, two classmates and I conspired to pull a senior prank on one of our teachers, the arrogant Dr. Prothro, whom we all despised. We had clandestinely planned the prank all semester long down to the smallest detail.

The night before our last class with Dr. Prothro, we sneaked in the building, climbed above the false ceiling, strung cables, positioned lasers, and tapped into the room's sound system. Then, we hacked into Dr. Prothro's computer and installed a graphics program we had written just for that occasion. After we did a practice run, all we had to do was wait and watch.

The following day when Dr. Prothro shut down his computer at the end of class, our plan went into action. The shutdown sequence triggered a command to our graphics program, and a 3-D hologram of a white horse appeared to come through the wall from the adjacent class room, braying like a donkey. The horse then turned around, aimed its hindquarters straight at Dr. Prothro, still braying, lifted its tail, and then disappeared as the computer shut down.

If the mediums at the séances wanted to use trickery, I was confident I could catch them.

While Victoria went on, I periodically kept an eye on the machine and saw words stream across the display that seemed to support her readings: *friend, twin, mother*. The messages all seemed about the same, a shout out from beyond but with important details about their lives or their deaths few people would know about. Once, I was astonished to see a pixelated image of an elderly woman, who was purportedly someone's grandmother, appear on the screen.

A short while later, a brief disruption gave me the chance to leave Victoria's table and slip quietly into another group. The host of this group was an older man who appeared to be around sixty, with a short-cropped white beard and wavy white hair that flowed just above his ears.

"Good evening," he said, looking at me. "My name is Chuck. For the time, I will withhold my last name. As I already told the others, by day I am the Chief Financial Officer of a medium-sized corporation—" He looked towards Victoria. "—but don't let that get around. Not everybody here welcomes capitalists." I sensed a rivalry between him and Victoria, perhaps friendly. As for economics and politics, I couldn't have cared less. "I will also decline to identify the company I work for, only because psychic phenomena are grossly misunderstood, and I don't want my credibility as a corporate executive jeopardized, at least not until I retire." He smiled. "I agreed to participate in Dr. Gibson's study— anonymously— hoping to help bring psychic phenomena into the mainstream someday."

When Chuck turned to face the others, I reached into the bag and plugged in earbuds and put one in my ear. He resumed talking to a middle-aged man whose reading my arrival had interrupted.

"There's someone with you right now," Chuck said. "I can see his aura over your right shoulder. Do you feel him?"

"No I don't." The man shook his head, staring at Chuck.

Two other people said they could see the presence, although I saw nothing.

"He wants you to know he's been with you all of your life and he never leaves you."

"What does that mean?"

I looked back and forth at Chuck, then the machine. I heard through the earphones, almost word for word, what Chuck said, but it wasn't like hearing an audio track. It was as if the earbuds were plugged into my own thoughts, like an inner voice subvocalizing words as I thought or read.

"He's your spirit guide. Some call it a guardian angel, but labels don't matter. He's in spirit form and stays with you to help protect and guide you. Everybody has at least one. It's just that few of us are aware of it."

"Guardian angel?" His grin was sarcasm.

"Yeah," Chuck said. "They're not just in movies about angels trying to earn their wings. Oh, and the wing thing—it's a myth. Cute, but a myth. Where they are, they don't need wings." Chuck looked beyond the man's head. "He's showing me a small child, maybe three years old, leaving a house alone, running toward the street. He called your name, and you stopped in your tracks to see who had called you, but there was no one else around, just as the car that would have killed you went by. I see you went back into the house safely.

He said it's time for you to know he was the voice that called you back."

"I actually remember that," the man said, the grin suddenly vanishing. "Vividly. But, how did you know?"

"I don't. He does." Now Chuck smiled.

"That was one of my earliest memories." The man's face was full of surprise. He shook his head as if in disbelief. "It was a man's voice, but my father wasn't home. Even so, I went into the house to ask my mother if she called me. She hadn't. I've never told that to anybody. Wow."

After that, Chuck gave several other readings. One, for a grieving young woman whose fiancé had been killed some years ago in the war in Iraq. Another, a young man had lost his father to cancer and wanted to know if he was at peace and pain-free. Then Chuck turned the remaining time over to the others to practice giving readings on each other. As of the time I left, they weren't doing very well at it.

Even so, hosts and visitors alike had given me a lot to think about: myths, skepticism, delusions, facts, surrender, acceptance. My thoughts were all jumbled up fighting each other. But, I couldn't deny what I had seen and heard and what seemed to have been confirmed by way of the machine. By the time the meeting was over, my thoughts were too jumbled to talk to Geoff. I had heard his unmistakable accent in the din of conversations and thus knew he was there, but I was no longer ready to talk to him about any of this. I left before he could spot me.

Chapter Twenty

MORE THAN A WEEK PASSED after the sessions with Victoria and Chuck, and I hadn't seen Geoff at all. That wasn't so unusual, but I knew he'd expect a reaction from me. In truth, I was avoiding him. My skepticism and long held beliefs about life and death were still intact. Sort of. I had no explanation for what I had seen at his research sessions, and I didn't think I would go to any more of them.

For the last few weeks, I had shirked some of my duties while I tried to understand Geoff's research, and most of all, its impact on my invention. Every spare minute, I had tried to hack into my own creation to find out what had gone on those nights with the readings and what I had seen on the computer screen.

On the surface, it seemed the machine was working. The crystal lit up, the screen displayed messages and images, and most importantly, the unit didn't burn up. But, I was no longer in control of it. Every attempt to get inside the machine had been thwarted as though the unit had its own anti-virus protection and I was the virus. I was extremely concerned the one-and-only Emorite xenocryst I had, that had proved to be the key component of the machine, was all used up. I tried formatting the disc to wipe out everything and start over, but was blocked every time.

On Wednesday morning, I knew Geoff would be in early, so I headed straight for his office when I got to work. Geoff was leaning back in his swivel chair, holding some papers and looking at them through dark framed reading glasses. He finished a page and flipped it before looking up at me. After some baseball talk about the Cardinals having a good year and what the chances were they might go up against the Dodgers in the World Series, I got right to the point.

"I'm not going to attend any more of your séance sessions." There. That wasn't so hard.

Geoff's reaction was simply to look at me over the top of his glasses without saying anything.

"It's taken away from working on my own research," I said.

"Wouldn't want to do that." His tone was flat, neutral.

"Plus, I don't know how they do it."

"They?"

"The mediums."

"Do what?"

"The shows they put on. Convincing, but—"

"Fake?"

"They have to be. 'Dead' is dead."

"You haven't seen enough facts to change your mind that there's something beyond death?"

"Facts? I haven't seen what the *facts* are. As I said, I don't know how they do it."

Geoff sat forward. "It's no weirder than that computer you've been working on for ages. In fact, they're much the same."

"How so?"

"The quantum aspect. In your own words, Simon, this tunneling effect you talk about is nothing more than stretched out waves penetrating barriers you normally wouldn't expect them to. Weird science, but it does seem to work. Sunlight tunnels. Why not thought? Why not consciousness?"

"We only know of tunneling happening with particles at the atomic level."

"There again. Your words, 'we only know.' At the present time. And we haven't always known that, have we? Tell me, Simon, how big is a thought?"

The best way out of a Socratic trap is not to answer the question.

"Is a thought, or consciousness, bigger or smaller than an atomic particle?"

"Neurotransmitters and chemicals in the brain have mass."

"They're just the lumbering freight trains that transport information. They aren't thoughts—or consciousness."

Again, I gave no response.

After a long pause, Geoff said, "Simon, I understand. It took me a long time to abandon my beliefs when I left the priesthood. My God, it was all I had known. I had second thoughts for years. I can expect no less from you."

I was thinking about thoughts as waves tunneling through our skulls, in and out. But, from where?

"Perhaps the time isn't right for you, Simon. When it is, the right teacher will come along."

"It's just that there aren't any facts."

"When facts are hard to come by, you sometimes have to go with the preponderance of evidence."

"That sounds a lot like faith."

"With faith, there is often a lack of evidence. Trust your eyes and ears. Trust your gut. You've seen the evidence."

"You're telling me, it's all real? Not some experiment to see how gullible people are?"

"All real."

Silence.

"Well, it's up to you. Every Friday and Saturday night, eight-thirty. Standing invitation."

All the way back to my office and then to my house, I thought about what Geoff had said, and the only explanation of the paranormal events, the psychic readings, I had seen was that thoughts must tunnel through something to get to us. If that's true, then maybe life does continue some place we can't see but isn't so far away that we can't receive signals from the souls who live there. There lay the paradox: where do the dead live?

Chapter Twenty-one

THE SUN SHINING THROUGH DRAWN CURTAINS in my room at Liberty falls too brightly on my closed eyes, disturbing me to the point of getting up. I have lain here well into the morning obsessed with what I just remembered. I must again ask myself, do I really want to remember what my mind has tried so hard to forget?

My memories are nearly impossible to believe. Can my own eyes lie to me? My ears, my brain, my rational faculty? I wouldn't entertain as fact for a moment that communication with dead people could be as convenient as placing a telephone call if it weren't for the machine giving its independent rendition of readings by the so-called psychics. If the machine had read-out word-for-word what the mediums had said, I could easily conclude the machine had become a mere recorder or voice-to-text translator. Instead, it didn't read verbatim as a transcript would, but instead as one might retell something unrehearsed, preserving the meaning but not in the same words or order. And to my greater astonishment the unit also displayed some crude images of people who had supposedly passed from this life.

If it were true the unit could receive communications from the dead — if it were true there is an afterlife — there can be only one explanation satisfactory to me. As Geoff had suggested, consciousness must ride on waves that can tunnel through the barrier—a barrier that is possibly a membrane of sorts—between the living and the dead, as sunlight does when it passes through the membrane of a green leaf and finds the shortest of many paths to stir chlorophyll, carbon, and water into an elixir that feeds the plant. Or when sunlight tunnels through closed curtains and eyelids, giving us dim and imperfect light, not fully blocked out. Perhaps the membrane between the living and the dead surrounds our entire universe and separates us from parallel universes. One or more of them could be where we go at death. If not preposterous, the idea is at least a fantasy I cannot fully support. Unfortunately, neither can I discount it.

At the moment, though, I have another problem: I can't tell Margaret about recalling these memories because what I want most from her is her signature on a release form. To get that, she must deem I have dealt sufficiently with the trauma of my life and my memory is restored—at least mostly restored. But if I tell her what I remember, she will surely think I am still crazy and won't release me. I'm in a kind of double bind, a Catch-22. If my memory isn't restored, I may never get out of Liberty. But, if I tell her what I have remembered, I still may never get out of Liberty. The best course of action for now, it seems, is to avoid her until I can figure this all out.

I run down a list of places to hang out to keep a low profile: not the television room, not the library, not the dining hall, not the grounds. That leaves the thicket. I can't lose by going there. I will either find solitude to think, or I might find Andrea there, a sheer delight of its own.

    I sneak as quietly as I can down the stairs, down the hallway, headed for the exit. When I encounter other people, I look straight ahead, thinking if I don't acknowledge their presence, they won't talk to me. My plan works until I run into Margaret. She is reading something on her tablet as she approaches me, her cane tapping with every other step. She stops in front of me and swipes the screen with her cane dangling off of her free hand, then props herself again with the cane and looks up at me.

    "Good morning, Simon. I haven't seen you for a while. I'm anxious to hear about your progress."

    Suddenly, I feel like a child caught in the act of something—telling a lie perhaps or stealing a cookie. "Progress? I haven't had anything to tell you." I have an extra hard time looking her in the eye. "Yet." Adding that word makes it less of a lie, implies I will tell her sooner or later.

    She looks back at her tablet. "Come see me when you do. I must be off."

    It strikes me then just how much space she's really giving me to work through this on my own. Now, I don't have to sneak out; I'll just go boldly.

The thicket is mostly shaded from the morning sun. Shiny droplets of cold dew cover the iron bench, so I shuffle down the slight decline to the fence, step aside some low cut bushes, and, finding a dry spot, lean on it looking down into the gorge below. The wind is still. The water rumbles steadily a hundred feet or more below my feet.

Behind me, green feathery ferns sprout from the thicket floor. At one end of the fence a potentilla bush has opened up its yellow blooms since I was here last. Some red poppies frame the other end of the fence. This is a good place to think.

After a while, thoughts abandon me to a blissful kind of inactivity, without emotion, without cares. Then Andrea's voice comes from behind.

"Hear that?" she says softly.

I turn to look at her. How glad I am to see her. At this moment, I could have wished for nothing better. "No. I'm sorry. I don't"

"Listen," she whispers, stepping closer. "The rhythm of the river."

I hear the river splashing, nothing more.

"Don't you hear it?" I shake my head placidly afraid of disturbing the sight of her. Her hair cascades to its full length framing her face, falling past her shoulders. Her eyes are closed; her skin looks soft and smooth; her lips curve upward in a sweet smile. "One, two, three. One *two, three,*" she says.

Still, I hear nothing and shake my head.

She steps next to me and leans over the fence. "Look, down there." She points, and my gaze eagerly follows. "Those three boulders in the water, staggered. Sometimes, the water hits them just right. Oom, *pah, pah,* oom, *pah, pah.*"

I see the boulders but hear only the rushing water.

"Like a waltz. You know how to waltz?"

"Actually, no—"

She takes my arm and leads me up the gentle slope, behind the bench where the ground is more level. "Dance with me, Simon."

"I can't dance." It's embarrassing to say. I've always felt too self-conscious bouncing up and down in time to music with arms up in the air and flailing all over the place.

"It goes like this." She takes my left hand in her right hand, and guides my right hand to her back. She's wearing a tank top and my fingertips touch her bare skin, warm, smooth, soft. She back leads me forward a step, starting with my left foot and counts, "One," then, shows me where to put my right foot to the side, then both together. "Two, three." Backward, side, together. Our feet shuffle on the ground for a while, certainly with me stepping on her toes; but she doesn't say a thing.

I don't get the hang of it. It's not as simple as one, two, three. I feel awkward and blame myself. I recall voting at the science and technology prep academy to have science fairs instead of dances and socials. If there had been dancing, it would surely have been dancing robots. Years later, I feel the vacuum of not having learned such social graces. Perhaps I would have known better how to explore things with Hannah if I had. Perhaps when I'm out of here, I still could — but, peculiar thing, I no longer want to. Now there's Andrea, here, close. From the moment I met her I've felt something different than anything I've ever felt before. I'm at a loss for words to describe it.

Suddenly, as if something grabs of me from the outside, I pull away from Andrea. "I've got to get back now." I hold on to her hands as I back up, dropping first one, then the other. I turn and leave without looking back.

Tonight after dinner, I plop into the chair and stare out the window into the waning light of evening, my mood also turning dark. All day, my thoughts have not wandered far from Andrea. Why did I bolt? In truth, I wanted to stay. Also in truth, I was afraid of messing up. I think I did, anyway.

A thought comes to me. I spring out of the chair, grab a flashlight, and pass swiftly through the dining room, picking up a plastic cup of water and an unwashed dinner knife from the sink and hurry back to the thicket. There, I pick yellow potentilla blooms and red poppies and nestle them against green fern fronds in the cup of water and prop the arrangement on the iron bench against a few rocks gathered off the ground. Then, I make my way back to my room.

The following morning before the dew is gone, I go back to the glade, hoping against hope to see Andrea and explain my foolish behavior: I'm sometimes at a loss for what to do or say. She's not there, but the flowers are gone. Two red petals have fallen from the poppies and lie on the bench; the rocks are carefully laid to one side. I walk through the glade to where it opens into her property, stop for a deep breath, then proceed all the way to her house. The wrap-around back porch is covered and open with two chairs and a round glass table in between. The French doors to the inside are closed. Lights are off. I knock at the door. There is no answer. The flowers I left for her have been taken out of the plastic cup and put into a vase sitting in filtered sunlight on a table next to the door. After a second unlucky knock, I turn to leave and see for the first time the panoramic view of the gorge and the tree-topped cliffs from her porch—unimpeded by brush as is the view from the bench. To the right, upstream there is a bend and shallow falls I hadn't seen before, large boulders jutting out of bubbling white water. To the left downstream, the river becomes a thick pencil line and the gorge seems to close.

And I remember the iron bench when I found it was dirty, unused and seemingly abandoned. With this view to be had, I understand why the bench has been unused. In the same thought, I wonder why Andrea has started going there lately. Synchronicity, perhaps. Or better, there was someone she has hoped to see. And what did I do? I pushed her away, fled from a dance lesson so that I wouldn't look silly. Perhaps I look sillier for having done so.

In front of a class of students eager to please me for a good grade, I'm as calm and eloquent as can be. That's my world, my element. Lectures about bits and bytes for beginners and quantum tunneling for my advanced students roll off my tongue as easily as the words of a poet when he recites his own verse. For, I speak a poetry of its own kind with rhythm, symmetry, and balance, and not the hollow memorized lines of an actor. But when it comes to talking to a woman, my words, my thoughts get tangled, and I end up looking like a fool. It hits me now that avoidance isn't the way to overcome difficulty. Engagement is, head on.

Then I hear it: the rhythm of the river, the water splashing off the rocks. I listen closely, one, *two, three.* One, *two, three.* Faint, but it's there. I look to see the source of this rhythm. An anomaly in the rock formation at the falls causes the water to swell, then break; swell then break. If I ever again have the chance to waltz with Andrea, I don't care how I look. I will dance all day, all night.

Just the way she showed me, I practice a few steps in time to the river. The porch creaks under each step. It's coming to me, the rhythm in my feet; it's not so hard. But, without Andrea here, I feel conspicuous, out of place, a trespasser, and I stop shadow dancing. Even so, I stay a while longer, looking at the river below.

I turn, looking for signs she might have come home, listening for the sound of a car pulling onto the gravel drive. But, the only sound is the rushing water.

I shouldn't stay any longer. I step off the porch over broken ends of boards, tattered from who-knows-how-many footsteps, how many years of weather, simple tongue-and-groove boards. I could fix them, if she would let me, if I could get out of Liberty Residence and come back with tools.

Down the steps and toward the trees a good distance away, I pass by the barn with the carnival equipment inside and briefly recall the first time I trespassed here. Perhaps Andrea discovered my footprints and that had led her to the thicket to see who had been there. I stop at the tree line for one last look before entering the thicket. No signs of Andrea.

On the way back, I sit on the bench and wait a little longer for her, hoping she will come home soon. This old iron bench, as comfortable to me now as any couch could ever be, has become a familiar friend. Today, it's warmed by the sunlight that manages to make its way through the canopy. I'm not sure I could hear Andrea's car from here. Maybe she'll come here on her own.

My thoughts drift, as they are lately inclined to do. I think of home.

As each day has passed, I've had a growing sense of restlessness, as if I should be doing something—not here, elsewhere. Back at Finial, teaching. Researching, in my office, in my greenhouse lab. With every memory, I've felt home pulling on me: the pull of sleeping in my own bedroom that still has the floral wallpaper my mother hung before my dad died; the pull of eating breakfast at my own table, the same round oak table with the thick fluted center pedestal I got in trouble for tapping with my toe at dinner time when I was a kid; the pull of drinking coffee from cups older than me, buttering my toast with knives just as old. I want to bring back those things so familiar, so comforting. I want my memory back and whatever else there was.

There was something else. I feel it; but I can't bring it in.

Just now, a tanager looking like a flame with its red-orange head and bright yellow body, swoops by me out into the open. Off towards the cliffs an osprey glides effortlessly like a kite above the river, probably looking for fish.

I've fished in that river before, further upstream where you can hike to the water's edge. Years ago, Michael and I used to go there for a guys' outing. The water is cold and clear as tap water. Michael put on rubber hip waders, stood in the stream, and whipped a weightless line guiding it this way and that, hoping the lure landed in front of a hungry trout, which usually happened for him. I don't like to be in water, so I fished from the bank further upstream. I cast my line, let it settle a little and slowly reeled it back, hoping to reel it by a hungry fish, which didn't usually happen. I stopped fishing, though, and told Michael it was because I don't like to eat fish and it didn't make sense to hook them in the jaw just to let them go. I always let him have what I caught; I just didn't like fishing.

I don't know why I would have been on a fishing boat in the middle of the ocean.

I get off the bench and go down to the fence where I can lean over and see in all directions: upstream, below me, and downstream. Sometimes I get that Zen thing about a river representing past, present, and future all existing at the same time. The Zen masters may have been early to realize the quantum effects of things being in more than one state at a time. Other times, the Zen thing doesn't make any sense to me at all. I can't get in a boat to go upstream and find Michael and me still fishing there.

Across the gorge lies a lost logging road. I've been up that road before, even though it's been officially shut down for decades. Michael showed it to me. We took his Jeep up the dusty road around hairpin curves to where it ended in a trail that went nearly straight up. At the top of the trail was a rock ledge where we sat, and Michael, while sipping one of many beers, described the geological processes that uprooted the layers of granite millions of years ago. Along the side of the ledge was a cavern. We'd never looked inside the cavern, I suppose now because there was probably little to find there except for sleeping snakes.

On the return trip, we wiped out. Michael had had too much to drink, and I shouldn't have let him drive. One of the curves was too sharp, not for the Jeep, but for a drunken Michael. The Jeep tipped over. Fortunately, we were seat belted in and the Jeep had rollover bars. With the help of a winch and a small fallen tree we used as a lever, the two of us set the Jeep upright again. I drove the rest of the way home.

We were lucky. If we'd wiped out a little further up, we could have gone off the cliff. A little further down and we could have hit huge boulders and one of us could have sustained some serious head injuries.

Head injuries. That rings a bell. I remember something.

I hurry off the bench and sprint back to Liberty, pounce on the door, and burst in running, then stop in the commons. "Has anyone seen Margaret—I mean Dr. Switzer? I've got to tell her something."

The TV group pauses the start of *Jeopardy* and looks at me funny. This is one of few times I've spoken to anyone here except for Margaret, for no particular reason. I just don't usually feel like talking to any of them.

"He does talk," the woman, Kelli I think her name is, says to a man next to her just loud enough that I can hear. Then she whispers she is going out for a smoke.

"I just saw her go into her office," one of the guys says. B.J. I think is his name, or D.J. Kelli nods and points down the hallway with the hand that's not clutching her purse. The guy holds the remote control as if he's about to hit the "Resume" button, but doesn't.

I take off running, forgetting to thank him. Behind me, the *Jeopardy* theme music comes back on.

Margaret's office is on the second floor. I take the stairs two at a time. Her door is open. I rush in, mouth running. "Margaret, I know where we met."

"Where we met?"

"When and where. The circumstances."

"Good, Simon. That's good progress. Why don't you come in, sit down, and tell me all about it."

This may be my ticket home. I can sort out the rest on my own later.

Chapter Twenty-two

I SIT DOWN IN THE CAMEL COLORED VELOUR CHAIR beside Margaret's desk, not in front of her. The warm incandescent lighting in her office is in sharp contrast to the harsh fluorescent light in the hallways. A table lamp with an off-white cloth shade sits on her desk and a matching floor lamp in the corner is aimed toward the ceiling. Books are neatly lined up on white painted shelves with gold tone pinstripe accents. The feeling is light, airy. The windows have the same sheer curtains as are in my room, and I think what a shame it is the windows are closed. I've always liked watching sheers blow in the breeze.

I'm not going to tell Margaret everything I remembered. I'm just going to tell her enough so that she knows my memory is returning and it's safe to release me now. What I remembered is this:

After overcoming the shock that my old family friend Geoff Gibson was doing paranormal research, I started going to his sessions regularly. At first, I wasn't sure what to think. Actually, I was sure. I was sure Geoff had "gone off his trolley," as he might have said if he'd been his normal self—at least the Geoff Gibson I thought I had known all of my life—which apparently he wasn't any more, or perhaps never had been.

I went to the next meeting, skepticism still intact, motivated by catching the fakers in the act.

The trick that had me stumped was how the machine displayed the so-called readings, sometimes with a pixelated image of the speaker. The trick had to be a variation of the old spirit trumpet ruse where an insider was causing the effects. However, taking control of the unit would have been extremely difficult because even I had been blocked from making any changes to it. And, no one should have known about its existence. What was more, I had kept the machine by my side night and day, so no one could have tampered with it. Except by Wi-Fi.

On that Friday night, I got there a little late and groups had already formed for their séances. I quietly slipped in with the machine in my book bag and found a chair next to a pillar in a dark corner so that I could clandestinely observe the shenanigans. I had also brought electronic surveillance equipment that could detect and block Radio Frequency transmissions, Wi-Fi, spying cell phones, Global Positioning Satellite transmissions, digital cameras, and much more. The equipment was small enough to be clipped to my belt and passed off as a cell phone. Before the evening was over, I intended to sweep the room.

My entry must not have been as inconspicuous as I thought, though. The host at the table nearest me, a woman I had seen there before, looked at me and gave me a slight smile without saying anything. I nodded in return. She turned her attention back to the group and talked them through several steps of meditation: inhaling a deep cleansing breath, relaxing, holding their hands palms up, etc. The effect was hypnotic, even to me.

"Visualize your thoughts as particles of dust in your cupped hands," she said. "Now, in your mind's eye, raise your hands to your mouth and blow the dust away, and with it, all the cares you may have had today." Sounded like good advice any day. "Make your minds like empty bowls. Ask for knowledge and understanding, then be still and listen very closely."

After a few minutes of silence, she followed up with some readings that sounded very much like the shout outs from the Great Beyond received by Victoria and Chuck: a mother who had died in child birth but had stayed close by her daughter, a man's buddy killed in a car wreck, grandparents who had lived to a ripe old age. The messages seemed to be universal, that they were all at peace and wanted to send their love. Simple enough.

At that moment, my stomach was on the verge of growling because I had skipped meals that day trying to hack into the machine. Refreshments were at the far end of the room, and there was still likely to be a nice quiet banana left. But, if I went to the snack counter, that might be the precise moment the host pulled some kind of trickery I would miss.

On the other hand, while crossing the room I might serendipitously catch someone else pulling a stunt, especially if I took the surveillance equipment with me.

I opted for the banana and clipped the spy detector to my belt.

While I ate, I eavesdropped on other groups. When I was finished eating, I moved around quietly from table to table, staying at a respectable distance, then went back to my chair by the pillar. The surveillance detector registered nothing, including the building's Wi-Fi, which I had earlier taken the precaution this time of temporarily blocking by using my administrative rights.

Back in my chair, I opened the book bag and looked at the machine inside. The purple spiral whirled in inner space as vigorously as ever, neither detected nor blocked by the surveillance device.

After a while, the nearest group stopped early for a break. They scooted their chairs back and quietly dispersed in different directions. The room was dark and I knew it would stay that way a while longer. I hated dark rooms except to sleep in, but took advantage of the darkness and ambled over to the vacant table and sat down as if I were a lingering group member. When I thought no one was looking, I crawled under the table with the surveillance equipment looking and feeling around for any kind of electronic device. Apparently, stealth couldn't be counted among my skills. As I crawled out from under the table, I saw a woman's legs and a cane, motionless, waiting.

"Good evening," she said. I stood upright, brushed off my knees, and tried to smile, although that had never helped me get by with a thing. "Can I help you find something?" she asked.

"No—No, thanks. I was just. . ." I paused, pointing underneath the table as if pointing were an explanation of its own.

"Whatever you're looking for here you won't find it with an electronic monitor." She looked at the device in my hand. I fumbled around putting it back on my belt, feeling as if I were about to be sent to the principal's office. She was patient, though. "Why don't you join us at our table when we resume instead of sitting over there by the pillar. We've got room."

She spoke with an accent I couldn't quite place. It was Germanic, not high German, possibly Austrian or Swiss-German.

I don't know what it is about accents. French and Italian accents, warm and slightly nasal, seem to draw us native speakers of English as sugary sweets draw ants. Germanic and Slavic accents seem harsh, impersonal. Perhaps that's unfair, but I think most North Americans would agree. It's not the fault of the native speakers of those languages, though. Maybe it's because of the way they've been portrayed in film and television for seventy years. Despite her accent, her tone and her smile were warm and welcoming. Her accent and her apparent warmth combined to create a push-pull effect on me. She motioned toward an empty chair.

"Thank you, but no. I'd rather stay here and observe."

"Observe? A reporter, are you?"

"No."

"I see. A skeptic, then, out to catch us? Well, I'm not certain if I should have you thrown out or invite you to stay." She looked at me a moment, almost playfully, almost breaking a smile but not quite, as if she were contemplating my fate for the evening. I couldn't tell. Even so, I didn't reveal I was there at Geoff's invitation and would stay as long as I darn well pleased. "I think I'll invite you to stay. You don't have to believe anything but your own eyes, ears, and common sense. You're welcome to just observe." She stared at me a moment longer, which caused me to look away. "When the time is right, the teacher and student will be united." That was the second time I had recently heard that phrase. She pivoted slowly with her cane and started to leave, then turned around. "My name is Dr. Margaret Switzer. What's yours?"

She didn't say what kind of doctor and I didn't ask. Philosophy maybe, psychology, sociology. For all I knew, her doctorate could be in cinema and filmmaking with an emphasis in special effects.

"Simon . . . Hensley." I omitted "Doctor" to keep it simple. Actually, I omitted it twice: once for computer engineering, once for physics.

"Si-mon . . . Hens-ley." I didn't know if she was mocking me or imprinting my name on her memory. "You're a teacher, aren't you?"

That'd be a good guess since I wasn't a reporter and I was *there* at a university. I suppose she could have thought me to be a student. Or, she could have heard or seen my name around campus. Or, "Did Geoff tell you that?"

"Geoff?"

I nodded across the room in Geoff's direction. She turned and looked, though in the darkness it was hard to tell him from anyone else.

"Oh, Dr. Gibson. No. No. Why would he say anything—No, I can feel that kind of energy coming from you. What subject do you teach?"

"*Subjects.* Computer engineering and physics."

"Yes. . . that makes sense. You're a man of science. You like for things to be concrete, solvable, provable." She paused, looking toward the ceiling. "Do you pace a lot when you lecture? I get that your students think you do."

"I suppose I do. It's almost involuntary. I don't think anything about it—"

"There is someone with you now."

"Someone?"

"A spirit . . . You used to play baseball, didn't you? In school, Little League, or something like that as a youth? I see you pitching." She leaned on her cane and brought her free hand up to her chin. She looked as if she were seeing something that wasn't there. "How do you connect with the term 'slider?'"

"Slider?"

"Yes. Is it a nickname?"

"It was for about half a season, long ago." She couldn't have known that, but, again, Geoff could have. Now, I wasn't thinking Geoff had conspired with her to defraud these poor unsuspecting participants, his statistical "data points." And now me. But, he was the only living person in my circle of friends and acquaintances who would know about that game, if he even remembered it.

When I had pitched for my Little League team, the Comets, I had developed a tremendous fastball through hard work and many hours of practice. Geoff had gotten me on the team the first summer after my father had died so that I could learn some badly needed coordination skills and teamwork. At that young age, my mind was nimble, but my feet and legs lagged far behind in agility.

My first attempts at winding up and pitching were so awkward that silence fell on the parents in the bleachers behind the chain-link backstop—the kind of spontaneous silence that signals when something is wrong. Perhaps they were stifling their laughter; maybe they were cringing inside. But, I felt their eyes upon me. And, I felt ridiculous. I kept at it, though, practicing every day throwing pitches to my invisible friend in front of the old oak tree in our back yard and letting the balls bounce off of the tree.

After a while, my fast ball became well known in our end of town. But what nobody had caught onto was I had also picked up a natural slider. Without trying very hard, I could make a pitch look like a fastball, then have it break left or right in the strike zone and suddenly drop. I had never before tried it outside my back yard, though. I guess I just didn't have enough confidence to.

"You struck him out," she said with a distant look.

"Yeah, a kid named Dylan." Dylan was the league's best hitter. Even at that age, the coaches, the parents, and the local paper were predicting he would go pro someday. And, the coach of the Comets, the team with the worst record in the league, had me up against him. I'll never know why.

"Everyone was expecting a certain pitch, but that's not what you did. A voice told you, 'Slider, slider.'" I had been afraid if Dylan connected with one of my fastballs, he would have knocked it out of the park. But, I didn't know what else to throw. Then, as I was ready to throw a fastball a voice called to me inside my head, and I changed my grip in mid windup to throw a slider. "I see three pitches, three swings, and he was out. I see him standing there with a shocked look on his face staring at you." She couldn't have been more right. And no one could have known that. No one, except for me, and I had never told anyone.

Goosebumps popped up on my arms and legs.

"The voice, Simon. . ." She still had a faraway look. "The voice was your father."

There comes the moment when the weight of a load will crumble even the strongest of foundations, especially when those foundations have just been blown away. Take, for instance, those old buildings sometimes seen on the news that are imploded when explosives are set off in the right order, in the right places. The building collapses on itself in just a few seconds. When the cloud of dust disappears, all that is left is a heap of rubble and a new landscape.

This was one of those moments for me. First, I couldn't disprove Victoria's readings. Then it was Chuck's readings I couldn't disprove. The people at those meetings seemed genuine. My machine, no matter how it did it, picked up the same messages the mediums were giving. I had swept the room for electronic trickery and found none. Now this. Margaret picked up on "slider" and the voice that had been inside my head.

I looked her straight in the eyes. She couldn't have been putting me on. She looked serious. There were no signs of a practical joke. She wasn't smiling. Then it hit me hard. "Holy crap," I said. A new reality just collided with me. And, if all of this spirit stuff were true, that meant I had invented the world's first mechanical device that could communicate with the dead. It had received the same signals as the brains inside the heads of these so-called mediums — psychics, whatever they wanted to be called. Sometimes you've simply got to surrender. "Holy crap," I repeated. I didn't take my eyes off of her nor did she take hers off of me. Her expression turned to one of concern, worry. She reached for my shoulder with the hand that wasn't on her cane.

"Are you all right?"

"Fine. . . fine." I barely got it out, then turned, grabbed the bag. "Excuse me, I've got to go." I ran all the way home.

Chapter Twenty-three

FOR THE REST OF THAT NIGHT and every spare minute for the next two weeks, I tried desperately to understand what the machine was doing. I skipped going to any more sessions until I had it figured out. So, once again, I went over the entire code line by line, character by character — this time without Hannah's help. If she had found out what I had been doing, she would surely have thought I had gone nuts.

What seemed to have happened was this. The machine had done exactly as it had been programmed to do: to simultaneously evaluate all possible solutions to a problem and arrive at the most probable one, learn from its environment like a human brain, use Hannah's intuition algorithm, synthesize thought, learn from its own experience, correct its own mistakes.

My hypothesis, therefore, was that by leaving the machine in the same building where Geoff's paranormal research had gone on, some kind of paranormal signals had tunneled through the xenocryst. The machine then set out to learn about those signals lacking human inhibition or fear.

Further, it had blocked out all other interference, an unintended consequence of programming it to interact with its surroundings while preventing the surroundings from causing multiple probable solutions to crash into a garbled mess.

As the purple spiral had spun restlessly over the last few weeks, the machine had learned how to home in on the communication waves that penetrate the barrier between the living and the dead, tunneling both ways carrying information. Then it converted those waves into the language and images of its environment and displayed them onscreen. The machine itself was indifferent. It was nothing more than a modern day telegraph, a new kind of text messaging or email service, or a new Skype.

The implications boggled my mind.

Dead people talking. What insanity! Life after death, life after life. What nonsense! Alive is alive. Dead is dead! All this talk of spirits and ghosts was the stuff of cheap fiction and bad films, right up there with zombies and vampires.

That was what I had always thought before going to Geoff's séances. Now, one moment I relinquished the old ideas, another moment I was still certain there was no afterlife.

But, seeing is believing. Margaret had said I simply had to trust my own eyes, ears, and common sense. Could I?

If a post-life life did exist, if the machine worked as I supposed it did, then the resulting effects on the world would be revolutionary. Science, philosophy, and theology would need to be re-thought in entirety. Naturally, though, critics will always find a way to refute challenges to their established ways of thinking. Apologists of old ways will quickly reject me and call me crazy or sorcerer, warlock, evil, occultist, anything and everything but the computer researcher I really am who stumbled into a totally unexpected portal.

Maybe I was delusional. Perhaps I'd had hallucinations. Or both. I made up a word for it: "delucinations." Yes. That's what they were. It couldn't have been real.

Still, if it were true there was an afterlife and if inhabitants of the afterlife and this life can really communicate with the aid of a machine I had invented, I couldn't begin to fathom the ethical implications for myself and for the world at large.

But I tried.

I got out a paper notebook and pencil, then began to jot down my stream of consciousness of benign uses for the machine.

History

Talk to great historical figures directly. Get the real facts from the original sources: Charles Babbage; Alan Turin; Joan of Arc; King Arthur; Genghis Khan; Hammurabi; Cheops to find out how the pyramids were really built. Why did Da Vinci write backwards?

Literature and the Arts

Did Shakespeare have a ghost writer (no pun intended,) as some scholars claim, Sir Francis Bacon maybe? Would the Bard like to write new plays? Would Bach write new fugues? Would Robert Frost write new poetry? What letters would Mark Twain write to the earth? What was Jane Austin really like? Vincent van Gogh?

Unfinished Works to be finished

Franz Schubert's Unfinished Symphony, Thomas Aquinas's Summa Theologica. Kafka's, Hemingway's, Dickens', J. R. R. Tolkien's unfinished works. Donald Knuth's "The Art of Computer Programming."

Equally as important: unfinished expressions from deceased loved ones, like my mom and dad. Give voice to everyone for unspoken sentiments, forgiveness, good-byes. Closure, reconciliation when there hadn't been time or opportunity.

Philosophy

Pick the brains of some of the greatest thinkers of human history. Who knows what they might have learned after death? Soren Kierkegaard. Jean-Paul Sartre. William James. Rene Descartes.

Seeking Advice

Would people in the west begin to seek advice from departed elders, like many people in eastern cultures do? With the machine, would it catch on here? Are spirits always smarter or wiser? Would people get a false sense of security and abdicate their responsibility for making decisions?

Crime-solving

Swear in murder victims under oath and they could identify their killers, or swear in dead witnesses and they could give testimony.

I put my pencil down and thought about that one for a moment. The dead don't lie, do they? Would the Supreme Court allow their testimonies?

Espionage — Political/Military/Corporate

Spirits may be able to get around to places where we physical creatures couldn't. Could they be recruited to spy?

After the list was finished, I added two of the most important people in human history I would like to talk to: Adam and Eve. Who were they really? Where did they come from? What was life really like for them?

I went outside the greenhouse for a breath of fresh spring air. At my feet was a tulip bed my mother had planted years ago and one I had done little with. Green shoots had broken through the fertile black soil— scouts checking to see if it was safe to come outside. As in so many springs before, their red blooms would soon open upward to catch the sunlight and dew while their roots drank from the rich soil's moisture. This was photosynthesis yielding simple elegance and beauty from the weird world of quantum effects.

The following morning, I went straight to Geoff's office and barged in.

"Okay, Geoff. You've convinced me."

"Good, lad. Glad to know I can still be persuasive. But... about what?"

"All this spirit stuff you've been studying." Had there been anything else? "Okay... I'm a believer. Life after death. Dead people can talk. All of that. I've given up my entire world view, and now I have to start over and develop a new one."

"Just like that? It took me years."

It wasn't "just like that," but I didn't want to tell him about the machine. I didn't trust anybody, not even an ex-priest-friend-of-the-family with that knowledge.

"Well, I'd say then I have been persuasive, lad. Although, let me persuade you of one other thing."

"What's that?"

"Go slowly. You're entering a world about which you know nothing. Even those of us who have studied it for years don't know the full extent. We know enough to know not everything is as it seems. And there are hidden dangers, plenty of them. Remember that."

I just listened.

"But this work is worth it. When I can document our research and arrive at a full hypothesis — and I'm so close — that proves once and for all our lives don't end here, people don't really die, and we can still talk to them, that we are all connected in some strange but beautiful way. It will change the world."

I could no longer argue against him.

"Look. Astronomers and astrophysicists continually monitor the heavens for signs of life elsewhere in the universe, even if it's only microbial life. Some of them hold that if humans receive signals or proof of life, especially intelligent technological life, that would be the biggest discovery in all of human history. I say that will be the second biggest discovery if I can document my findings and *if they can be repeated by others.*"

Just then, Hannah walked by. I hadn't seen her in weeks. I abruptly excused myself and rushed to catch up to her.

"Hannah," I called out, slowing down, suddenly feeling foolish and realizing how it must have looked as if I had something urgent to say. "I haven't seen you in a while. How've you been?" I wanted badly to tell her about the results of our work, about the success we'd had together. I almost did. "I just wanted you to know—" And, I thought better of it. "—that I appreciate the work you did and. . . I've missed working with you." Although that was true, I didn't know if it was too personal or too strong a hint.

I could swear she blushed. "Thanks. I'm running late. I've got to go." She turned and left, never one to stay and talk unless it was all business.

Running late, or just running? Was it the other professor she was running from—the one from her old school—and the scars she bore, or was she running from me? Perhaps she was running from something else. Herself, maybe. Or maybe I'm just not that appealing, to her or any other woman for that matter. There may never be a chance to see if we could have other successes, too, or give it a try. I didn't know what else to do, to say.

I went back to Geoff's office. "Sorry. I haven't seen her—"

"Of course, of course." He waved a hand dismissively. "I remember what it's like to be young, Simon, even if I wasn't technically available at the time." His tone became serious. "Look, these are serious matters we were talking about. Just be careful."

That night I had been working in the greenhouse until I was so tired I could no longer think straight. I locked the door thinking how easy it would be for a burglar to break the glass or bend the aluminum frame and get right in. For that reason, I didn't keep anything of extreme value out there.

I went inside, locked the back door, and slogged with heavy feet to the bedroom. I managed to pull off my shoes and pants before falling into a deep and dark, dreamless oblivious sleep.

Sometime later, a blinding streak of light hit my eyes as startlingly as a glass of cold water. Then I heard my name. When I sat up, the light went away, but I noticed the machine was on. I opened it, but had to shield my eyes against the light from the screen.

"Simon."

The voice was my dad's. Even though it had been more than eighteen years since his death, his voice was unmistakable to me. When my eyes had adapted to the light, I looked at the screen. Before me was a crystal clear image of Dad as I remembered him, not pixelated, not washed out. He had been a thin man, tall and rather ordinary looking, but a beautiful sight to me. His hair was shaggy, just over the tops of his ears, and slightly messed up. He had worn glasses, and Mom had always made sure the frames were in style over his protests. He had thought function reigned over form, but had always given in. In life, he brushed his hair once each morning and said that was good enough. If it got messed up during the day, he did nothing about it.

"Dad." My voice quivered. "My God, Dad. I've missed you. Is this real? Am I dreaming?"

"It's real Simon. You've found a way to get through to us. You're a hero over here."

"Hero?"

"Simon, millions of people desperately want to talk to their loved ones again. On both sides, there where you are and here. They've got things to say. And now it looks like you may have made that possible."

"By accident. I wasn't looking to do. . . *this*." I pointed at the machine with an open hand. "Wait. How do *they* know about the machine over there? I haven't told anybody. . . here."

"Word gets around fast. Thoughts even faster."

"So, somebody's watching me?"

"Everybody has somebody checking in on them now and then. It's part of the plan."

"What plan?"

"It's too complicated to get into. Suffice it to say, there is a plan."

"And my machine is a popular idea over there?"

"Very popular."

"What's it like. . . you know. . . *over there*? Do you have a body? A home? How do you get around?"

"Simon, it's fantastic here. We don't have bodies in the physical sense, but we do have independent consciousness. We don't hurt, and we don't get tired. We travel by thought."

"By thought. So, where you want to be is where you are?"

"You are where you focus your attention."

"If you don't have a body, then why are you wearing glasses?"

"I'm not. You just see me this way so that you recognize me."

"How's Mom?"

"Doing great. We've been together every minute since she arrived. We've had a lot of catching up to do. She let me come to you first since she had fifteen years more with you than I did."

I wanted to ask him a specific question, one that had been on my mind recently. In life, Dad was an Asperger's guy like me. He was not always very emotive, and he didn't smile much, except at Mom and me. But I always knew he loved me from the way he'd often lift me up onto his lap as he sat on his three-legged stool in front of the black slate workbench in his greenhouse laboratory. He showed his love by showing me the world of biology hidden deep below his microscope, by explaining the things I saw. That tiny world of plant cells, human cells, nuclei and mitochondria, purple stains, miniature organisms — that was his world, the world he shared with me. I could sense his great satisfaction in doing so. And, I loved him for it.

That was then. Tonight while I had him around, I needed him to share something else about the world he now inhabited. "Do they have Asperger's there?"

"The Asperger family, like Hans Asperger? I haven't run into them."

Dad could sometimes be so literal as to seem obtuse. "No. Asperger's *disorder*. You know, like me. . . and you."

"I knew what you meant. I was just messing with you. You sometimes take me too literally. To be truthful, son, I've never thought of Asperger's as a disorder. We Aspies just have a different way than Neurotypicals of viewing and dealing with the world. Just different, that's all. But, to answer your question, no. We communicate mostly by thought and understanding each other's intent. That pretty much eliminates communication difficulties and social awkwardness, don't you think? Words aren't necessary, so they never get in the way."

We talked for a long time. Then, Mom appeared. She was worried I wasn't eating and sleeping properly and that I hadn't gotten married. She and Dad would like to have grandchildren, even if they couldn't be together physically.

Then Dad said, "I'll check in with you again now that I can."

Mom said, "Good-bye for now, Simon. I love you."

That quickly, they were gone. I said, "I love you both, too," but the screen was already black.

I lay back on top of the covers. The clock said it was three a.m. Outside a neighbor's dog barked, the street light cast a faint glow on my window shades, and that was about all that was going on. It was a normal night. For the rest of the world.

But, I had just talked to my dead parents. Why couldn't they have lived? Was that part of *the plan* — this unknown complicated plan? I supposed the plan had so many probable outcomes for every decision we make, each outcome with so many probable consequences that if we tried to imagine a fraction of them our heads would swim.

The plan had taken the only two people I had ever loved and had left me alone.

My parents had had something special: each other. And now, they were together again; I was happy for them. They'd had a love I'd always thought would evade me, the kind of love that made them happy just to be with each other. They hadn't gone out a lot, and I'd seen them dance only one time, at a wedding party. The band played *Color My World* and the lead vocalist sang, ". . . I realize just what you mean to me. . ." Mom held onto Dad's neck; his arms wrapped around her waist. Dad's feet barely moved and had no rhythm, but Mom didn't seem to mind. They looked at each other the whole time. When the music stopped, they stood there for a moment holding each other. He kissed her lightly. Then they had come back to our table holding hands.

Will I always be consigned to a life alone?

Chapter Twenty-four

ON THE FOLLOWING FRIDAY NIGHT, I went to the session bursting to tell Geoff about my experience with Mom and Dad, yet utterly reluctant to do so. My emotions were a see-saw. What had happened was so incredible, yet I wasn't ready to make known my invention. I still wasn't a hundred percent positive I hadn't had a hallucination, or best case, a dream.

I got to the meeting room during the social time, and the crowd was just beginning to build. I went over to see Geoff, still unsure whether or not I would say anything about the machine. Before I could say much, Margaret came into view. Geoff looked her way and then asked me, "You met Dr. Margaret Switzer last time, didn't you? Wonderful lady, tremendous psychic." He tried to get her attention by waving, but she didn't see him. "She's an MD, you know."

"An MD? No, I didn't know. And yes, I observed her group."

"A psychiatrist. She founded a psychiatric hospital just south of town, Mt. Liberty Residence."

"Never heard of it."

"She and her staff deal with extremely difficult, non-violent cases of mental illness."

More people shuffled in, and the room got noisier. I had wanted to ask Geoff some questions but didn't want to shout to be heard. Obviously, he was a believer, Margaret too. Apparently then, his research had been overall positive. What had he learned? I had never been one to accept overly broad answers to questions, such as "Take my word for it," or "Trust me." I had always needed more depth, more meat on the bone. So, I had to ask.

I tapped his elbow and leaned in, stepping further away from the crowd. Geoff followed me. "Has your research shown why some people are really good at readings and why others don't receive anything at all?"

"That's what we're trying to find out. But I've got some ideas that'll be going in my paper when I write it," Geoff said.

"I overheard Margaret tell someone psychic communications are as natural as breathing, and everyone receives them at one time or another. If that's so, why don't we know it?"

"It's a little complicated." He pursed his lips. "But here goes. The human brain has an exceptional talent at constructing and interpreting our reality for us. It fills in some blanks for us so we don't have gaps in our perception, and it filters out what it thinks we don't need to be aware of. The psychic signals— I prefer to think of them as waves—are typically filtered out. We're too busy with other things."

"If they're so important, why are they filtered out?"

"In terms of survival, they're not that important. Look, if you were equally aware of all the sensory input around you—if you had all five senses on high alert at all times—you'd go stark raving mad. Add to that a sixth sense. So, the human brain has learned to filter out the vast majority of sensory input and focus only on what matters most at the moment. In psychology, we call it selective gating. That's generally thought of in terms of visual input but can be thought of in other ways as well. Psychic input tends to be on the periphery of our perception, so it's easy to ignore. Or, alternatively, and I think this happens more often than we know, we regard them as our own thoughts.

"There are some fascinating theories that could help explain psychic phenomena beginning with this point: no one has ever been able to describe consciousness with any scientific certainty. Some scientists believe consciousness is a quantum process, like that computer you've been building for years. Some researchers think the human brain has lattice microtubules in the cytoskeleton of brain neurons that have the ability to tunnel within the brain communicating with other neurons, running multiple processes in parallel. In other words, thinking along different lines simultaneously, finding the shortest path through the brain and settling on what we think is the best answer. Add to that, recent experiments show brain waves can be received outside the skull through brain-computer interface devices that are being used to help stroke and spinal cord patients manipulate prosthetic devices."

"Some of that I tell my students. But, you make it sound like the brain is just a mechanical device – a peripheral you can hook up to."

"Or, quantum computers are devices that act more like brains than we ever thought."

"What does that have to do with your studies of psychic phenomena?"

"Ah, lad. . . that's where science gets elegantly weird. Quantum consciousness *could* mean human consciousness can exist in multiple states at the same time, past, present, future." He paused for a moment looking at me to see if I got it, which of course I didn't. "Life. Death. Both. Something in between."

"Alive and dead at the same time? Are you kidding me?"

"Absolutely not. Think about the communication with spirits you have witnessed. Their bodies are biologically dead. Their consciousness just exists in a different state, the same consciousness they had when their bodies were alive. Some theories, not necessarily mine, suggest that information from the brain appears to survive outside the body. If that's so, in the cases of near-death experiences, consciousness first transforms into a different state, leaves the body temporarily, then returns. Now that I think of it, multiple states of consciousness could also explain déjà vu." He got a faraway look and paused before continuing. "One feels as if he or she has experienced something before. Maybe he or she did in a sense, all at the same time. Perhaps one is presented with multiple situations, outcomes, and instantaneously chooses one and the others vanish, yet leave a residue like a real experience that's soon forgotten. . . It's just a thought. . . Anyway," he lowered his voice to where I could barely hear it above the din of the room. "I think I am close to demonstrating we are all connected to a larger reality, like collective consciousness. If these theories are right, quantum information from our brains may be handed off to the universe upon our deaths. Or, all of the parallel brain waves may collapse into a single state and one's identity is preserved—"

"Sounds like you're describing a soul." I looked away for a moment. "You know, Geoff, this is way out on the fringe of legitimate science."

"I'm using the techniques of legitimate science to construct a sound hypothesis and test it. That's why I'm holding these sessions, to experiment and build on the work of the pioneers in this field and take it in a new direction: explaining psychic readings."

"There'll be a lot of scoffers. A lot of reputable scientists criticize those theories of consciousness. I've read about them and some of their predictions haven't held up under scrutiny."

"True enough. But, the jury is still out. Remember, at first, the Big Bang Theory was scoffed at. The very name was pejorative. Who's scoffing now?"

"Quantum consciousness still doesn't make complete sense to me."

"Of course not. It's all too new and beautifully bizarre. If it makes sense to you, you don't really get it. If it doesn't, you're perfectly normal."

"I understand the laws of mechanics at work inside machines. . . but inside humans?"

"Well, talk to Margaret. She has a different take on it. I'll let her tell you her story." Margaret was standing at the refreshment counter with a cup of coffee talking to an older gentleman. Geoff waved at her again. "Margaret, over here."

Margaret joined us. After a couple of minutes of polite talk, Geoff went off to greet other guests as they shuffled in then came back carefully carrying three cups of steaming hot coffee wedged in a triangle formation in his hands. After giving a cup to Margaret and one to me, he took a sip and abruptly veered off of our small talk. "Margaret, why don't you tell Simon in your words how you came about your psychic abilities. While you do that, I'll mill around."

Margaret seemed pleased at the suggestion, and we slowly migrated to a corner of the room where there were several arm chairs. I set the machine in the book bag on the floor while Margaret took a seat. Then, I scooted a chair up and sat down facing her.

Chapter Twenty-five

"It was a long time ago," Margaret said, "1985, after my final, final in medical school at Üniversität Zürich. . . sorry, University of Zurich—"

"Ich spreche ein wenig Deutsch," I told her. "I knew what you said."

"Sehr gut." She gave a raised-eyebrow nod. "Anyway, a number of my classmates and I pooled our money and rented a cottage in the mountains for the weekend. They asked me to pick up four bottles of Chateau Lafite-Rothschild Bordeaux 1982—"

"Okay, I don't speak wine."

She tapped my leg playfully with her cane. "The good stuff—in bottles with corks, not in boxes. Anyway, we were so poor after all those years in school. And to think we were finished. We were ready to toast the lives ahead of us. Well, after picking up the wine, I was on my way up the mountain road toward the cottage in my brand new, little red Alfa Romeo Spider convertible Father had given me just a week earlier for a graduation present. The road was steep and winding. It was dark. I mean, forest-in-the-mountains dark. From out of nowhere, a deer jumped in the road right in front of me. When I woke up thirty-two days later, I found I had gone off the road and landed on top of a three-story house below, which probably saved my life. But my leg was shattered and I had severe head injuries." She pulled her hair back and traced a scar the shape of an upside down horseshoe with her finger. In the dim light, I had to lean in to see the scar.

"I can't imagine," I said.

"But wait, there's more." She set her cane against the arm of the chair and scooted forward. "I don't usually talk about this so soon after meeting someone. . . but, Geoff asked." She folded her hands on her lap and straightened her posture. "During the coma, I had a near death experience." She said it with a straight face and paused.

I crossed my legs and braced my elbow on the arm of the chair.

"I did," she said, crossing her heart. "God's truth, already."

"Let me guess. You saw a bright light and a voice told you to go to it."

"Cliché, isn't it?"

"That's what they all say, right?"

She thought about it for a second or two. "I suppose if that's what you expect to see, that's what you'll see. But, that's not at all what I saw." She paused again, looking at me. "Shall I go on? Yes?"

I nodded.

"I saw a place I was approaching—and it was well lit." She gave me a look as if to tell me to hold my comments until I heard the rest. "Colors were bright but didn't glare. The closest thing I can compare them to are those LED Christmas lights. There were a lot of people, I suppose I should say spirits but they looked like people, standing around in clusters, not mingling, just standing in groups talking. As I got closer, it looked like a big meeting room or reception hall. Not much different from this room except there were no tables or chairs. The floor was covered with bright red carpet—"

"The red carpet treatment."

"It wasn't like that. It was like wall-to-wall carpet. Anyway, nobody paid any attention to me, until a group of five or six cut through the crowd and came toward me. I took it they were there to greet me. When they got closer, I recognized them: dear friends and family who had passed away. I knew I wasn't there to stay, just to watch—"

"That'd be reassuring."

"You'd better believe it." She smiled and feigned a sigh before going on. "Behind the big open area was a wall that divided it from rooms with windows. They were like offices with people in them sitting at desks."

"Desks? What were they doing at desks?"

"What you normally do at desks. Work."

"That's supposed to be heaven? Work?"

"What do you suppose they do there? Sing in choirs all the time? Strum harps?"

"I hadn't really thought about it."

"Would that be heaven to you?"

"I couldn't carry a tune if one crawled into my pocket. So, point taken. What do they work on?"

"Same things as here. They study. They learn. They research. Do you think—?"

"Wait. Who told you all of this?"

"I wasn't told anything. . . I just kind of understood it all." She leaned toward me. "Do you think all of our marvelous ideas and creations originate with us?"

"You mean to say our original ideas aren't really ours?"

"Not all of them. Even Sir Isaac Newton said he saw farther because he stood on the shoulders of giants. Those giants may not always technically be alive." She studied my face closely. "You may think I'm crazy, and I don't blame you. For a while I thought so, too. That's why I decided to specialize in psychiatry—for self-help."

"So you psychoanalyzed yourself and determined you're not crazy?"

"Not I alone. I went to counseling for two years because of the trauma. . . and because I began to receive messages out of the blue. Spirits came to me. I didn't ask them to. Worse, the messages were for other people. At first it was the people I knew then it became anyone who was around me. It's never gone away." She took a sip of coffee looking at me over the cup. "And, before you ask, I am *not* delusional. And, that dear Simon, was the beginning of my psychic powers."

"How would a head injury be responsible for that?"

"I don't know. Perhaps it rearranged brains cells, or made them more sensitive. Perhaps the injury had nothing to do with my abilities. Maybe they would have come anyway. Maybe it was the near-death experience that changed me."

"Hmm. Psychic psychiatrist. Has an alliterative allure to it."

She pursed her lips and tapped my leg again with her cane. "I see already it is past time to start," she said.

We stood up. I said, "It's all. . . *so* hard to comprehend, so hard to take literally. It's so incredible." I threw away her empty coffee cup and stayed with her as we walked slowly toward her group in silence.

Then I stopped. She turned and looked at me. "Can you teach me how to do this psychic stuff?" I asked.

I stayed with Margaret until after the break when I went across the room to join another group that had caught my attention. There was more light there, and I preferred it. The host said her name was Drew, and she invited me to join them. I was immediately drawn to her and thought how easy it would be to believe anything she said. She was in her mid- to late-twenties. Her skin was smooth as caramel, and an unusually provoked thought told me it would taste as sweet. I shook off the thought like a pitch I didn't want to throw. Thick dark hair swooped over her ears and was tied behind her head. Her eyes smiled when she smiled, and I liked that very much. So much, in fact, I kept looking at her eyes. I must have smiled, because she smiled an even broader smile and I just about melted. My eyes darted away, but only for a second, and I was looking back at her again.

Then I noticed. In this light her eyes looked as if one were blue, the other brown, a condition I'd heard of before called heterochromia. Funny, though, I had to look hard to detect the difference.

As the session opened, the group sat silently, looking expectantly at Drew. The room was filled with a soft hum of conversations. Slowly, Drew picked up a pencil and scratched some notes on a legal pad. She put the pencil down and sat perfectly motionless, trancelike, for a minute or two with the palms of both hands flat on the table, a distant look in her eyes.

Suddenly, she began to speak. I'd expected a soft soothing tone. Instead, there was an intensity, urgency. She wrote something on the paper. "I sense a name. . . beginning with C or K. I'm being directed to ask about someone whose name begins with a C or K. That spirit was close to someone at this table. Does this make sense to anyone? I think it's a mother, grandmother, sister, aunt. The name begins with C or K. And this person had an illness and was sick for a long time. Does someone have a relative or close friend whose name begins with C or K?"

I glanced as surreptitiously as I could at the machine inside the bag on my lap. The screen was blank; the crystal barely lit up.

"I feel it's a feminine energy and female name. Carol, Carly, Carla, maybe spelled with a C, maybe a K, or maybe two different names like a first and middle name. Carla Kay, Carol Kay. Karen, Kerri. Does that ring a bell with anybody? One initial may be for the first name, the other for a last name. When spirits give me initials, they want me to pay attention to it. So I have to keep coming back to it. The initials may be theirs, or someone they're with, or someone you both know who has either passed or is still here but is a connection between the two of you. Does that make sense?"

I frowned, recognizing a basic fortune-telling technique I'd read about. With any given group of five or six people, the chances that one in the group knew someone with a name beginning with C or K was a near certainty. Then, the fortune teller gets the person to fill in the blanks, while the fortune teller makes high probability generic guesses and sweeping general statements.

"Yes. I know someone—" a woman said.

"Who was she, please?" Drew asked. Her soft eyes had turned strange, intense.

"She was my grandmother—"

"Did she live with you? Did you live with her? Live near her? Did you spend a lot of time at her house?" Everybody had a grandmother they wanted to be near.

"No—"

"I thought not."

And there was the old trick, the disappearing negative. If the subject had said "yes," the response would have been, "I thought so."

"Still, I see something about a house. Were you with her at her house?"

"No—"

"At your house, your mother's house? I still see something about a house, but we'll go on." Of course. Everybody has a house of some kind.

I glared at Drew now, disappointed and glad I hadn't fallen for everything she'd said. "Has she passed? I sense she has already passed or is close to it. She has or had an illness. Did her name begin with C or K? I'm directed back to the letters. When I'm given the letters, they mean something, and I can't ignore them.

They don't always spell a name or a word, but they're given to me for a reason. They ground us to something the spirits want us to know."

I peeked into the backpack again. Nothing. I looked up. Drew had mastered the look of compassion and dished it out in heaps on this poor woman.

"Her name was Kathryn," the woman said.

"Spelled with a C or K, please?" Drew asked.

"With a K."

"That tells us what the K is about. Whenever spirits give me initials, they don't want them ignored. And, they keep bringing me back to them until we figure it out. Initials are too powerful, and receiving them is a powerful message. Do you understand what I'm saying? Spirits can't always speak directly to us and we can't always receive directly from them. So they give us signs to connect us to the messages they want to give us. Does that make sense?"

"I suppose," the woman said.

Drew went on. "She had or has an illness. Has she passed? If she hasn't, she's in danger of passing soon. She—cancer. Did she have cancer? That may be what the C is about. I keep being directed back to the C."

"She passed away about two years ago. She had a heart attack and died."

"Was she at home when she died or in the hospital?"

"She died at home, suddenly," the woman said.

"That makes sense. That's what the C stands for, cardiac or coronary. And she must have had coronary disease for a long time."

I felt myself scowl. Keep going, Drew, I thought, and with enough wrong guesses you can eventually get her to tell you her whole life story and you can take credit for it.

"Whenever I'm given a letter," Drew said, "it means something. Spirits don't give me messages that don't mean anything. And the house... she was telling me she died at home."

She finally got something right.

"She is here with you tonight," Drew said. "She wants you to know that. She wants you to know you can still communicate with her. When you get those warm feelings and fond memories, she wants you to know she's sharing them on the other side. You have something of hers. Right? Something she left behind that was important to her and to you. What is it?"

I checked the machine again. The screen was a complete blank.

"I can't think of anything," the woman said.

"A necklace, bracelet, watch, ring, piece of jewelry, or something. Could be costume jewelry or real gems. Do you recall what it is?"

"No. She never really gave me anything. Not much anyway." Disappointment colored her expression.

"Nothing? She's telling me she gave you something very important," Drew said.

"She moved away when I was very young. I got toys and dolls as a little girl but nothing beyond that. She didn't have a lot of money."

"Did she give your mother a necklace or bracelet or something similar? I see something around a woman's neck, something sparkly. Could she have given your mother a necklace or some jewelry. Did you play 'dress up' with her or your mother's jewelry?"

"No. I never played 'dress up' with their jewelry . . . I had a doll with a necklace when I was a little girl. But, my grandmother didn't give it to me."

At least this subject was making Drew work for it.

"She's pointing at a doll with a necklace. That's it. You got such enjoyment playing with that doll, and she got such enjoyment watching you play. That's what she wants to say. She wishes she could have been a bigger part of your life after she moved away. She wants you to know she can still be a part of your life. She will always be near you. Whenever you want a hug from her, just think warm thoughts about her and she'll be there."

Drew swallowed hard and took a breath. "I'm getting a message for someone else. A name beginning with T or D . . ."

I slipped out quietly and went to an empty room down the hall. When I got there, I checked the machine for loose connections and battery power. Everything was fine.

When I went back in, I kept my distance from Drew.

I stayed behind to talk to Geoff after all the people had left. I didn't know how I was going to tell him what I thought without revealing my machine. But, I had to try.

"That Drew's a fraud."

"That implies you must believe the others are real." Geoff rubbed his eyes. "But yes. Brilliant one, that Drew."

"She's a phony." To my relief, he didn't ask how I knew, perhaps because it was late and we were tired.

"I know. I hired her." Geoff laughed. "She's my control, my placebo. She's in on it, the research, that is. And, oddly, when we get reviews back from participants, it's surprising how many people think she gave them a great psychic experience."

"Oh, she's pretty good at it, all right. But aren't you concerned about the ethics of giving fake readings? People go home thinking they've really heard from the spirit of a loved one. Do you think that's right?"

"Maybe it's a gray area, but people choose to come here of their own free will, and I don't make them any promises. If they get comfort, well, it's no worse than what they get from those 900 numbers that charge by the minute. And, Drew doesn't dispense advice." He thought for a moment. "Maybe it does go right up to the line. Maybe it crosses the line a whit, but I rather don't think so. Anyway, it's all in the name of science. I've got to have a placebo to have a legitimate study. If there's any breach of ethics, it's mine, not Drew's. She's just doing what I pay her to do."

"So, it's buyer beware in the realm of psychic phenomena?"

"Especially so."

After the meeting broke up around midnight or a little later, I walked home. It was cold outside and the wind had started picking up. I had seen some strange things over the last several weeks and was now past denying their validity. A new world had been opened up to me, literally a new world, and I should have been analyzing the radical and sudden changes in my world view. But, not on this walk home.

    I couldn't get Drew out of my mind. I knew nothing about her, only what Geoff had told me a few minutes before. Maybe it was the warm timbre of her voice when she had spoken or her airy whispers that lured me. Maybe it was her posture, poised but relaxed, or the way her slender fingers had draped over the flesh of her folded arms, or the way she had brushed an errant strand of dark hair over her ear with her fingertips. Maybe it was the way she had moved effortlessly across the room, gently stirring the air leaving traces of her perfume that I couldn't name, but nonetheless made me want to go with her. It could have been all of that. It could have been something more.

    The wind picked up again, but luckily for me, it was at my back. I hurried. Half a block away from home, there was the splintering crack of a large tree limb overhead that came crashing to the ground. I jumped out of its way just in time and continued on.

Chapter Twenty-six

WITH ANOTHER SEGMENT of my recent past complete and neatly filed in my mind, I waste no time going to see Margaret to tell her about it. Maybe with this revelation, I can finally go home. But less than half an hour later, I trudge down the hallway back to my room disappointed again. Margaret said it's wonderful that I remember how we met at the séance sessions. I left out the parts about the machine and what I told Geoff about Drew and other incidentals that shouldn't matter to her for the moment. When I asked her if I was well enough to go home and finish recovering there, she thought it best if I stayed a while longer. She thinks there's more I'm better off dealing with here. Apparently, she knows something she's not talking about. When I asked what it is and why she just doesn't tell me in order to jog my memory so that I can expedite getting out of here—actually, I said expedite my return home—she said that would be cheating and wouldn't do me any good. So, here I stay. For now.

Chapter Twenty-seven

FORCING YOURSELF TO REMEMBER something forgotten is nearly impossible; at best it's very difficult. Memories simply don't appear on demand like cable TV. They sometimes pop into your head spontaneously. Like this one did just now: the pencil Drew used during her placebo reading was the eraserless kind. Just like the one I found lying on the ground next to the bench in the thicket.

I kept that pencil, forgot about it; and now I can't find it. This room isn't that big, and I don't have much stuff here, so it shouldn't be too hard to find. I rifle through the bureau drawers and find nothing. I search under the bed, feeling around with my hand. It's not there. I give up looking and pull out my best pair of khakis to change into. When I unfold them, the pencil drops onto the floor. I snatch it up, finish getting dressed, and head out the door towards Andrea's place. Or, Drew's place.

I pass through the thicket, glancing momentarily at the bench to see if Andrea is there and stop at the tree line, peering through at her house unsure of what I'll say if she's home. The last time I saw her, I ran away like a scared little rabbit. This time, she'll have to chase me away.

My heartbeat quickens a little and butterflies flutter in my stomach. But, I go on, clutching the pencil in my hand, knowing that returning it is simply an excuse. Some people seem to need excuses to do what they know they should do anyway. That includes me today. I should just run up to her, tell her I'm sorry I bolted the other day and let her know I really want to get to know her, I'll hang around a while if she'll just let me. But, that approach lacks finesse. I've never understood why you can't just say what's on your mind, openly and honestly, especially when it's about the important issues such as relationships. I've been told that's the Aspie in me. But, no matter how I would say it, my feelings are the same. Michael once told me it's really important to use finesse with women, especially early on in a relationship. I don't really have finesse. At least I don't think I do. But, I guess some people need excuses, others need finesse.

When I get closer, I see she is squatting on one knee in front of the back porch with ear buds in, listening to something while she churns a bed of rich black soil with a trowel. The flower bed runs the full length of the porch with flowers blooming in shades of red, blue, purple, orange, and yellow.

I don't think she hears me come up behind her. She's wearing cutoff denim overalls with a white tee shirt underneath; her hair is pinned to the back of her head in a ponytail bob; her fingers are caked with dirt; bare toes dig into her flip-flops for balance. She couldn't be more beautiful in a Versace gown.

I put the pencil in my hip pocket, step a little closer, and circle around so that I approach from her side. "Andrea," I call. She looks up and smiles. I smile back. Soil encrusted fingers pull the earbuds from her ears. I crouch to her level.

"I was just in the neighborhood." I smile sheepishly. What a transparent line. So much for finesse, but I'm making this up as I go along. "Thought I'd stop by."

"If you weren't dressed so nicely, I'd have you help me. This is the very last of my spring planting." She carefully lowers a petunia into its new home and with her fingertips gently sculpts the soil around its roots into a firm little mound. "It's almost too late in the season for planting flowers."

"What counts is that it *isn't* too late. Right?"

She smiles while she continues to work. "Right. It takes time and effort to cultivate a beautiful garden. You've got to be patient. You know, life is a beautiful garden." She looks up at me and I see them. Blue and brown. The most beautiful eyes I have ever seen.

"I like flowers," I say. "But I don't have much finesse with them."

"You've got to have the right match: flowers, soil, location, and timing. Then give them tender loving care. You know what I like about these?" She points to some tall foxgloves loaded with dangling bell shaped blooms in purple and white. "And these." She points to daylilies, bright yellow and orange flowers leaning way out of long grassy leaves. "When the blooms die, you can pick them off and new ones come right back, fresh and vibrant. They always give you more than one chance at a beautiful garden."

Andrea picks up the trowel and sets it on a tray that has several small pots of flowers waiting to be planted. For a moment I envy them, knowing that soon her hands will gently hold them. She brushes the dirt off of her hands and sets her hair loose to fall to its full length and shakes her head a little. She rises gracefully with the tray in one hand.

I move to the steps. When I sit down, the pencil reminds me of its presence by poking me. Andrea comes over to sit next to me, but not close. I pull the pencil out and twiddle it in my fingers a bit before saying, "I remember how we met the first time." I hand her the pencil. She frowns quizzically as she takes it and puts it in her bib pocket. "I found this on the ground by the bench before we met . . . the second time. You used one like it at Geoff Gibson's séance research session."

"I like pencils without an eraser. They force me to think more carefully before I write something." She shifts her weight to one side and tilts her head to look at me. "I'm glad you remembered. I remember. You were there observing."

"And you were there—"

"Acting." She laughs a tiny laugh, and a smile remains on her lips.

"I'm glad your part was just an act."

"I've known all along about you being there. I wanted to say something, but Margaret told me to let you remember on your own. Do you remember anything else?"

"It's still a blur, but the fog is slowly lifting. I was beginning to piece together that you must know Margaret—living next door and being at the research sessions. What I'd like to know is, how did you learn to do your act?"

Chapter Twenty-eight

ANDREA TOLD ME on our last visit about growing up a "carnie," as she called it. There was a sparkle in her eyes, a sweet expression on her face, wistful, longing — the kind that comes from retelling beloved memories and wishing for a return even if only temporarily to a simpler time, a feeling I have sometimes had since the passing of my mother. She recalled being home schooled while crisscrossing the United States, Canada, and Europe, caravanning with trucks hauling the pop-up circus. And she, the only child of the handsome tuxedoed emcee, magician, and animal trainer and his glamorous assistant and musician, both now gone, like me was left alone.

But, that day, we ran out of time, and it got dark before she could tell me what her dad's new scheme was for his loquacious daughter.

Now, there is time:

Before Andrea was even a teenager, her father had dreamed up another new act featuring her called "Drew The Seer." Andrea had a small tent of her own with a flap that could be pulled closed behind a customer. Inside, there was a small round table with a table cloth that festooned onto the lumpy canvas floor.

There were also two chairs: hers, a cheap reproduction of a throne that engulfed her small body, and the visitor's, an uncomfortable old wood slat folding chair to entice customers not to linger.

She said not a word and let her father do all of the talking until it was time to start her act. She had a gift, he barked out to curiosity seekers outside her tent, a miracle that had given her two different colored eyes and with them the ability to see what others could not. "Step right up, look in the eyes of Drew the Seer and let her read your soul, your past, your present, your future." He said the same thing in every town, every county, every province they visited. And for ten dollars each, she performed her miracle.

I ask her, "How did you know what to say?"

"By reading a lot—books, horoscopes and, believe it or not, fortune cookies. Then trial and error. At first, it was very scary for a twelve-year old girl. I would rather have sung the *Star Spangled Banner* and try to hit the high notes before a stadium of eighty thousand people. It was that kind of scary."

But she practiced and practiced, and it quickly came to her. She practiced on the truck drivers. She practiced on the little people husband-and-wife clown team, the guy who made the funnel cakes, the burly guys in shirts with cutoff sleeves who drove the tent stakes into the ground, calling them all into her tent one at a time and putting on the airs of an eastern mystic and rolling her r's. She even practiced on the Chinese acrobats her dad had hired that summer who didn't understand but a fifth of what she said. And she came up with the same formula she had used at the séance research: talk fast; talk over people if you have to; be indistinct such as using letters or initials instead of whole words. Or, use words that "sound like" another word that might be meaningful. Ask a lot of questions to induce the person being read to provide information and then use imagination to build on what they said. Use the double negative, that is, ask questions that she could respond to with either, "I didn't think so," or "I thought so." And most importantly, sound confident no matter what.

"One thing I have learned, Simon, is that real readers are specific. They make specific references, use real names. Sometimes they don't get it quite right, but it is close enough to be recognizable. But even with real names you have to be careful."

Andrea says years ago she had learned of a fire at the National Personnel Records Center in St. Louis that had destroyed nearly 18 million military records for U. S. Army and Air Force service members. She demonstrates how that could be used.

"I'm getting something, Simon." She puts fingertips to both temples as if she had a headache. "Someone is with you now. Wait. . . I'm getting his name. It's Richard." She rolls her r's. "He went by Ricky. He wants you to know he is with you to protect you. Yes. . . I can feel that he is a protective spirit. Yes. He was a soldier. He died in World War II. I can see his full name. Private Ricky Mullen. Oh, I just lost him."

"But with his military rank and full name I could go look up his service records—"

"Yes, Simon." Her fingertips go back to her temples. "Ricky wants you to know that you may not be able to find his service records. He's showing them to me in flames. There was a fire. Yes. . . a fire involving military records that were burned and lost forever. His records may have been among them. He wants you to try, though, for validation. Oh. . . I'm getting how he died. He says it was at Iwo Jima. I see it. I see him. This is horrible. It's such a dark and dangerous place. There are explosions, gunfire, blood, death. I see bodies. I see him get shot several times before he falls into mud. Oh my God, I can't stay there any longer." She closes her eyes, shudders, then calms down and opens her eyes becoming perky again. "Just like that," she says.

"Wow, you're good. I knew you were faking and you almost had me believing."

"That was the idea. Except it was supposed to be for entertainment only and not to defraud anybody. Admission to 'Drew the Seer' was only ten dollars. And people came to our carnivals to have fun. I didn't think a thing of it until one day an elderly man came up to me."

The man, she says, wore a gold wedding band on his right ring finger. He had just lost his wife of over sixty years and could barely speak without tearing up. Andrea was almost eighteen at the time and well-practiced at fake readings. The man sat stoop-shouldered in front of her, looking down, hands clasped almost prayer-like. He just wanted the comfort of talking to his wife, he said. His health was failing and he wanted her to know he was not far behind her and he wanted her to be there for him when his time came.

The man's sorrow pierced Andrea, she says, and she choked up listening to him. This wasn't entertaining, she thought. There was no fun in this. She didn't know what to say and just wanted to give him back his ten dollars. Instead, she began to speak and couldn't believe the words coming out of her mouth.

"Lester," she said. The man hadn't told her his name. "Phyllis wants you to know she is waiting for you." He raised his head. His eyes reddened and glistened, his chin quivered. Andrea says she really saw Phyllis, not with her physical eyes, but in her mind. And, not an old Phyllis, but a young one, around thirty. "Red hair," Andrea said to Lester. "Oh, she's a radiantly beautiful redhead." That made him smile for the first time. "In a yellow sweater—Lester," Andrea said, faking reproof, "that's what you liked about her the first time you met, wasn't it?"

Lester attempted a short chuckle that came out like a sigh. "Guilty," he said. "But that wasn't all. She was as beautiful inside as outside. She was a teacher. Loved children. Raised ours and taught hundreds of others. Loved every one of them, too. Well, almost every one."

Andrea stops the story there. "After Lester, I told my father I was through. No more 'Drew the Seer.' It freaked me out."

"I'll bet you didn't really stop, did you?" I ask.

"I stopped the act. I stopped taking money—until Dr. Gibson hired me for his research. But, I couldn't stop receiving messages. I didn't know what to do with them or about them. To be honest," her tone becomes somber, "I thought I had gone a little crazy."

I know the feeling.

"Can you stay?" she asks. "I've got a few more flowers to plant, then we can have lunch."

Chapter Twenty-nine

IT'S DARK NOW. My room feels so closed in after spending the afternoon and evening outdoors with Andrea. I'm still thinking about how graceful and tender her hands looked as she set the last petunias in the ground and gave each one a good long drink. After that, she washed up while I waited on the porch in a rocking chair, rocking slightly in the shade of the house. She returned with a tray with all the makings for sandwiches and a pitcher full of lemonade cold enough to make our glasses sweat. I watched her lissome fingers place deli thin slices of turkey breast on top of dark green leaves of lettuce, ruffled and overhanging a slice of bread, followed by thick slices of Swiss cheese she carefully arranged while apologizing it wasn't Comté or Beaufort, two types of French cheese I had never heard of. Then she drizzled some spicy mustard across the arrangement and topped it with another slice of bread. She delicately cut the sandwiches in half diagonally. Andrea had to have seen me smile. At home, when I make a sandwich, I just slather mayo onto the bread and slop on a few slices of lunch meat. This was a feast.

We talked about everything, we talked about nothing, until the lemonade was gone, until the sun went down.

Once again time ran out.

As I have said before, to force yourself to remember something is at best extremely difficult. Even more so if there were good reasons for forgetting. But, now, I've got to try. I can't spend any more time here at Liberty. No one should have to cut short life's great pleasures once they're found. I don't know if this is what being in love feels like. I've never been in love before. If this is it, I like it.

I could just leave, go out the back door, make my way through the thicket, across Andrea's property and out to the highway where I could either hitch a ride back into town or walk, then come back for Andrea. Or, maybe Andrea would take me home. Except, it wouldn't be fair to Margaret to leave without giving it one more good try.

Difficult or not, I've made up my mind. I'm not leaving this room until my memories are fully restored, not to eat, not for any reason. I don't know how I'll do it, but I'll do it.

Yes, I do know how: hypnosis. Just as Margaret had done.

I lie down and place a fingertip on my forehead, feeling its warmth. The warmth spreads as if gentle waves of warm bath water were pouring over me. From my head to my toes. I'm at the top of the stairs now. Slowly, I walk down them, counting: one, two, three... I'm at the door to the unknown room. I go in and sit down. This time, I demand answers. This time, I remember.

Chapter Thirty

THE NIGHT I HAD MET DREW THE SEER, I hurried home from the session with the cold wind at my back. After narrowly avoiding a collision with a falling tree limb, my thoughts returned to Drew, or rather, Andrea. I wanted to see her again and knew I must somehow.

The wind gusted even more harshly. At the back of the house, the metal greenhouse door rattled. Before I got all the way onto the porch, my thoughts switched briefly to Hannah.

My attraction to Hannah had never felt like this feeling I suddenly had about Andrea, yet I had known Hannah longer. And, my hints to Hannah, my attempts to suggest we could change our relationship when the time was right, went unnoticed, deflected by disinterest. Perhaps I was to blame for her cool indifference. Perhaps I hadn't used enough finesse. Perhaps if my father had lived he could have given me a few tips. Computer engineering and physics were simple compared to understanding women.

When I got home, the warm air inside felt good on my face. The cold had made my eyes water and my nose run. I hung my coat up and kicked off my shoes.

My thoughts bounded away from humanly matters. In the last few weeks, the very way I had always looked at the world and the universe beyond it had been revolutionized, uncomfortably so, and I didn't know what to think about it. I'm not the kind who likes a lot of changes I didn't plan for myself. On the other hand, I must admit, when I did plan changes, I was impatient to see them put into effect. But, these sudden changes in my world view, my understandings of science, philosophy, and theology had come at me too fast to sort them out and assimilate them. Rejection would have been my normal reaction; but as the man of science I prided myself in being, I had to accept the weight of evidence.

There was too much on my mind right then. I took my clothes off, tossed them onto the chair in the corner of the bedroom and slipped under the covers for a nice cozy night's sleep, perchance to dream. But sleep didn't come.

After a while of staring at the waves of moving geometric patterns on the backs of my eyelids, an idea came to me. I should try to make an outbound call through the machine to my father and get some fatherly advice. What good was the machine to me if I couldn't do that? I got up, pulled the machine out of the bag, and then stared at it, lacking any idea of what to do. Before, the machine had blocked all my attempts at input. But, I'd give it a try.

"Dad," I said looking at the screen as if it were a human face. Then I thought, how would they, *over there*, know whose dad I was calling? "Dad. This is Simon. Simon Hensley. I'd like to talk to you."

A face appeared but it wasn't Dad's. It was a total stranger with a kind looking face, old with deep-set smile lines around soft-looking eyes, slim but with slightly sagging jowls. His rumpled hair was gray and thin on top.

"Who are you?" I asked.

"My name is Philippes Legrand—"

"I was trying to get through to my dad."

"He couldn't make it. I'm afraid he was busy attending other duties." This didn't feel right, but I went along with it. "You don't know me; I died long before you were born. In France. 1587 to be exact, during the War of the three Henrys." He spoke with no accent. Spirit thought must work that way.

Instantly, an image was displayed onscreen. Pale, bluish-gray bodies stained with blood, stripped of their clothes and dignity, were piled knee-high in the streets outside of medieval-looking stone buildings. One building looked like a palace. Naked men dangled from nooses. A body was tossed out of an upstairs window like so much refuse. Loot was carted off. Dogs barked. Soldiers with spears and swords were stabbing unarmed people. Not even babies were spared. "It's the Louvre, the St. Bartholomew's Day Massacre," Philippes said. "There were over thirty years of the French Wars of Religion, fought by zealots on both sides. I saw them all. Wars in the name of piety."

A torrent of revulsion ran through me. I wanted to look away but was held captive by the repugnant images. Eventually, I said, "Go away." Instantly, Philippes' face returned, calm and almost pious.

"No. Not that easily," he said.

"What do you want?"

"I'm here to warn you."

"About what?"

"Are you aware of what you're about to unleash?"

"Unleash? Yeah. A whole new way to view the world and life and death. A way of giving hope to billions of people that our lives don't end just like that." I snapped my fingers. "Nor do the lives of our loved ones. And we can stay in touch with them, learn from them. Possibly — probably — get help from them, which is what I was trying to do with my dad until you popped in." I looked at the clock. "It's two-oh-nine a.m. Maybe you don't need sleep, but I — "

"Sleep? You think that's important? You don't get it, do you? You are about to change humankind's entire understanding of their place in the universe."

"So did landing a man on the moon."

"And undermine nearly all of the world's major religious and philosophical systems. The first thing that will happen is the church will demonize you. Talking to the dead is unholy they will say. It has been thought to be of the devil for millennia. Do you want people to think you're of the devil?" Of course I didn't. All of this metaphysics stuff was new to me, and I wasn't even persuaded of the existence of a supreme evil being. Even so, I didn't want to be equated with him, or it. "Scientists will denounce you as a kook or a fraud."

"The church has been wrong before, and they adapted and survived. There doesn't have to be inherent conflict with the church because of showing that the afterlife isn't what we've been led to believe. It's no different than changing their understanding of the earth's place in the solar system. Remember Galileo? I'll simply have to prove some things. And. . .

and scientists will give in before the church does. So, don't threaten me with how I will look."

"Then how about this? Undermine the authority of the world's religions and the values they represent, you will set off chaos. Sheer, utter chaos. People won't know what to believe anymore, whom to trust. Morality will decline."

"I couldn't disagree more. You're selling people short." But, he may have had a point. I could turn on the news any day and see how low humans could sink. I thought about it some more. "Maybe I should introduce it gradually."

"Or not at all."

"What are you saying?"

"Consider your idol Charles Babbage—"

"How did you know about Babbage?"

"I know more about you than you think. You've made quite an impression over here. But, as I was saying, Babbage was so close to having a working computer he never completed, fortunately."

"Fortunately?"

"Timing is everything, Simon. Think what may have happened if he had succeeded making his Analytical Engine so short a time before the bloodiest war on American soil, the one you call the Civil War, and just a few decades before the first of the two most vile wars ever fought in human history, World Wars I and II. Suppose he had given the world a working computer to help analyze, strategize. The wrong sides could have won. Millions more people could have been lost."

"But Alan Turing developed a computer that helped win World War II—"

"Forget Turing. He would have been inconsequential if the other side had had a working computer before him."

"Well, then, maybe wars could be averted with a little understanding from 'beyond.'"

"It is commendable that you focus on what you think will be the positive outcomes. For every positive, there is also a negative. It's almost like Newtonian physics, the equal and opposite reaction." He may have had me there. "If that's not enough, go public with your machine and you'll be a marked man, I promise. There are many who will want to control your machine for their own purposes."

"Such as?"

"Controlling information — and opinions — is power. Dictators, governments, religious authorities have used that premise forever."

I rolled over on my back and rubbed my eyes, then turned back towards Philippes. "What are you suggesting?"

"Destroy your machine."

"You're nuts. No, I'm nuts for listening to you!" I slammed the machine shut. The xenocryst glowed brightly.

No matter how hard I tried, I couldn't get back to sleep. I had no idea who Philippes really was, where he really came from and why he really came to me other than to scare me. But still, he'd made some good points.

From childhood on when I had envisioned building a small room temperature quantum computer that could run processes in chunks, my thought was to provide the world with a machine that could be programmed to observe the world and learn like a human brain but work much faster and more accurately than classic computers to provide such things as medical diagnoses and perform medical procedures too intricate for human hands, to process climate data in order to understand climate change and mitigation in real time, to better understand genetic connections to disease, and a litany of other improvements for humanity. My dream had become a partial reality with the introduction of Michael's Emorite crystal; but what it had learned was totally unexpected, and now I find maybe unwelcome. I wasn't ready to believe Philippes, but if I had believed him, then my machine could cause as much or more harm as good. And I would be responsible.

Philippes' axiom, however, had a ring of truth to it. Not all probable outcomes of an event or problem are necessarily good. I wrote at the bottom of the page entitled "Uses:" *For every probable use, there is an equal and opposite probable abuse.* Then, I wrote some down.

ABUSES

Religion
Would actually talking to Jesus, Mohammad, Moses, Buddha, etc. undermine or affirm religious beliefs, morality, compassion, benevolence?

Psychological/Emotional
How will people react to a new view of life after death? Would it give them greater peace? Less concern for health and safety, or more? Would they see life as

something continuous? Would life become more valuable, or less? Would death become less dreadful?

Social/Political
Would the dead try to influence society or politics? Hitler trying to revive the Third Reich? Again, did the dead lie, conspire, cheat?

Miscellaneous
Steve Jobs could tell us what amazed him so much his last words were, "Oh, wow."
Military, governmental, corporate espionage if spirits worked in collaboration with the machine's owners.

OTHER CONSIDERATIONS

Unintended Consequences

This was the biggest, perhaps the most serious category yet. But, by its very nature, this category would be empty until the consequences were encountered.

By the time I arrived at the realization that Philippes' concerns were predicated on the computer being reproduced in numbers, which meant there would have to be more xenocrysts than just the one I had, the sun was up and I needed to get ready to go to work. Philippes was either a crank or he must have known there were more xenocrysts in the same manner that he knew more about me than he had the right to know. I quickly resolved to press Michael the next time I talked to him to find out how abundant the supply of xenocrysts was.

Chapter Thirty-one

IN THE AFTERNOON OF THE FOLLOWING MONDAY, I went to the lounge in the activity center at Finial U to get a jolt of caffeine to perk me up. In a nook off to the side of the student lounge was a row of vending machines that dispensed chips, nuts, candy, soda, bottled water, breath mints, fruit, you name it. If it could go in your mouth, a machine had it. And one even dispensed the potion I was looking for, a cold cappuccino.

Just the other side of the nook's wall was a wobbly table with two chairs. The machines' humming made a curtain of noise that blocked out distractions, so I sat down there, reached into my bag and pulled out my work laptop, leaving the xenocryst machine in the bag. I logged onto the Internet and looked up the War of Three Henrys and found this:

In the sixteenth and seventeenth centuries, in total Europe had a hundred years of Christian wars, Roman Catholics and Protestants against each other battling for religious supremacy, which equaled power and control and riches. The wars started only a few decades after Martin Luther's Reformation movement in 1517, which had challenged the authority of the Roman Catholic Church. Wars at that time were often fought along lines of religious loyalty more than loyalty to the state. Thus, religious persuasions led to wholesale killing. The War of Three Henrys was the last of more than thirty years of religious wars fought in France in the late sixteenth century.

While I read from the screen, a hand started waving in front of me to get my attention and a voice faded in. Hannah had come up to my table. "Dr. Hensley, you must be deep in thought." True enough, I could get that way. Actually, I could sometimes get so focused that I blocked out everything else for hours.

It had been a long while since I had talked to Hannah, other than trying to get her attention in the hallway when she was always in a rush, and I couldn't remember what our last conversation had been about. But, I was certain I still hadn't told her about the machine's strange new powers. Now there she was, books in hand, and a few feet away one of her girlfriends appeared to be waiting for her. Not long ago, I would have been silently begging her to sit down, hang out with me, and talk about something other than algorithms. Nevertheless now, I simply wished to return to my reading.

"How's your program?" she asked. I knew she meant "our" program. "Anything new?"

I was trapped. I couldn't lie. What should I tell her? Yes, it works like a charm and, by the way, it calls on dead people? Glibness is not one of my strong suits. My life has been filled with incidents of wit of the staircase, those instances when you think of the perfect thing to say — but only after it's too late.

"I'm still tweaking some things here and there." I supposed that wasn't bad. "Nothing new to report." There it was: "to report" were the operative words.

"Well, let me know if you need me to do anything." She joined her friend and they walked away together.

I returned to the article about the three Henrys.

The warlords were three men named Henry. One was Henry III, King of France and a Roman Catholic; one was a Roman Catholic fanatic and leader of a Catholic alliance The Holy League; the third was a Protestant Huguenot.

The three Henrys invaded each other's territories killing and stealing. Matters got worse when Spain sent troops to support the Catholics, England sent troops to support the Protestants, and later Germany made two forays into France to support the Protestants, one unsuccessful, one successful.

The King of France was eventually assassinated by a priest. The Protestant Henry converted to Roman Catholicism so that he could be crowned the successor to the French Throne. He was later assassinated by a Catholic fanatic.

Assassinations, massacres, expropriation of property. Wars that killed thousands. Horrors in a wrapper of piety for the sake of power and privilege. Some historians claim the religious wars had determined the balance of power in Europe for the last five centuries.

What power it is to control religious thought! And with power come privilege, prestige, and money.

Was that Philippes' point in dragging me into wars that were settled centuries ago? Was it that history shows people's cruelty and depravity when it comes to forcing groupthink onto others and the barbaric extent to which the jealously powerful will go to keep their power? I wasn't about to invite him back to clarify.

But, that was then. This was now. People are supposed to be more civilized, more tolerant now. Still, what if Philippes were right? What would I be responsible for in the wake of a sudden shift of the world's views and values?

Then, an idea came to me. With half an hour to go before my next class, I closed down the computer, quickly shoved it into my bag and ran to my office, scribbled a quick note saying today's session had been moved to the Hippodrome amphitheater and trotted off to tape the note to the classroom door.

The amphitheater was a legacy feature of the campus from a time decades ago when Finial University was still a liberal arts college. Upon transition to a science and technology institute and the elimination of the performing arts, there had been a big debate about what to do with the amphitheater. Donors who had contributed handsomely for its upkeep naturally wanted to see it maintained and used for its original purpose. Others had preferred demolishing the amphitheater to open up space for future development of a science building. In the end, it had been cheaper to maintain the amphitheater in some form rather than to raze it, fill it in, and construct a building that hadn't even been proposed yet. And so it stayed.

The amphitheater was not large. It had six rows without seats terraced up the side of a hill at the northeast end of Finial's campus, the farthest point away from the noisy streets. An acoustic shell rose above the concrete podium. Each row was two steps deep, grassy, and retained by rough cut granite blocks.

As a concession to the science building supporters, statues, busts, bronzes, and reliefs of great contributors to science had been erected on the top row and the area had been paved in cobblestone. Honoring solely science figures had sparked its own controversy, so as a concession to the liberal arts donors, monuments of contributors to the arts and philosophy had been added later. That spat had occurred years before my time. The compromise had rubbed some the wrong way, but it seems you can never please everybody. As for me, I saw no conflict with great notables of all fields and all times co-existing side-by-side. The amphitheater became a millstone to university administration and so it was later developed into a botanical garden just to make use of it. Over time, it had come to be used mostly for runners going up and down the terraces.

I had run these terraces myself with Michael for a while every morning when we were still students. I would run from my house — then it was my mother's — to the dormitory where Michael had stayed. We would start out running up and down in the amphitheater and from there run three miles before coming back. And, it was easy to hurt yourself running the terraces because of their odd spacing. Up wasn't so bad. Going down was the risky part.

One time on a cool spring day like today, I had twisted my ankle going down but had managed to make it up again right behind Michael.

"Stop." I breathed heavily. "Gotta give my ankle a rest."

Michael bounced up and down running in place while I braced myself against a statue to stretch my Achilles.

"What chaps me," Michael said with a cheeky grin, "is that there aren't any statues of geologists here." He smacked the back of Galileo's head who was peering through a bronze telescope. "We have our rock stars, too, you know."

"Funny." My ankle throbbed. I let up on the stretching. "Name one."

"You wouldn't know him if I did."

"Isn't that the point? But, try me, anyway." Stretching my Achilles wasn't doing any good, so I sat down on a granite block and rubbed my ankle.

"Okay. Friedrich Mohs."

"Nope. Don't know the name."

"He devised the hardness scale for minerals. How about Benjamin Franklin Mudge?"

"Nope."

"A former mayor of Lynn, Massachusetts who moved out west and became the first State Geologist of Kansas."

"Okay, let's go." My ankle had settled down. We took off running again and left the plaza of statues behind us.

"Hey, what can I say? Geologists are down to earth guys who don't get much limelight." I groaned at him and kept running.

Now today, I thought the presence of the likenesses of great minds of the past, Newton, Einstein, Turing, Plato, Pythagoras, Da Vinci, Galileo, Curie, Edison and others watching over us, made the amphitheater a good setting to pose an important question to this class of brilliant young minds.

I sat on a granite ledge waiting with my feet pulled up. One at a time and a few in pairs the class arrived. They must not have known how sound could carry in an open air amphitheater. I didn't catch who it was, but one student said, "Wonder what's going on?"

Another said, "Something's up. It's not like Hensley to be spontaneous."

"Or fun."

"My allergies are killing me," followed by three sneezes in a row.

"Maybe he's going to make us run the terrace if we don't give the right answers."

"Over my dead body."

"With your body, Christopher, you'd be dead in no time and we would be running over your dead body." They laughed, although it was true, the pudgy Christopher was out of shape and always seemed to be snacking on something. But, he was very sharp, and in truth, I hoped for his insights.

When they'd all settled in, they were seated in much the same order as they usually had been in the class room: the more alert and responsive ones in the front, the shier ones behind them.

"Look around you," I said, making a sweeping gesture toward the statues with an open palm. "These are people who were ahead of their times, whose ideas, works, inventions, changed the world forever." Most of them looked around. "Is changing the world a good thing or a bad thing?" The majority, like me, dreamed of changing the world someday for the better. Whether or not change was good, they seemed to agree, depended upon the outcome. "Then, let me open this for discussion. Can you think of human inventions or developments that have turned on humankind?"

I would have been shocked if someone hadn't brought up all things that emit carbon: furnaces, car engines, factories and plants, followed by nuclear energy and nuclear weapons, the low hanging fruit. Those topics came up right off the bat.

For the next forty-five minutes, we wandered through a dense forest of human inventions that could go wrong, which was just about everything humans had ever invented. Even the discovery of fire had a malevolent side. Medicines for blood pressure can stop a heart; drugs to treat pain can also addict; governments and institutions that can free people can also enslave them. One student, who was usually so quiet I couldn't recall her name, pointed out that since the Industrial Revolution machines that had been meant to free us from labor had made the masses dependent on the machines for their livelihoods and had addicted consumption-based economies to the fruits of the machines' production.

Even the lowly saddle stirrup was guilty of malevolence. While the stirrup allowed horse riders to easily mount their steeds and ride more comfortably, it also gave firm footing to the medieval warrior horseman to lodge his lance solidly into the chest of his opponent.

The printing press allowed for the proliferation of books and education and the eradication of illiteracy. But knowledge set loose required more knowledge and more technology. Technology always requires new technology to replace the old in an unending chase. The list went on and on.

"So is it fair to say," I asked, "that for every use of an invention, there are unintended consequences, possibly even an equal and opposite abuse?"

From the front row, Christopher said, "Maybe. But the abuse is *potential* abuse. If every time an invention was used the equal abuse was triggered, nothing would ever get done and we'd end up back in the stone age. In most cases, the abuse occurs only a fraction of the time. The common element in all of those scenarios is the human element. It is only humans who can use a human invention for bad purposes."

That was the kind of answer I'd hoped for from Christopher. But I was seeking true north on this. "Now let me ask this: If you as engineers or designers invent something or work on a team that develops something, are you personally morally responsible for misuses of your product?"

No one jumped in right away. I let the silence work on them psychologically awhile to squeeze out an answer while I looked up at the plaza of statues. A slight breeze moved the limbs of a bush in front of Thomas Edison. He appeared to be looking at me. Then the bush hid him again. Madame Curie seemed to be awash in a yellow glow. It was just the angle of the sun, I reasoned. I pulled my attention back to the people in front of me.

Christopher was saying, ". . . if something's used other than the way it's intended to be. The knife that butters your bread can also be used to stab someone. Should knives be banned?"

Behind him to the left, Lauren said, "X-ray equipment saves lives, but the radiation is also harmful."

Voices began to blur. From the back row someone said, "I have an offer to go to work for a defense contractor to develop smart weapons systems. If I can help with designs that minimize the loss of life, it's a good thing." "You're still responsible for the lives those weapons take." "I think you're just rationalizing because the defense industry pays well." "I can definitely see both sides." "It's the lesser of two evils." "But the lesser of two evils is still evil!" "But if you intend for it to do good. . . "

On the back row all the way to the right sat Philippes, legs crossed, hands folded and laid on his lap. I couldn't believe my eyes. I looked away and looked back. He was still there, dressed in old fashioned clothes as I imagined someone from sixteenth century France might dress. I closed my eyes then opened them squinting. The class was still there talking, but I couldn't hear them.

"Are you going through with it?" Philippes asked in perfect unbroken English. His voice was all I heard now.

"Going through with it?"

"Proceeding with your machine. Making it available to the world."

"If you've been here all along, you've heard the conversation. Good and evil depend upon one's intent. I intend only good things. So, yes. I'm 'going through with it.'"

"If you do, you'll live to regret it." And he was gone. From kindly old peasant soldier to scaremonger just like that.

When I looked around, the chatter had stopped and people were staring at me. "Who were you talking to, Dr. Hensley?" Christopher asked.

My thoughts were jumbled, my tongue was twisted. All I could get out was, "That's all for today."

Chapter Thirty-two

THE DISCUSSION IN THE AMPHITHEATER SETTLED NOTHING for me, and I couldn't get Philippes out of my mind. Midday, I went home a little freaked out and burrowed in, just the machine and me. Along the way, I had the creepiest feeling I was being watched or followed. When I looked around, there was nothing unusual going on. Just the same, I felt a shadowy presence around me, something dark, unnerving. When I got home, I locked the doors, including the greenhouse door, and made sure the windows on the first floor were also locked.

In the refrigerator there were three raw hot dogs, six slices of bologna, two fingers of milk in the bottom of a half-gallon jug, two sticks of butter, applesauce in a jar, half a dozen eggs, and shoved all the way to the back was a single bottle of Blue Moon Michael had left that would simply stay there unopened until the next time he came for a visit. Or until I threw it out. In the cupboard there were half a loaf of whole wheat bread and two packages of Ramen noodles. All of that meant I didn't need to go out for a while.

After settling down a little, I melted some butter in a skillet and fried two slices of bologna to make a sandwich and took it into the living room with the remaining milk poured into a glass and sat down to watch television. The Science Channel and National Geographic had nothing good on, and there was no baseball on ESPN. That feeling of a tenebrous presence returned and creeped me out. I muted the television and got up to check the doors and windows just to be sure they were still locked. Later, I checked them again, and still later, I checked them again until I finally convinced myself of the irrationality of checking every few minutes.

While I stared at all the motion on the television, my brain was an overcrowded chamber with thoughts too impatient to wait on another one. I thought about the machine. Then came thoughts about Hannah, Drew, dead people. Back to the machine. Something on TV triggered a thought that fizzled out altogether. Then, back to the machine. One thought would rise like a soap bubble, then pop. I clicked the remote.

On one of the movie channels, there was a high speed car chase. Two cars leap frogged past each other with occupants hanging out of the windows shooting guns. It wasn't my kind of movie and I left the television muted, but it reminded me of a time a few years ago when Michael had test driven a brand new Camaro and had stopped by my house shortly before noon on a Sunday to show it to me. He'd been thinking about trading in his rock crawling Jeep for something with a little more flair that "the ladies would like."

We went west out of town into the flatlands of farm country where carloads of families were returning home after church for Sunday dinner. The road was a two-lane state highway in pretty good shape.

Michael passed the car in front of us. "It's time to see what she's got." He stepped on the gas.

"Acceleration is good." Too good as far as I was concerned. Michael kept accelerating, passing, accelerating more, car after car. When I looked at the speedometer, I thought it said one hundred fifteen miles per hour. I felt like screaming at Michael, but at that speed, I didn't want to startle him, so I kept my mouth shut all the way back to my house.

Michael could be reckless like that sometimes, throwing caution to the wind, whether in pursuit of thrills, profit, or discovery. In a rare admission, he had told me once he'd lost all of his money playing Blackjack in Las Vegas while at the same time owning a sizeable stake in a solar panel company that went broke. One hair away from bankruptcy, he had hit it big in an investment that had bailed him out. I surmised that, too, was blackjack.

But, this was the first time he'd ever been reckless when I was around. "What were you doing!?" And, it was the first time I had ever raised my voice to my friend. "You could have gotten us killed!"

"Relax," he said with a grin. "I knew what I was doing." I wasn't so convinced. My insides quivered and I suddenly had to go to the bathroom. Michael walked around the car inspecting it and looked under the hood.

"So, are you going to buy it?" I wanted to know because if he were to buy it, we'd have taken my car any time we went somewhere together from then on, or we'd have gone separately.

"Nah. Rock crawling is more fun." I couldn't have agreed more.

Even today, my pulse quickened just thinking about it. But in like manner, I now wondered if it was time to throw caution to the wind and test this machine of mine "to see what she's got."

Calling on spirits was a new thing to me, and I still wasn't sure how to go about it, especially after encountering Philippes. Should I simply open the lid and start talking to whomever I wanted? I didn't know if I had done something wrong the last time when I got Philippes instead of Dad. It was worth trying again.

I didn't leave the house for two days; I had lost track of time and didn't know what day it was until around midnight on Saturday and realized that Geoff might still be at his usual research session. I had some incredible things to tell him, but I hadn't told him about my machine and didn't know how to explain what I had to tell.

When I got to Geoff's meeting room, he was by himself stacking chairs along the far wall and didn't notice me. He was startled when I walked up to him.

"There you are, Simon. I wondered what had become of you—"He looked at me closely. "You look tired. Are you all right?"

"Yes. Fine. I think. Why? Do I look that bad?"

"No, no." He set down a chair he had been holding. " I looked for you last night and again tonight and wondered where you were."

"I've got some incredible things to tell you."

We crossed the room to a pair of upholstered chairs facing each other. Geoff was right. I was tired, exhausted really. But, I was energized by excitement. Geoff would surely think my news was good.

As if I were making an announcement, I said, "I no longer have grounds to be skeptical about all of this spirit stuff—communication, I mean. The evidence is overwhelming. As a man of science, I've got to go with the evidence."

"That's great news." But, his expression didn't match his words. He looked at me intently. Geoff is one of few people I can look at directly without being uncomfortable. But, the intensity of his gaze concerned me.

I told him I'd had the experience myself. I had talked to spirits. Hundreds of them. I began to name some: Da Vinci, Michelangelo, Mark Twain, Kafka, Nikola Tesla, Bertrand Russell, Carl Jung, Isaac Asimov, Jane Austen, Mozart, Beethoven, Benjamin Franklin, Emily Dickinson—"

"Go easy, Simon."

"Emily Dickinson said in retrospect she should have thought more about her life than her death. And Shakespeare. He ignored me when I asked if he had actually written all of his plays. But he told me if he were alive today, his next play would be about a soldier away at war in Afghanistan who gets a letter from his girlfriend back home. She tells him her feelings for him have gone cold since he's been gone and she must break it off with him. He writes her back, and says he felt the chill in her letter, but not to worry, he has an Afghan to keep him warm at night. In true Shakespearean form, it ends tragically when—"

"That's all good, Simon, but—"

"And Charles Babbage. Strange thing. He was cheerful, amiable, unlike his reputation. He told me that waiting a hundred and sixty years to be recognized wasn't as bad as it seemed. Time flies when you're dead—"

"Okay, Simon. Stop."

"I thought you'd be pleased." I had expected smiles, maybe laughs, giddiness, a slap on the shoulder, fist bumps, something.

"I am. Of a sort. A breakthrough like that is highly unusual. Normally, it takes time, a lot of it, and patience." I was tempted to tell him about the unit but didn't. "But, you should beware. There are malevolent influences all around us. You must be careful. Did you say an invocation before you began these communications?"

"I don't believe in prayer. I've been open about that."

"I still have some of my Catholic roots, and I begin every session with a prayer asking for divine protection against harm. It's imperative, Simon. You don't know who—or what—is out there. Heed my words." He raised his hand and for a moment I thought he was going to make the sign of the cross. Instead, he patted me on the shoulder with a gentle touch, a fatherly touch, a priestly touch. But not a pat of celebration. "Come. Help me slide these chairs over to the wall and I'll give you a lift home. You should get some rest."

Afterward, we made a silent trip in Geoff's silver Volvo and pulled up in front of my house.

"Heed my words," Geoff said, as if he knew what my thoughts had been.

I went straight inside and heeded his words—to get some rest.

Physically, mentally, and spiritually exhausted from the onslaught of new things, I plopped onto the bed fully dressed. The machine was wide awake and whirling away on the night stand beside me.

The lines between dreams, imagination, thoughts, and—I hesitated to think the words—*real* communication with spirits of the dead had blurred. I still had difficulty believing any of those contacts with the dead was true. But, if they weren't, what did that say about me? And if they were, what to make of it I left to sort out another day. For now, a good night's sleep was in order. I closed the lid of the machine and shut my eyes. But only for a moment. Instantly, the screen started blinking wildly, the light leaking from around its edges causing me to open it up again.

What happened next, I would blame no one for calling me crazy or delusional for believing it was real; but I swear it was.

When I reopened the lid, in front of me was the face of Henry David Thoreau, immediately recognizable because of sad eyes and neck beard. He moved backward until I could see his full length; but he never looked straight at me. He silently gestured for me to follow him, and I found myself on the steep, tree-lined, sandy slope of Walden Pond a few steps away from his cabin in the woods.

In the silence, I had a long look around. Through what chestnut, hickory, oak, and pine trees that remained after the surrounding forest had been almost completely logged out in his time, the sun shimmered off of the crystal clear water and lit up the space where we stood.

I sensed his dismay at the plundering of the landscape. "They've grown back, you know," I said.

"The trees that is." I looked over at him, but he wasn't looking at me.

Thoreau breathed a sigh. "Yes, I know. I've kept a watch over them all of these years."

"It's mostly maples and pines now, though." I had been there and knew this to be true.

"Indeed. A wonderful rebirth." Thoreau turned and headed into the cabin. "Come in, if you please."

I followed him into the one room shack. It was surprisingly comfortable. There was a table, a wood stove from which hot winter fires had long been extinguished, a firewood box, empty except for splinters and remnants of bark, a closet with no clothes, a cot with a blanket and pillow, two chairs, and a small writing table. He offered me a seat and took the other one for himself.

"I was very happy when I lived here," he said. "I had all the necessities of life and the luxuries of solitude and, most importantly, the time to write."

How similar we were. From his own eloquent writings I knew that Thoreau had been obsessed during his life with collecting data, sometimes to his own dismay; and he had been content to work alone, although he cherished time spent with his frequent visitors, even as he was warm and hospitable with me now. Thoreau had seldom looked anyone in the eyes and by most accounts was awkward in social situations. Whistling and talking to squirrels and chipmunks had been easier for him than talking to women. For me, the language of computers was the simpler.

Yet, we were also so different. Thoreau was repulsed by the trappings of 1840s modern society that many had already begun to see as essential. Whereas, for all of my life I had embraced modern technologies and felt that invention was necessary to accompany humans into the future to provide for an ever-increasing world population with proportionately increasing demands for food, clothing, shelter, medicines. There were not enough acres around wooded ponds for everyone to live as he did.

"Then why did you leave?" I asked.

He took the question with no obvious surprise. "My experiment was over. I proved one can live quite happily with less than modern society had given the illusion of requiring. It's all, life that is, about achieving harmony: in your surroundings, in your livelihood, in your pursuits, and I now must add, in your relationships. But, the time came that necessitated my return to town." I looked out the open door and onto the rising landscape Thoreau had seen every day during his experiment and knew why he had loved it so much. He couldn't have known in his day that this pond had been carved out by swirling meltwater from a disappearing glacier thousands of years ago. I wondered if he'd learned that now. What he did know in his time that was just as true today was the water was fresh, clear, and cool. "I still needed money and worked various jobs for that purpose. But, my real work, the work that I lived for, was my writing, and I carried that love until the end of my days." I had a sense of how hard it must have been to leave here and return to town.

"Which ended too soon," I interjected, though one could always wonder why he had died so young if the lifestyle he had promoted was so healthy. Out of respect, I didn't ask.

He nodded a thank you. "I'm glad to know you think so."

"Mr. Thoreau—"

"Henry."

"Henry, why am I here?"

He didn't hesitate, as if he had expected the question. "Your work, Simon. You are doing difficult work, complicated work. Ahead of your time."

"Are you saying I should stop?"

"Not at all. I have no province to suggest that to you. Neither did I stop nor slow down modernity in my time. I merely reacted to it in my own way, which I never advocated for everyone, although I think everyone would have been the better for it if they had lived as I had. But, even I left here after two years two months and two days. My aim was merely to inspire those unfortunate souls like me who, finding their lives unsatisfactory, could simplify and pursue more spiritual meaning if their lives slowed down and their thoughts and attentions weren't so tied up in the pursuit of gain."

Thoreau was a good and honorable man. I knew from reading he had abhorred the fast pace of his time, excruciatingly slow by our modern standards. For him, the coming of the railroad, among other things, had sped the motion of life to a spiritually unhealthy measure. He, like me, preferred walking wherever he could. Walking gives you time to think, time to notice. Yet, it was that same train that took him back and forth from his hometown to Harvard where he got a first class education grounded in the classics that had prompted his philosophic pursuits and taught him to write so well. I wondered if he saw the contradiction the way I did. And, if he were alive today, I surmised he would gladly take the train he had once abhorred rather than a jet airliner. He might even learn to drive a car, even if he left it in his garage most of the time.

"Then what are you saying?" I asked.

"The future will come on time, Simon. There's no need to rush."

It seemed as though his message was from Ecclesiastes: a time to depart, a time to experiment, a time to return, even a time for modernity—it can't be stopped, anyway. Perhaps he was simply saying modernity belonged to the future. But, I could see no bright line between now and the future. I didn't know how his message affected me. Maybe I was overanalyzing and all he was saying was find some kind of balance.

I headed out the door thanking him for his hospitality. Underfoot, twigs crackled. Startled birds fluttered off into the overhead branches laced with blue sky.

"And, Simon." I turned around. He stood in the doorway. "Learn to dance."

Puzzled by the abrupt shift, I didn't know what to say.

"I've learned it can be a useful skill if you aspire to finding a wife and having a family, that I never had, other than my family of woodchucks, gray squirrels, and crows." He swept his hand out in a gesture as if to include the whole forest. "And, learn when to put aside talk of your work, the facts and information so dear to you is so dry to others. Remembering that will go a long way for you."

There it was, what he really wanted to say to me. There, too, is a time for dancing, a time for simple talk.

After bidding Thoreau a second farewell, I made my way up the embankment where upon reaching the crest the sweet mellow sounds of a violin passed by my ears. Mozart's Violin Concerto Number 1 drew me to a chamber where there sat a lone figure playing without sheet music to prompt him. I approached the violinist at first from behind. His hair was gray, longish, and unkempt in a Bohemian sort of way. A bushy moustache was the most prominent feature of his face. I recognized him immediately. He continued to play until he came to the end of a section and his violin struck a final note. Without saying anything, he pointed with his bow to a chair indicating I should have a seat while he waited, holding the violin upright resting on his thigh.

I was the first to speak. "Professor Einstein, what beautiful music you played."

What I knew of the great physicist came from reading three biographies of him when I was a child. Despite my admiration for him, when I had taught his theories in my classes I had purposely avoided tagging his name to them as much as I could. His name had been so often invoked as a sign of brilliance, or sarcastically a lack of brilliance, that it had become cliché. And, most people don't know what they think they know about his theories.

"Music was a lifetime joy of mine, Professor Hensley. Mozart wrote such beauty as can only be plucked from the universe like the bloom of a lush red rose plucked from its stem. Such magnificent beauty surely cannot come from within a living person." He placed the violin back under his chin and played a couple of trills, then rested it on his leg. "The work you will one day tire of, even as I did. But how can we ever tire of beauty?" The great professor paused for a moment, looking at me.

If I had known I would meet Albert Einstein, I would have expected to see him in front of a blackboard scrawling out chalk symbols, solving equations that explain our existence or some other high-minded theory that was beyond me, not playing a violin. I looked at his violin case on the floor beside his feet and saw he was barefoot as he was reported often to have been while walking the sidewalks of Princeton.

"Achieving beauty was the true purpose of my work with atoms," he said, "although it didn't always turn out that way."

"But your theories are elegant in every way."

"Spooky stuff. If you think you get it, you don't get it. Even I didn't believe some of my own theories."

For a moment, nothing was said.

"Professor Einstein, why am I here?"

"Such a deep question, Professor Hensley. I can't answer that. Only you can discover the answer."

"I mean why am I here, right now, with you — not that I mind. I very much enjoyed hearing you play." From the way his nose crinkled, I realized he knew what I had meant and his reply had come from his odd sense of humor, the same humor that captured him in a photo sticking out his tongue.

"Your work, Simon—" He seemed serious now "—May I call you Simon?—Your work picks up where mine left off—"

"I wouldn't say anything of the sort. I'm just a computer and physics teacher."

"You have stumbled into something unintended, haven't you?"

"You know about my machine?"

"If I didn't, we wouldn't be talking, would we? I also know how inventions and theories can be turned on their heads, even those made with the best of intentions. My search for universal beauty at the atomic level, trying to find symmetry that would explain everything that exists led to the world's worst nightmare: its ability to self-destruct. And I have regretted it ever since."

"Are you saying I should stop my work?"

"Goodness no. That's not up to me. I would simply say to you don't forget to look for beauty. Always and at the same time while you work. And most importantly, be aware of how your work can be turned on its head so that you don't live to regret it." He began to play the violin again while I watched his fingers glide over the vibrating strings until he stopped and held the violin under his chin while he spoke. "Play the piano for your girlfriend."

"Piano? Girlfriend?"

"You do play piano, don't you?"

"Yes. No. Sort of." He couldn't have known that I had taken lessons as a child.

"Try learning some Chopin or Liszt. Irving Berlin got it right." There was a glimmer in his eye that, if I had known him better, I would have said was a look of mischief or playfulness. "The ladies love it, Simon, when you play for them."

I thanked the great professor for the music and conversation and told him I must be on my way, although I had no idea where I was going.

I didn't have to wait long. A sign said I was entering West Orange, New Jersey. Soon, I entered a very large, ultra-modern looking, single story building. The space inside was open and brightly lit without glaring. For as far as I could see ahead, there were workstations without walls, people in clusters or working by themselves, some chatting, some appearing to study. It looked as if a speck of dust had never been allowed to settle there. An unusual kind of contented industriousness filled the air.

"Come in and look around awhile." The voice was Thomas Edison's. "I'm glad you could come. We're very proud of the work we do here."

After the last two encounters, I knew not to bother asking why I was there. I would simply get some vague response that it was about my work. Everybody seemed to know about my work, a portable quantum computer that had gone haywire and did things no one could have predicted, least of all me. So far, nobody had an answer for what to do about it.

"What are they doing over there?" I asked. His eyes followed my gaze to where two figures stood in front of a white board. Each one had on a small helmet with hundreds of tiny wires sticking out, and in an exaggerated way they held their hands behind their backs. In front of them was writing I couldn't decipher, and as they talked, high level mathematical symbols spontaneously appeared on the white board.

"Oh, that's going to be one of my proudest inventions." He beamed like a new father. "We call those 'thought conversion helmets' for now. We'll come up with a snazzier term eventually." He chuckled at that. Thomas Edison being snazzy. "If I can perfect them, they will one day replace pencil, paper, word processing, and so on. The helmets are lined with sensors that pick up brain waves and transmitters that project those brain waves onto a medium at the speed of thought." He took my arm and turned me around. "Look over there," he said pointing. In the opposite direction were two more figures with similar looking helmets. "Those helmets project musical scores. We're very close to getting them to play and record music as a composer imagines it. The implications of these thought helmets will be astonishing for writers, poets, novelists, composers, movie makers. If I can figure out a way to project those waves over long distances, they can even replace email and instant messaging." He started us walking towards a couple of chairs where we sat down.

"In my time in the world, I had over a thousand patents," he said. "My favorite invention was the phonograph. I have only two regrets about it. First, that I didn't think of inventing stereo. But, I was completely deaf in one ear and hard of hearing in the other, so stereo was immaterial to me. The second, I wish I had found something snazzier to say for the world's first recorded words than 'Mary had a little lamb.'" He bent his head back and gave a hearty laugh.

"Your favorite invention wasn't the light bulb?"

"I can't take all the credit there. I didn't invent the light bulb, I merely perfected it so that it could reliably and economically light up the world. The phonograph brought music, enjoyment into people's lives. That's what my work was about: making people's lives better."

"Perhaps, then, I should ask you about my work."

"Oh, yes. Your computer. Go right ahead, that's the reason you're here."

I knew it. As I had thought, everybody seemed to know about my computer. I didn't bother to ask if he knew what it did. He would just tell me the same as Einstein had. "Should I continue with my work? I've been told there are some really serious downsides if my machine is abused."

The world's greatest inventor talked about tenacity, working long and hard hours until he and his researchers got it right. He spoke of inspiration and perspiration.

Then I said, "But you gave up on your research of x-rays."

"Don't talk to me about x-rays. I am afraid of them."

"But, they have done so much good for medicine."

"I concede the point. . . provided they are used by trained experienced people. One of my researchers died because of x-rays, leaving behind a wife and two children. The cost was too high for me."

I had clearly hit a nerve without intending to. The face that'd had the gentle smile of a humble, yet proud man as he spoke of his accomplishments turned a bit dark, a bit dour. His bushy eyebrows drew down into a frown that I took to be a look of concentration, thoughtfulness. Perhaps he had become lost in a sad memory.

"I make things that are good for people. I'm proud to say that I never invented a weapon."

The look on his old face told me that he was uncomfortable with this line of discussion. I should have left it alone. Nonetheless, I had to know more. "But in your time, you advised the military to use science for its purposes and you helped them. And the company you founded, General Electric, makes components for war machines and sells them all over the world. Doesn't that make you responsible?" I recalled the discussion I'd had in the amphitheater with my students. "At least in part? Indirectly?"

What a careless statement I had made! I wounded him. Deeply it appeared. Some guest I was in that strange world. I hadn't asked to go there; but I was there, and I had offended. And a double-edged sword it was I had swung. The great man's inventions had helped the world in thousands of ways, millions, billions of times. What offense I may be inflicting on the world with my one-and-only invention!

The kind face that had a short while ago lit up with delight at the chance to talk about his inventions turned away from me, glum, crestfallen. He stared at the floor and covered his eyes with his hands. I saw then that he wept. A moment or two later, he looked up.

"I'm sorry," I said. "I wasn't thinking."

"It wasn't your words that offended. It was the grim fact of history." He shuffled to his feet, a little slowly at first. Vigor gradually returned to his expression. He walked us back towards the thought conversion helmet researchers and the others. "But, I keep my eyes on the prize." The look of a good kind of pride returned to his face.

"What will you do with these inventions?"

"Inspire."

I recalled Margaret's words when she had told me that not all of our fine ideas were original. At that point, I hoped the inventor would turn prophet and promise a weaponless future when people could co-exist with their similarities and differences and not hold a knife to each other's throats. "Can you inspire a weaponless future?"

"One can always hope."

We stood side-by-side in silence. I felt immense trepidation at what I was about to ask. "Mr. Edison. Do you think I should continue my work?"

"That isn't my place to say."

"Should I give up?"

"That isn't my place, either."

Thomas Alva Edison walked me to the swinging double doors that opened into the foyer of the ultra-modern building. Ahead were large glass windows that looked out into a grassy area with bright sunshine. I thanked him for his kindness, apologized again for my thoughtlessness and stepped through the door.

"One more thing, Simon." I turned around. "I don't know why I feel compelled to say this to you, but a man's best friend is a good wife. Farewell, and always strive to do good." He waved and closed the door.

I didn't know how I had got there or why, but I summed it all up in my head before leaving. Thoreau had just wanted to slow down and have time to write, but wished he had made time to learn how to approach a woman. Einstein had simply wanted to find beauty. Edison had been driven by wanting to make things to help improve people's lives. None of them had known how far-reaching their work would be, whether the consequences were intended or unintended. None of them had aspired to greatness. Great things had just happened because of them. All of them were Asperger's guys. Or, so they have been retrospectively diagnosed.

When I woke up, I was slumped in a chair in the living room still dressed in clothes from the previous day. My neck and every bone in my body hurt. The machine had fallen off my lap onto the hardwood floor at my feet. It, too, was in sleep mode; the screen was dark and the crystal barely glowed. I closed its lid and tucked it away in an empty drawer in the buffet in the dining room.

For the next several days, I carried on trying hard to put that night's events out of mind, although I knew that before long I would have to come to terms with them.

Chapter Thirty-three

AROUND THAT SAME TIME, the world's preeminent critic of artificial intelligence, Sir Howard Ainsworth, a renowned British scientist, was in town for a lecture series hosted at another university. The octogenarian scholar should have retired ages ago, in my opinion. Nonetheless, I had always wanted to have a conversation with him and hoped his visit might afford me the opportunity.

His views were well known that "artificial" and "intelligence" were in direct contradiction to each other. "Intelligence," he had written in his most famous essay *Figment of Imagination*, "and therefore consciousness as well, is a natural phenomenon shared to one degree or another by animals, and only by them. Intelligence arises from a flow of chemicals and biologically sourced electrical impulses transmitted from one or more differentiated brain cells to one or more other differentiated brain cells. In other words, rocks can't think; neither can a puddle of water nor a stalk of asparagus. Likewise, machines will never be able to think."

I had always thought differently. Intelligence, to me, was the ability to organize information, rearrange it, synthesize it, and communicate it, whether or not that information was transmitted to and from brain cells or to and from logic gates in a computer. Now, considering what I had learned from my machine, the topic of intelligence proved to be deeper, broader, and far more complicated than I had ever imagined. And that had left me with the only logical conclusion: neither Sir Howard nor I had it right.

Nevertheless, Sir Howard's lecture was exactly the kind of event I thought Hannah would enjoy, especially if she got to meet Sir Howard in person. Tickets were thirty-five dollars each, which included dinner. I bought two, intent on asking Hannah to go with me, but not before performing due diligence and finding out there was no policy against a personal relationship with Hannah now that she was no longer my graduate assistant nor a student in one of my classes. The easy part was done.

The rest was new to me. At the academy I had attended and later in my undergraduate years, I had been so much younger than my classmates and so engrossed in schoolwork that I had done little socializing, except with my buddy Michael. In truth, I had never been on a date. The mysteries of science were no greater than the mysteries of a woman and often times less so. And, many women, I feared, would find me very dull, I had concluded, because I didn't know how to do small talk very well. And, that brought up the specter of rejection. What if Hannah told me "no?"

It was upon me then that I must make a compelling case for her to go to the lecture with me. I could have called Michael to get some advice—he was good at that sort of thing—but, I wanted to do this on my own and I didn't want to admit my inadequacies. So, I came up with a plan.

It began with getting a copy of the announcement which had a photo of Sir Howard from the waist up, his thick shaggy white hair slightly tousled, wearing a striped tie and tweed jacket; bullet points of lecture topics; and the day, date, and time. Then, the plan called for me to show the bulletin to Hannah, make the case that this would be very interesting and in stark contrast to what she and I had worked on, followed by asking her to go with me.

For days ahead of time, the bathroom mirror at home became the stand-in for Hannah as I practiced what I would say and how I would look saying it. I tried different phrases. *What are you doing Friday night?* No. That was none of my business. *Would you like to go out?* Too general and didn't seem very smooth. *Would you like to go to dinner? Oh, by the way, there's a lecture before dinner?* Or, *How would you like to go with me to a lecture?* Or, *Are you busy Friday night? I know of a good lecture we could go to.* Or, *If you're not busy Friday night, I've got two tickets to a lecture.* I practiced several ways to ask over and over until it seemed like second nature, knowing that the right phrase would come at the right time.

The plan, brilliant by my standards, was thought up on Sunday night. By Tuesday, I had caught only one glimpse of Hannah in the hall with her friend and had seen her one time sitting on a bench outside a classroom. I resolved to go up to her then and ask, but a sudden case of nerves got in the way, so I turned and left. Wednesday, I didn't see her at all. Thursday was my last chance to ask because the lecture was the following night. I went looking for her and found her at a table by herself in the student activity center.

"Hi, Hannah." She set some papers down, smiled, and looked at the clock on the wall. Here was the moment I had practiced for. I was ready for this. "I would like to invite you to attend a lecture Friday night." I laid the bulletin on the table in front of her. "Sir Howard Ainsworth is in town—"

"I've read some of his works." She looked the bulletin over.

"I've got tickets," I said, taking them out of my shirt pocket to show her. She scrutinized the bulletin long and hard as if she were taking in each and every bullet point. After moments of nerve shattering silence, she looked up at me.

"I'd love to go." And I had been afraid of rejection. She held the bulletin in front of her with both hands. "Can I take my friend Logan?" she asked without looking up.

My brain froze up just then. I didn't know what to do. I just stood there, holding the tickets out in front of her. "Logan?" I had never heard of her speak of a boyfriend before now. "Uh. . . yeah, sure." She took both tickets from my hand, and I let her. Had she not understood that I was asking her out? Hadn't I asked the right way after all the time I had spent practicing?

Hannah looked at the clock again and scooped her things up hurriedly. "Thanks, I've got to run, I'm late." She took off, and I just stood there for a while, wondering what had just happened.

Fiasco. That was the only word to describe what had happened. Though confused by Hannah, I couldn't be upset with her. But, I could be plenty upset with myself and even cringe over the mess I'd made. Aspies, according to so-called experts, lack a natural instinctive interpretation of social signals, and that causes us difficulties in relationships. They claim we don't always catch subtleties of expressions, as when someone is angry at us or when we have talked too long and have bored someone; they claim we don't understand sarcasm, and we take the things people say too literally. In this case, it seemed it was Hannah who hadn't caught the subtlety of my invitation, and so far as I knew, she was neurotypical. I needed to straighten things out right away.

Late that same night, I decided to go by Hannah's on the way home and talk to her about the tickets and what my intentions had been. She lived not far from me in an apartment in the back of Mrs. Albright's house, one I had passed by countless times in my life. I would simply go there, knock on her door, and explain I had meant to ask her out on a date, despite her prohibition of getting involved with faculty. I mean, people meet where they meet, don't they? If something is promising, what does it matter where they meet? Who wouldn't see that reasoning?

There were several routes I could take going home since this part of town was laid out in rectangular blocks one-eighth mile by one-twelfth mile. The distance was the same no matter where I made ninety degree turns. One of those paths took me right by Hannah's place; so it was no great effort to go there. However, eleven p.m., I admit, was a little late to be dropping by in most instances. But this wasn't an ordinary instance, not to me.

The air was chilly, and the wind started picking up a little, but I didn't notice until I turned a corner into the wind. All I could think of, though, was what I wanted to say to Hannah—that somehow I thought I was developing feelings for her and wanted to give a relationship a try. That was a big step for me, revealing myself however eloquently or poorly I said it, becoming vulnerable to her apprehensions or rejections.

Three blocks off of School Street and two blocks further down, I came to the block Hannah lived on just four-and-a-half blocks from my house. In front of Mrs. Albright's house there was a lot of commotion: blue and red police car lights—spinning strobes, lighting up the street and tinting the clapboards of neighbor's houses. Then the lights went off. I hurried and hid behind a thick tree across the street. A police car was parked in Mrs. Albright's driveway. Another one was parked on the street and sat there running with a cop in it.

Mrs. Albright was outside in her nightgown with a sweater thrown over her shoulders; her thin hair, done up in loose ringlets, was flat on the backside. She stood next to Hannah, smoking a cigarette and doing most of the talking. From my position, I could make out most of what they were saying, but with the wind blowing past my ears, I couldn't hear everything.

Hannah had returned home earlier in the evening, she told the policeman in reluctant fragments coaxed by Mrs. Albright, and had found her apartment ransacked. Her books were scattered all over the floor. Drawers had been dumped out, and it seemed to her as if special attention had been paid to her undergarments because of the careful way they had been smoothed and laid out on her bed. Kitchen cabinets had been rummaged through. Her medicine cabinet had been emptied onto the floor. It seemed from Hannah's demeanor and apparent impatience with the whole ordeal that she would have preferred that Mrs. Albright had not called the police.

"Nothing was taken, officer," Hannah said. "My place was just messed up a little. Can't we just forget about it and go on?" Hannah asked.

"Hell no, I'm not forgetting about it, dear," Mrs. Albright said, looking up into Hannah's face. "This is my house and I want the person who did this to be caught and have to pay for it." Mrs. Albright was small and feisty — and shivering.

"But, nothing is missing?" The policeman asked Hannah. She shook her head. "Consider yourself lucky. This stuff happens all the time with less happy results."

The policeman went inside while I watched, still hidden by the tree. After he returned, he stopped and wrote something on a sheet or a pad on his clipboard.

"I want somebody to pay for this," Mrs. Albright said, sounding a bit demanding.

"The only property damage," the policeman said without looking at her, "was a jimmied lock, ma'am. There's not much to pay for."

"But still," Mrs. Albright, said pulling her sweater tighter around her. "It's the principle."

"I'll write up the report. That's all I can do. If anything else happens, call us." By then, the other cop had left. The officer put his hand over the earphone in his left ear, turned his head, and pressed the button on the microphone attached to his shoulder. "Seventy-three Beat... Ten Four... We're through here, will be en route in a sec...Ten-Four, Ten-Eight." With that, he left. Mrs. Albright turned and headed briskly, almost stomping, toward the front door.

Suddenly, the tickets and a botched date request didn't matter as much. I was about to step into the street to cross over and try to console Hannah just as a sporty little car zipped right in front of me and whipped into Mrs. Albright's drive. A young woman with long legs and short hair hurriedly got out of the car, went up to Hannah and hugged her. She looked like the friend I had seen Hannah with in the halls. They talked quietly for a moment, then turned toward Hannah's apartment. The friend wrapped a consoling arm around Hannah's shoulders as they strode toward the door. The only thing I heard was when the wind relented as Hannah said, "I know who did this."

I watched as the friend held the storm door open, then followed Hannah inside. I wondered for a moment if my instinct to be helpful had actually been grounded on true selfless compassion or if I had secretly held the desire to be gallant and if my chance to be gallant had just been whisked away by Hannah's friend. Either way, a sense of helpfulness became helplessness. With nothing more I could do there, I set out for home.

On the way, the wind picked up ferociously, and when I got close to my house, the greenhouse door banged loudly and I could hear it from two houses away. In front of the door lay shattered little pieces of tempered glass reflecting light from my neighbor's porch. I knew it took more than wind to break tempered glass. It would take repeated blows from a hammer. Inside the greenhouse, the equipment cabinet had been turned over spilling my oscilloscopes and analyzers onto the concrete floor, breaking them. Next to them, Dad's old microscopes and stereoscopes lay broken. The kitchen door had been pried open.

    I went in cautiously and paused, quietly listening before going further. The house was dark with just enough light coming in from the corner street light and the moon to give the night's washed out colors enough chroma that I could see to get around. I went through the house checking everywhere until I was confident I was alone, then went to the kitchen to turn on the lights. I stepped in a puddle and slipped, nearly falling. Milk from the refrigerator had been poured out onto the floor. Cereal, coffee, and bread had been thrown into the white mess. Cupboards were flung open, one with the door ripped off its hinges, dishes and glasses smashed on the floor. I wiped my feet with a kitchen towel and moved on. Clothes were strewn in the bedroom and hallway, books thrown around in the living room. In the bathroom, toothbrushes, a razor, wash cloths, and towels had been thrown onto the floor. Toothpaste had been squeezed out on the vanity top. A bottle of aftershave was broken and dumped into the toilet. This was more than a random break-in. This was personal. But why?

    Then it clicked inside my head: the shadow figure. Hannah had just said to her friend that she knew who had broken into her apartment. She had to have meant the shadow figure I had seen the night Michael came to visit, the one who was demanding to know "Hensley's secret." I ran across the house to the dining room and pulled open the buffet drawer where I had earlier left the machine. To my relief, it was still there. At that moment, I resolved to never let the machine out of my sight.

In truth, nothing valuable was missing, but that was only part of it. The point was the intrusion! The violation! The uninvited plunge into my intimacy! No one had the right.

But how would anybody know to come to my house? Why me? Something was terribly wrong. Hannah must have told my secret to the shadow person. How could she? I had trusted her. Now, somebody else knew, somebody willing to go to extremes, somebody who wanted to take my machine away from me. Someone wanted to patent it, to reap the rewards, to steal my place in history, to make money, lots of it, off of my invention.

But, no one could know about the machine's special capabilities. I hadn't told anyone. "Philippes! Philippes!! Are you behind this?" I couldn't see him, but I felt the presence of malevolence. "Get out of my life, you bastard! Leave me and my machine alone!"

I took a baseball bat out of the closet and used it to poke through the scattered debris that was my belongings and took a couple of air swings, defying anyone to come near. But, when I stopped shouting, there was only silence. And me.

After seeing how lightly the police had treated the break in at Hannah's despite Mrs. Albright's interventions, I decided not to report the crime at my house. Police saw much worse things every day. If someone were badly hurt in a car accident, the police were there. When there was a bank robbery, or a shooting, or a hostage situation, the police were there. Cops didn't care much about someone breaking into my house and stealing my sense of security.

Anyway, a broken door was easy to replace, and I pledged to myself I wouldn't wait long to fix it, perhaps on spring break, which would be coming soon. My mother's broken dishes are another thing. They had been a wedding gift to my parents. Often when I had used them, I thought about the thousands of meals she had fixed for me and felt the love she'd put into each one, even if the meal was just sandwiches or a casserole. Quiche was her favorite, which she sometimes made on weekends when she had time. It wasn't my favorite, but I never complained, and I would have given anything to have another helping of her quiche now. I swept the broken pieces of ceramic memories into a dustpan.

I mopped up the milk, put clothes back on hangers, books on shelves; I cleaned, organized, and restored order. I held onto and looked at my dad's microscopes for a long time before finally accepting they couldn't be fixed and put them into a plastic trash bag with the broken dishes.

By the time I finished cleaning, fractured beams of early morning sunlight streamed through my front windows and made slices of airborne dust. I leaned the broom and mop against the refrigerator, left overflowing trash bags in the middle of the floor, and went to bed.

When I woke, it was two hours before Sir Howard's lecture, and I had no tickets. Regardless, I got cleaned up, changed clothes, and went out through the greenhouse, stepping over chunks of glass that hadn't been swept up yet, to the detached garage where the Jeep sat dormant. I opened the garage door and got in the car. The near-lifeless battery strained and pulled the engine slow and hard until it seemed as though it would peter out altogether. Then suddenly the engine whirred and started up. I backed out with the wipers on to brush off the accumulation of dust.

Unlike people, machines usually react predictably. The car, with regular maintenance, occasional use, and a little gasoline could be depended on to take me anywhere I wanted to go. People, on the other hand, say one thing and do another, such as pledging confidentiality about your life's work. They swear to an unseen god you can trust them. But don't turn your back.

I drove to the auditorium to buy a ticket at the door. On the way, I recounted what I really knew about Hannah, which in truth wasn't much. She was from Minneapolis and didn't like the extreme cold and relentless snow there. From her blonde hair and fair complexion, I deduced she must be from Scandinavian ancestry. But, she had said her last name, Tuttle, was English even though it was a contracted form of the Scandinavian word for the god of thunder, Thor, and a word meaning "kettle" or "cauldron." She had said her ancestors must have been cauldrons of thunder to be so named.

That seemed so unlike her. She had always been quiet, studious, and reliable—which I had taken to mean contemplative, trustworthy.

Quiet people, I have found, often have qualities attributed to them by others in absence of a real knowledge about them: They are stoic. They have inner strength, nobleness, intellect, wisdom, trustworthiness—and the big one—an air of mystery. *Still waters run deep* some people say about the quiet ones. But through years of observation, I've learned that quiet people may have none of those qualities. They may simply be quiet.

In school, I had known a fellow who sat in the back corner of every class, kept to himself, and rarely spoke more than a few words. One teacher kept after him to join in and speak up. When he finally did, it became apparent why he had rarely spoken. He couldn't string together a full coherent sentence.

Maybe my attribution of trustworthiness to Hannah had been founded erroneously on her quiet behavior.

I arrived at the auditorium with time to spare and dawdled on the way to the door with my hands stuck in my coat pockets. It wasn't clear to me yet what I would say to Hannah if I ran into her—especially in the presence of her friend Logan—whether I would ask whom she had told about the machine, or whether I should show concern about the break-in, or whether I should clear up my intentions about the tickets.

By themselves, in pairs, in groups, people of all ages passed right by me and filed in dressed for an evening out. Men in suits dug in their breast pockets for tickets; women dug in their purses as they approached the flight of wide concrete steps that led to a terrace. The double glass doors of the atrium were held wide open by people in line. Just inside, a young man and two young women I presumed to be students dressed in tuxedoes and white gloves were collecting tickets. I stopped at the base of the steps. Warm air rushed out of the doors and mixed with the night air. There was excited chatter about a world luminary coming here to talk. Discussions and disagreements had already started.

    I changed my mind. I no longer wanted to hear Sir Howard. I didn't want to see Hannah. I hurried back to my car and went home.

Chapter Thirty-four

THE FEELING OF BEING VIOLATED by an intruder into my home didn't go away. Even restoring order, organizing, replacing books on shelves categorized by subject, alphabetized by author, hanging shirts in the closet grouped by sleeve length and then by color didn't help.

After a semblance of order was restored, I stayed in the rest of the weekend.

Early on Monday, an email blast told me I didn't have to go to work that day and that classes would resume Tuesday afternoon. There had been another of those insane school shootings that seemed to be all over the news recently, this time at the same nearby university where Sir Howard had spoken on Friday night. I'm sure it was pure coincidence because I don't believe he'd said anything so provocative.

I switched on the news to get the latest report. Of course, parallels were being drawn between this shooting and earlier shootings, in particular one at an elementary school where the shooter had been previously diagnosed with Asperger's Syndrome and the suggestion that Asperger's had been *the* contributing factor. Now, it seemed everybody wanted to look suspiciously at Aspies as if they were mass murderers in waiting. Nonsense. Asperger's had nothing to do with it. Asperger's Syndrome is a difference, not a disorder. A homicidal maniac is a homicidal maniac no matter how his brain functions. Evil is evil. Taking life is evil. I had never had a single thought about taking a life.

The thought of evil recalled the image of Philippes. I didn't know what to think about him. Was he malevolent, or was he a messenger? With these questions in mind, I realized I had begun to accept him as real. The thought caused me to shudder.

I looked back at the television. The news was depressing, as usual. I turned the television off and left it off.

By Tuesday, I regretted not having stayed for the lecture that night to look for Hannah. I hadn't spoken to her or heard anything since the break-ins. Worried for her safety, I walked over to her apartment to check on her.

Mrs. Albright was a widow, and it seemed to me, she had always been old and had always lived there. She wore the same type of clothes all the time: loose fitting dungarees with the cuffs rolled up two or three inches, a belt cinched around her thin waist causing the waistband to mushroom over it, and a tucked-in short sleeve, button-down floral shirt with the collar buttoned.

Whenever I had seen her, she was smoking non-filtered cigarettes and wheezing, and her patchy front yard was littered with butts that hadn't burned out completely, left to be shredded by the lawn mower next summer. Mrs. Albright was nice enough. She would always speak if she was in the yard when I walked by and she tended to go on and on, as if she hadn't talked to an adult in ages. Although I never looked directly at her, I would sometimes stop to talk through the chain link fence even though we had little or nothing in common, other than she had known my parents when they were alive, just as she knew everybody around there or something about them. Every neighborhood, I supposed, had a busybody like Mrs. Albright. Her English Bulldog, Chip, was always there, too, drooling, panting, and standing on his hind legs while balancing himself with one front leg against the fence, the other air-clawing at me. They were a matched pair.

When I got to Hannah's, Mrs. Albright was in the front yard smoking. I asked her if she'd seen Hannah, if Hannah was all right.

"Oh goodness. Haven't you heard?" She seemed eager to tell something.

"Heard what?"

"It's been all over the news."

"I haven't watched the news. It's all bad stuff or politics. But, I guess that's redundant." A creepy feeling rushed over me. "But, what has been in the news?"

"Did you know her well?" She cocked her head to one side.

"Did?" Past tense. "What happened?" Now, I looked straight at her.

"Oh my. You don't know, do you? Honey, she was killed yesterday morning. Real early. Before sunrise. So tragic," she said shaking her head and blowing out smoke followed by a loose sounding phlegm hack. "She was so young, had it all in front of her—"

"What!?"

"Yes. And the police came by here and everything. They were here just the other night when her apartment was broken into. Now this—Well, I told them I didn't really know much about her, she'd just rented here a short time." She took a drag on her cigarette and without flicking the ash clutched the cigarette in her fist with the ash pointing upward. Her bony elbow was supported on the other arm that clung to her tiny torso. She talked with her mouth full of smoke. "I told them, she was one of those *les*bians." She raised her pitch on the first syllable and drew it out. "I never have understood that. You couldn't tell by looking at her. I didn't know until I saw her kissing another girl in front of her door late one night. And not just one time. Again and again. Right on the mouth, for a long time, not just a peck, you know. And they had their arms all wrapped around each other like vines. She called her friend, 'Logan sweetheart.' If my Marvin was still alive, he'd never allow a thing like that. She'd have had to move." She drew on her cigarette again. I was too stunned to say anything. "But I need the money, and hey, it's a new day and age, you know—"

"How did she die?"

"—I guess you just gotta get used to it, they're everywhere." She shook her head again and let her cigarette dangle. For a fleeting moment, Mrs. Albright seemed pensive. "Shook me up pretty bad."

"What? Her being a lesbian or—never mind." I was getting impatient now and agitated that Mrs. Albright seemed more concerned about Hannah's sexual orientation than her death. "How did she die?"

"Oh, it was a hit and run accident. The driver got away. She was out jogging by herself. You think you're doing something good for your health, then this. She'd be better off if she'd stayed home and smoked a cigarette that morning."

"She doesn't—didn't smoke."

Mrs. Albright took a long hard puff from her cigarette and tossed the butt, still glowing, on the ground. "I'm just saying. . ."

At that moment, I was hit by two colliding revelations, the first that explained why Hannah had been so aloof with me—and I had been too dense to see it. The second, more important and shocking, that Hannah was dead. My stomach turned.

"Thank you, Mrs. Albright," I said abruptly and took off running towards campus, leaving her and her cigarettes in peace. I didn't stop until I got to Geoff's office. But he wasn't in. I ran up the stairs taking them two at a time, down the hall to his classroom and burst in without thinking. Heads looked up at me. I was breathing heavily, unable to speak. Geoff came over to me from the table where he had been reading a newspaper.

"We're having a test," he whispered, then guided me by the shoulder back into the hallway. "Simon, you look shaken." Of course I did. I was having a panic attack. I was hyperventilating and my stomach felt every fiery shot of adrenaline coursing through me. "Sit over here." He led me to one of the wooden benches that lined the inside wall. "Try to calm down. I'll get you something to drink." He left for the vending machines at the end of the hall and returned with a bottle of water. When I didn't reach for it, he set it on the bench beside me. He looked at me for a long moment, then said, "Do this." He cupped his hands over his nose and mouth. "Now breathe into your hands. Slowly. Keep pace with me." I watched him and kept pace.

When my breathing returned to normal, Geoff said, "I take it you heard?"

"Yeah. Hannah's dead." I couldn't get the rest of the words out that it was my fault. Philippes had to be involved in this, too. I just knew it. But I hadn't said a thing to Geoff about Philippes or the machine, and all of that was too much to get into now right now. The machine was involved, too. It had to be. If only I had never invented the damned thing!

"You just now heard about Hannah?"

I nodded.

"That was a couple of days ago."

I nodded again.

"What else have you heard?"

"About Hannah?"

"About your friend Michael."

I could tell Geoff was holding something back. "What about him?" More adrenalin shot through me, then the weighted feeling of dread fell on me as if someone had dropped onto my shoulders.

"Maybe it should wait." He looked at me with sorrowful and worried eyes.

"What should wait?" I said barely above a whisper, although I felt like shouting. "If there's something I should know, tell me now."

"I think it's better if we wait—"

"No—now, Geoff. Please."

For a moment, there was dead silence in the hallway. The kind of silence you get when you plug your ears. Geoff put a hand on my shoulder. "I'm afraid Michael is also dead. I'm sorry to be the one to tell you."

"How?" My eyes filled and I couldn't help it.

Geoff hemmed and hawed around, but I made him tell me what had happened to Michael. He told me Michael's remains had been found below one of those jet burners they used for blasting holes in the ground for spallation out in the desert where he'd been working. The only thing further Geoff said was Michael's body was not intact. Not intact. There was no need to guess what that meant. Foul play hadn't been ruled out, and an investigation was ongoing.

I felt sick. I was going to throw up. I stood up and paced in circles, disoriented, trying to locate the restroom, which hadn't moved. This was worse than hearing about Hannah. It was all my fault. And Philippes'. Geoff sensed what was about to happen and aimed me in the right direction. I took off running.

When I came out of the restroom, Geoff was standing just outside the door. He asked if I was going to be okay. No, yes, no, I don't know, I told him. My ears rang. There was pressure in my head. These surroundings should have been familiar, but they seemed foreign. I knew I worked there. I knew I had walked these halls many times. But I felt as if I were inside a bubble and had glass jars over my ears—or better yet, that I was inside a snow globe, at the center with glass walls all around me, and everything outside was smaller than they used to seem and colors were faded and Geoff's voice was faint and far away. Nothing seemed real.

I said an abrupt good-bye and ran home.

When I got there, I slammed the door shut behind me and stood in the middle of the living room as it spun around me. I stumbled up the stairs and into my old room that had inexplicably been left alone in the burglary. There on shelves and on top of the dresser were my old baseball trophies and scholastic awards. This room had always been a safe place for me, and I looked to it now for protection. I leaned on the dresser with both hands and at my feet spotted an empty Blue Moon box Michael hadn't thrown away. I swept it aside with my foot.

Then I lurched, almost as if in a spasm. It was my fault. All my fault. They were dead because of me. I screamed, "Michael! Hannah! Hannah! Michael!" Their names were trapped in an angry, roaring spiral of thought, and I yelled them at the top of my lungs. But, no one was there to hear my words. No one was there to explain it to me. No one was there to comfort me, calm me. No one would ever again come through my door and visit me. And, I would have nowhere to go. Their deaths would forever be on my conscience.

Inside my snow globe I heard distant screaming and pounding and more pounding. Then, my fist broke through the lath and plaster wall. When I pulled my hand back, my knuckles were skinned and bloody, but I couldn't feel them. Then, I slid down the wall to the floor in stunned silence and stayed there.

Chapter Thirty-five

AFTER MY SENSES—and the feeling in my hand—came back to me, I carefully replaced the peeled flaps of skin on my knuckles and struggled with my left hand to bandage them. When I was finished, I rushed out the front door and down the steps to leave and go anywhere rather than staying there.

Overhead, clouds were rolling in choking out the sunlight and bringing on a chill. Their flat shadow lay on my driveway and partway across my neighbor's house as I backed my Jeep out of the garage. Just before I got to the street, a two-tone red and white Mini Cooper pulled up behind me fast and stopped abruptly, blocking me in. I braked hard to avoid hitting it. The door opened and Margaret Switzer got out with help from her cane.

"Simon, I'm so glad I caught you. I've been trying for days to call you at work, but your voicemail box is full, and I don't have your cell number."

She was right. I hadn't been to work since last week.

"Is something wrong?" I managed to get out.

"It's getting chilly out here." She looked at the sky. "Do you mind if I invite myself in?"

I helped her up the stairs and onto the porch. Inside, she made her way over to one of the armchairs in front of the cold, soot blackened fireplace. It was the chair my mother had always sat in with a little lamp table to one side where Mom had laid her glasses and whatever book she was reading at the time and an iced tea or a mug of hot chocolate. I had used that chair very little since her death. One side of the navy blue upholstery was faded from afternoon sunlight bearing down on it through the west windows; the arms were threadbare. But I had never had the heart to throw it out. I sat opposite Margaret.

"I haven't seen you at the research sessions lately, Simon."

"Yeah, I know. I've had a lot going on."

"Have you seen enough to accept the communications we've been studying? Or are you still not convinced?"

"It's not that. I've just been busy." In that chair, she reminded me of my mother. I hadn't noticed before, but her hair was about the same length and color, her size and stature about the same as my mother's. A thin white glow tinted in rose along the edges outlined her shape. I had never believed in auras before, but I thought I was certainly looking at hers just now.

"Simon, your mother came to me the other day."

It was strange, but I felt my mother's presence. It was nothing like the visitations I'd had through the machine or what I had witnessed at the sessions. It simply felt as if my mother were there in person.

In life, my mother had had something in common with Margaret. She'd been a licensed clinical social worker and had worked in a family practice helping people solve emotional and mental problems.

With me, my mother had always been very kind and patient. She knew my differences at times made it difficult for me to process some things emotionally that were so easy and natural for other people. She knew that my childhood outbursts weren't temper tantrums; they were emotional overload. She could always calm me, not by words or by giving in, rather by simply being there for me, reassuring me with her presence. When I was little and needed her to, she held me on her lap. When I grew too big for that, she hugged me. Eventually, I learned self-control and got along fine, that is, until earlier today. Nonetheless, her presence had always been reassuring.

"She's worried about you. She has been sensing a disturbance in your aura for some time."

"Tell her I'll be all right."

Margaret looked away as if she were listening in on someone else's conversation. "She's telling me that she knows you have suffered a loss and are taking it hard. She wants you to know she'll be with you and she'll send you some comforting energy."

"Do you know what happened, Margaret?"

"I heard you lost two friends. I'm so sorry."

"Did Mom know that was going to happen?"

"No. She just knew there was some kind of trouble."

"Did she tell you anything else?" I was fishing to see if Mom had told Margaret about the machine. "Does she know anything else that's going to happen?"

"It's complicated. Over there, spirits can see and know some things, sometimes more than we do here, but they can't see everything. It all depends on their level of advancement and their purpose. They have their work to do. Just like here. Some are there to guide us and they have the privilege of knowing more about us than the general population of spirits."

"So she doesn't know anything else?"

"Like what?"

"Anything."

"She didn't let on like she did. That was all she said." But Margaret wasn't ready to leave. When someone is holding back something there is a certain feeling in the air. Margaret was holding back.

There were two times in my life when my mother had been obvious in holding something back from me, unable to find the right words. The first time was when she had told me about my dad's sickness that would eventually take him. The second time was when the sickness had taken him.

"There's something else, isn't there?" I asked.

Margaret hesitated then spoke as if she were talking to my mother. "Let me have a few moments alone with Simon, please. . . I'm sorry, I can't tell you. . . I know you're his mother, but it's something private. . . Just a few minutes earth time, please. . . Thank you."

We waited. I wasn't sure what for. Then Margaret said, "She's gone now. I have another message for you, Simon. This one is from Benjamin, my personal spirit guide." She paused as if she were waiting for a reaction I didn't give her and then went on. "Benjamin has been with me all of my life, and he's a powerful and good soul. I trust him." I wondered if a spirit guardian were the same as a guardian angel, if such things really existed, and if I had one. "The first thing you must understand is that a psychic usually but not always must pass along the readings she gets.

That's just one of the rules. This isn't going to be easy, Simon. I'd give anything not to have to pass this one along." She stalled until the oppressive silence made me squirm. "Your life is in danger. Somebody is going to try to kill you. Soon."

There it was. I was next. "Do you know who? When? How? Why?"

"That's all I got. I wish I could tell you more."

Margaret still didn't get up to leave. She dug in her bag and pulled out a pad of paper and a pen. "Do you take any medications?" she asked.

"No—vitamins. That's all. Why?"

She quickly scrawled something on the pad, tore off the top sheet and gave it to me.

"What's this?" I asked.

"It's a prescription for Xanax, one milligram. Two weeks' worth. Have this filled and start today taking one each day." She must have sensed my hesitation. "It will do you good."

I thanked her, and she got up to leave.

"I need a hug," she said. That was what my mother had always said to me whenever she felt I needed a hug. Margaret wrapped her arms around me. "Be careful, Simon. Pray for guidance and protection. I'll pray for you." She took my face in both hands and pulled me to her to kiss me on the forehead, just as my mother used to do. I realized then how wrong first impressions can be.

As she pulled away, I stood on the porch and watched until she turned the corner. My hand churned nervously, crumpling the prescription Margaret had just given me. Once inside, I threw it across the room.

That was it. I'd had enough! Dead people lecturing me about war, religion, and power. Telling me to learn to dance, look for beauty, find a good wife, strive to do good. Friends being murdered. Now a death threat against me! All because of a soulless machine that talks to spirits.

I ran into the garage, got a ball peen hammer, and with it pounded the xenocryst until my grip turned to putty. The unscathed crystal glowed, taunting me, like the glaring eye of a Cyclops, a Cyclops of my own creation, one I had come to fear and hate. From the nearby tool chest, I pulled out wire cutters and clipped the leads going into the computer.

"That should do it," I said aloud.

But for good measure, I set the machine on the workbench and swung the hammer like a bat, sending the machine flying across the garage and onto the concrete floor.

I stood over the machine breathing hard until my breaths slowed down, then scooped it up and took it into the greenhouse where I set it down on the counter and sat on a stool and laid my head to rest.

"Mom, Dad. I wish you were here." Such a simple wish. That wish carried with it the flavor of a bygone time when life's problems were so simple Mom and Dad could fix them. After Dad died, Mom had her share of coping to do for herself, but when things got tough for me, she always knew how to "fix" me with a gentle touch and a dose of clarity, teaching me how things in life really were and helping me to reason through them. It was she who taught me in my adolescence that things shouldn't always be taken literally, problems aren't always black and white, people aren't always predictable. Gradually, I began to see the light that it was logical to expect others to sometimes react irrationally. Thus, there was no real breach of logic. There were merely probable alternatives. How I wanted her clarity now to make sense of all the irrational things I had seen.

The machine began to flicker, fast and brightly.

"Simon, we're here." It was Mom's voice. "Both of us." Two faces looked at me through the cracked display, yet their images were perfect, unblemished, except for their worried looks.

"Mom, Dad." But, I had cut the wires, destroying, I thought, the connection to the computer. Instantly, I realized if the xenocryst programmed with my algorithm could tunnel through the membrane into the hereafter, tunneling through to the computer a few inches away was no great feat. "I need your help. I don't know what I've gotten myself into."

"Honey," Mom said. "It'll be all right, whatever it is. You just wait and see. Remember what I always told you, 'When the going gets tough—'"

"I know, I know. 'You must be on the right road.' But, this is different, worse than anything I could imagine."

"What is it, son?" Dad asked.

Just having both of them there made me feel better. "This machine. It's causing trouble. Big trouble."

"You mean the same machine," Dad asked, "that's allowed us to talk again after all of these years? How can that be trouble?"

"It's caused people to die. My friend Michael. And Hannah." Mom had known Michael, but neither

The Iron Couch

one had known Hannah. I had to ask, "Have you heard anything about either of them?"

"No," Mom said. "I'm sorry we haven't."

The screen went black and silent. For a moment, I thought we had lost contact. Then Dad came back. His image was as clear as ultra-high definition television, even through the cracked lens. I studied his face. I hadn't thought about it before, but it was the same face I had seen as a child. They must not age over there. His facial expression betrayed little emotion—it seemed professorial—yet I could feel a soothing father's warmth coming from him and knew that it was real. "Mom's going to see what she can find out about your friends. She's made some connections here. While she's gone, let me share some thoughts with you, if that's okay?"

"That's why I called on you."

"I can sense your dilemma, son, but as much as I as a father want to hand you the answers and make all your problems go away, I can't—simply because I don't know what is right for you."

"Margaret said we all have spirit guardians who help us at times like this. What about that?"

"We do. But, it's not always easy to contact them directly. They're an aloof bunch, but they're always there. They talk to you in ways so subtle it's often easy to miss what they say. They can guide you only if you can listen to them."

"That's what I'm trying to do. Can you put me in touch with mine?"

"Sorry. Only they determine when or *if* they will make direct contact—"

"Dad, that sucks."

"But, remember, they're always there. You can always talk to them, no restrictions. You simply have to be attuned and listen very closely to hear them. That's the hard part. And remember this, too: When help comes in the least expected and most unusual ways, it's probably help from your guardian."

"But, what about now? I think I'm in serious trouble."

"Did you ever read Plato's *Republic*?"

"Of course. It was required reading for Philosophy 100. But what does that have to do—?"

"Did you understand it?"

"I got an A on the test."

"That's great, but it doesn't mean you understood it. Do you remember the Allegory of the Cave?"

"Barely. That was a long time ago, and philosophy wasn't my major."

"Let me take some license and retell it in a way that may apply to your situation." At that moment, Dad seemed to slip comfortably into the dual role of an educator and a storyteller. I felt as if I were once again sitting on his lap in the greenhouse laboratory while he had explained the mysterious worlds I had seen through his microscopes. I listened closely as he spoke. "Plato wrote an allegory of the world as he saw it. The world of perception in which you still live, and through which I have passed, is like a cave, according to Plato, from which its dwellers cannot easily escape and cannot easily see out. They think they see clearly, but they see each other in the same dim light, unaware it is but a reflection of the greater light. Of the world visible to them, they see nothing but shadows of objects cast on the walls and don't know the source of illumination that created those shadows."

"By 'illumination' you mean...?"

"Metaphorically, knowledge, wisdom, and understanding. And darkness is ignorance and misunderstanding."

"Or the misapplication of knowledge," I said.

"Well put, Simon. I think human history is full of examples where knowledge was turned on its head and worked against its original purpose and against humanity."

"What can I do to prevent that?"

"Nothing."

I had wanted to hear there was some scheme, simple or elaborate, that would allow me to proceed with development of my machine and prevent abuses from occurring.

"Suppose, now," Dad said, "one man escaped the cave, thus becoming enlightened. Suppose further, he returned. Would a good and just man wish to keep his fellows in darkness, or would he prefer instead to show them the illumination and lead them out of darkness?"

"I suppose that people of good conscience would try to lead them out just like I try every day to illuminate my students."

"And, I am sure you do it well." He smiled at me before going on. "Imagine still, if the others would not learn—that is to say, you could not enlighten them regardless of how hard you tried. Would it be just to consign them to total darkness?"

"Hardly."

"Then, let's put this all together. You asked what to do about your invention. It's capable of doing great good and bringing enlightenment or bringing great harm. You rightly intuit that others want to stop you for their own purposes. What would one who thinks himself to be good and honorable do?"

"So, what you're saying is a good and decent person who can shed light that allows people in darkness to see the truth has a moral obligation to do so?"

"I don't say that. Plato did—at least the ones who see should lead those who don't. If they don't want to follow—"

"Even if it's to my peril?"

"Plato didn't address peril, and he seemed to be a little averse to it himself. You're on your own there deciding what to do. But, it does seem Plato saw the world as being full of ignorance and false impressions and that only a few people saw things as they really were. Whether or not he was right, I'm not here to judge. Plato thought they were the people who should have been the leaders who led the followers out of the dark cave. But, neither am I in the position of judging anyone's morals. I want to be clear on that."

Good. I wasn't ready to declare it to be a moral requirement that I should share my machine with the world, if that's what Dad was getting at. There wasn't time to think it through and continue our dialogue before Mom returned with word about Michael and Hannah.

"They are both fine," she said, "Trusted souls are helping them adjust to the transition; it was so traumatic and unexpected for both of them. But, they're in good company."

"Can I talk to them?" I asked. "I need to apologize to both of them."

"I already asked. Neither one is ready to step forward yet. It's just too soon. You've got to understand."

"Tell them I'm sorry."

"I will," she promised.

"We've got to go for now," Dad said. "You think about what I said. Okay?"

After they left, I mulled over what he'd said and still didn't really get what I was supposed to do.

Dad had invoked the teachings of Plato for a reason. Perhaps it was because Plato was one of the founders of western thought and the founder of the world's first institution of higher learning; or perhaps it was that Plato had taught abstracts. And, the world I had ventured into was about as abstract as it got. Or, perhaps it was because Plato's method of working through a perplexing problem was to bring in good thinkers, pose the question, and let them reason through it.

I could find out for myself. I could use the machine to bring in a good thinker and see what he might have to say. "Calling Plato. Plato, the great teacher of Athens. If you can hear me, I need to talk to you."

My call was met with silence.

I waited. The xenocryst didn't do anything remarkable. I called again. "Plato, if this gets through to you, please, I could use some help."

The screen lit up. The light inside the crystal whirled manically.

"Here I am. What can I do for you?" The voice was unfamiliar, but the crystal clear image was remarkably like the bust of Plato I had seen many times before on the covers of books and in encyclopedia articles which showed him with a thick full beard and thick hair combed forward onto his broad forehead.

"I'm sorry to disturb you, Mr. Plato."

"It's no disturbance. If it were, I simply wouldn't have come."

That simple thought humbled me. I hadn't thought about it, but it made sense that just because the machine could get through to them didn't mean they had to reply at my beck and call. And Plato had chosen to answer my call.

"What should I call you? Plato, Mr. Plato?"

"You may call me Aristocles, or you may call me by my nickname, Plato."

A moment of doubt or perhaps caution edged its way in. "No offense, but how do I know you're the real Plato?"

"No offense taken. I encourage your skepticism. Wait right here and I'll be back in a moment."

While he was gone, the reality set in that if he was who he said he was, I was having a conversation with Plato — student of Socrates, teacher of Aristotle. In English no less. I didn't speak a word of Greek, and I was sure Plato pre-dated English. Thought must transcend language. But I would have to put off marveling at the notion for now. Moments later, he returned with Mom and Dad.

"It's the real Plato," Mom said.

The Iron Couch

"You can trust him," Dad said with a scholarly nod.

They both left quickly. "Love you," Mom called from a distance.

"So, Plato, I've got a dilemma."

"I know."

"You know about my dilemma?"

"Indeed I do. You have stirred up a lot of excitement here. But, I hasten to add, also a lot of ambivalence for fear it could go either way, that is backfire."

"That's what I need to talk to you about. What am I supposed to do?"

"What makes you think I have the answer?"

"I don't necessarily. But, maybe you could help me arrive at the right answer."

"Do you think all questions have a right answer?"

"Perhaps not. But, we may first have to arrive at several probabilistic solutions and collapse them down to the most probable correct answer. Right now, I'd rather just cut through it and settle for a better answer than I've got."

There was silence for a moment before Plato spoke again. "All right, that's a reasonable starting point. Consider this. If you had borrowed a knife from someone and he asked for its return, would it not be right to give it back to him?"

"Of course."

"Suppose you knew he had lost his mind and intended to kill someone with it. Would it be right to give it back to him then?" Somewhere in the back of my mind, I realized I was experiencing, firsthand, a real

Socratic dialogue. The enormity of it struck me hard. "Suppose further, upon your refusal, he determined to break into your house and steal it back from you. Would you have any responsibility for its misuse?"

"Maybe. If I hadn't secured it properly."

"In that case, would it not be better then, to cast the knife back into the fires from which it was forged, so it could never be used to kill?"

"I guess so — Is that the only option? Couldn't it be hidden until it's safe?"

"Only so long as our hypothetical madman, or others, didn't discover its hiding place. Do you know of a place so clever no one would ever find it? Before you answer, bear in mind, 'ever' is a very long time."

I thought about the analogy for a while. Then I said, "We seem to have switched from merely keeping the knife away from the madman to hiding it away forever, or destroying it. But are there to be no knives in the world? Knives can be used for good purposes. Talking to you, for instance, and my parents."

"You look to me for an answer. I can give you only perspectives, choices." A fat lot of good it did to call on Plato. "I'm sorry if I've disappointed you. That's just the way it is."

"Philippes seems to think introducing my machine to the world will cause religious, philosophical, moral, ethical chaos that will disrupt societies as we now know them. Is he right?"

"I can't say that's an inevitable conclusion. There are so many possibilities it's virtually impossible to say. I also can't say that wouldn't happen. All breakthroughs challenge something, and reactions are unpredictable at times."

"But this one is big. Really big."

"Yes. I agree. I don't feel I've been much help to you today, Simon. I am sorry. But before I go is there anything else I can try to help you with?"

"Yes. One other thing. Who is Philippes Legrand? Is he for real? Is he a good guy or a bad guy?"

"I don't know this Philippes. I must leave it to you to decide."

With that, Plato was gone. Shortly after, that strange snow globe feeling came back.

Chapter Thirty-six

I HAD TO GET OUT OF THERE. I knew where I wanted to go, where I needed to go. Up into the hills off of the Granite Passage logging road there was a trail where Michael and I used to hike and explore. Michael had discovered that place before we met in school and told me it was where he would sometimes go for solitude. It was there he told me of his passion for geology and earth sciences and talked about the various layers in the granite formations across the gorge. That place is where I hoped to find some solace.

South of town at the second exit after the highway stopped looking like a city street cluttered with shopping centers and car dealerships and big box stores, apartment complexes, multiplex movie theaters and medical centers, where sanity returned, I turned off onto a county road and a few miles later headed into the trees. In daylight, the road looked like a swath cut through the greens and browns of the forest. At dusk, the landscape turned to charcoal gray etchings.

On the way, my thoughts turned to Hannah and what Mrs. Albright had told me. If Hannah had only known how much courage it had taken for me to insinuate my interest in her, perhaps she would have had the courage to tell me about herself. Yet, I understood Hannah's need for privacy, and I would have been honored to be counted among her friends. Perhaps I hadn't insinuated clearly enough.

And Michael. We were total opposites. Few would have guessed we'd ever become best friends. He was gregarious and funny, had an easy manner around girls, and had liked to party. And, he was nine years older than me. That hadn't stopped him from being the first person in my class to accept me. Others had thought I was some kind of child prodigy, which is a euphemism for oddity. But after Michael had become my friend, others gradually warmed up to me and stopped staring at me and talking in hushed tones when I came around.

The rest of the night could have been lost in memories, but my attention had to return to driving. The turnoff to the trail I was looking for was marked by two distinctive trees on the left that were just far enough apart for my Jeep to pass between them without tearing off the mirrors. It was fully dark now and I had to strain to see them.

A sharp left, a pause to shift to four-wheel drive, and I was off and up. I had been there many times before in daylight, but this was the first time after dark. This trip, the trail seemed like a metaphor for life: an uphill climb, getting scraped and banged on the way, seeing ahead only as far as the cones of my headlights allowed, and coming to an abrupt end, uncertain of what lay ahead, even though I thought I knew.

At the edge of the headlights, a forked tree came into view to the left. That was my stop. I set the parking brake and got out. One trunk of the tree was nearly horizontal, just below waist high. On the other side of the tree, the landscape leveled out and there was a flat rock ledge that overlooked the Glaser River gorge several hundred feet below. The ledge was about half the size of my living room. To the right, the hill continued its ascent, but at the bottom of the rock wall was a cavern just deep enough to crawl into, high enough to sit upright. If I'd had to, I supposed I could take shelter there.

A mist that coated everything with a dull layer of moisture settled in fast. Overhead, light from a near-full moon filtered through airborne droplets. At times, the light was diffuse. Other times, the fog was so thin it simply formed a halo around the moon. Clear patches let in some twinkling stars.

Looking out from earth to what I could see of the heavens, I tried to think about the big questions, such as the meaning of life. And, why all of this was happening to me and wondering why it had to involve Michael and Hannah. But, it was no good; I couldn't think straight.

Instead, I remembered a time when Michael and I had taken off on foot from this very point and made our own trail through the forest until we stumbled onto an abandoned logging camp. The shells of dilapidated shacks remained, leaning and tired-looking. Even a pile of half-rotted logs that had never made it to the saw mill had collapsed in on itself. A lumberjack's leather harness with rusted rings lay on the ground. All were signs people had come, taken what they wanted, and left, leaving only decay behind.

My mind clogged. My brain shut down. Something came over me, something uncontrollable. I yelled into my own echo, "What do you want from me!?" I had tampered with something that should have been left alone. I had stirred up something, and because of me, Michael and Hannah were dead. "All you great spirits, where are you now?" First, they had come to me uninvited. Then I went to them. Oh, they were so happy then to talk to the living. I had been warned. Philippes had told me I would be a marked man if I persisted. I didn't understand why. "Now you have left me alone." Alone on that ledge. I could have thrown the beastly machine into the gorge below. I could have jumped with it. But then, someone could perhaps have found us and the monster would live on.

I opened the machine. "Dad — Plato, someone." Instantly, Philippes' face popped up. His lips moved but I couldn't hear him. "Jesus, God. Help me." I slammed the lid. The crystal glowed and whirled like mad. I sat down on the hard moist granite, hyperventilating in fits of rapid shallow gasps, my insides on fire from adrenalin. I pulled my knees up with the machine wedged against my chest. I stayed there a long time with my arms and head resting on my knees wheezing loudly. After a while, I remembered what Geoff had showed me and cupped my hands over my mouth and nose, breathing into them while trying to maintain a slow count. One-one thousand. Two-one thousand. Three-one thousand. I got to over three hundred — one thousand before my breathing returned to normal.

When my head cleared a little, I recalled what Plato had said about returning the offending knife to the fire from which it was forged rather than letting it do harm. If I could have, I would have stuffed the crystal back down the hole out in the desert, the hole deep as Mt. Everest was high and leave it there for eternity. But there was no Michael to show me where that hole was.

Time got away from me sitting there on the ledge. The ghostly moon had moved two-thirds of the way across the sky. Exhaustion set in every one of my muscles, but I didn't want to risk driving downhill backwards on the fog-moistened trail in the dark to go home.

I crawled back through the crotch of the tree and went to the car to get some emergency supplies: an old stadium blanket, a sweatshirt, an emergency candle and butane lighter. In the front cupholder there was a partial bottle of water.

The air was early-spring cold. I put on the sweatshirt and crawled into the front seat, which angled upward with the hill's incline, and pulled the blanket over me. Soon, I was asleep.

But not for long. Dreams kept waking me. Recurring dreams where I was falling but just before hitting the ground I woke up. Even awake I had that falling feeling. Maybe it was the angle of the car. Maybe it was a premonition. I drifted off again.

Morning came. I took the water bottle and worked my way out of the car and over to the ledge. The sun was at just the proper angle to reflect off the rock wall to my right in little pinpoints that flickered when I moved my head this way or that. I knew why Michael had loved this place so much. There was a quiet strength here. The wind stirred the trees. If you dared to look over the ledge, the river below was silent and seemed motionless. Yet, there it was: the patient victor, soft and fluid, that had held on and had worn its path through the cold hard granite hills.

Suddenly, all was quiet like those moments when life throws you in the midst of turmoil and an eerie, unexplainable calm comes over you, a calmness not born of the restoration of order and control, but rather calmness that is a capitulation to the uncontrollable. Or perhaps it was simply a pragmatic solution since the only thing you could really control in those circumstances is your own reaction.

I was thirsty and raised the water bottle to my mouth. Water sloshed and ran down my chin. I wiped my chin with my shirtsleeve and recapped the bottle. Water sloshed again inside the bottle. Back and forth. I tilted the bottle one way then the other, watching the ebb and flow. It was like an ocean in a bottle, tide coming in, tide going out. It was also like finding a message in a bottle.

Something inside my head tugged on me, but I felt it in my chest, too. It was hard to tell if an idea had come to me from deep within or from deep outside of me. The feeling churned my insides. I had to go to the ocean; but, I didn't know where.

Chapter Thirty-seven

LATER IN THE DAY the eerie calm remained, but an unsettling sense of detachment also set in. That snow globe feeling had come and gone many times in the last few days, and now it was back with a vengeance. I felt as if I were present but distant from my surroundings. Sounds were muted and hollow, again. The glass jar effect.

In my car, I plodded along the freeway towards the airport with lines of traffic passing me on the left and on the right. Mountains stood in the periphery at the horizon. Sparse herds of cattle that usually grazed on both sides of the freeway whenever I had driven this way before went unnoticed if they were even there that day.

When I got to the airport, I paid sixteen dollars for one day in the satellite parking and took the small bag containing the machine with me to the shuttle stop. A couple was already there, complaining about the wait. "It's been twelve minutes already. We could have walked there in this amount of time." "I told you we should've gotten up earlier." "Oh, Rachael, don't start now." "What do you mean, 'Don't start?' We're going to miss our plane. . ." Their useless chatter drifted away. I watched cars coming and going.

Other people came, and when the shuttle finally got there, everyone got aboard, some banging their suitcases against the metal steps on their way up. The driver stopped at every terminal and let people out in their little groups while I stayed on, no destination in mind, until the bus eventually stopped at the farthest terminal, and I was the only one left. The door opened and the air smelled of exhaust fumes.

A voice spoke, but I didn't hear it well. It spoke again.

"Sir, if I don't let you out here, the next stop is back at the parking lot." The speaker was the shuttle driver.

"What?"

"Is that were you want to go, back to satellite parking?"

"Satellite—? No. No. Here is fine—Sorry—Thanks."

The airport was jam packed with young travelers, whom I thought to be college students on their way to spring break vacations, bustling, clustering, flirting, and constantly prattling. I, on the other hand, had followed an urge, a notion, an intuition that had taken me there with nowhere to go. And now I was out of ideas. Going there had felt like the right thing to do, but it increasingly seemed like a bad idea.

From a few yards away, a burst of laughter and cheering erupted from a group standing beneath an arrival/departure board. I went toward them.

"I'm going to South Padre," I overheard a young woman say. "Where're you guys going?"

"Ft. Lauderdale," a smiling guy said, doing a fist pump.

"Cancun." That announcement brought cheers and loud woo-hoos.

"Key West."

"Jacksonville."

"I thought about going to go to San Juan," a blonde woman said sounding a bit affected as if she were bragging. "But, I've already been there. . . last winter with my parents. The tropical weather is simply marvelous any time of year."

I shot her a glance and remembered from a geography lesson long ago that the Puerto Rico Trench, just off the northern shore of San Juan, was 28,000 feet deep — almost as deep as Mt. Everest is high. It should make a suitable grave for the xenocryst and the machine. The board showed that Flight 5511 was scheduled to depart non-stop for San Juan later that day.

There it was. The reason I had been led there.

The bubble that had surrounded me all morning dissolved quickly and my senses returned to normal. Maybe that was because of the clarity of deciding on a destination.

I found the way to the ticket counter where a rope line with maze-like square corners was filled with passengers, winding their way slowly toward the counter. People of all kinds were there: the presumed spring breakers, families with babies and small children, lone travelers. Pulled off to the side was a young woman with a Yorkshire terrier with its head stuck out of a soft-sided zip-up carrier. Agents told the woman that she couldn't board with her dog. She protested that she had called ahead and had gotten permission. They argued, but there was no doubt she wouldn't win.

A young couple who appeared to be married split duties. He went ahead to get a boarding pass while she filled out a name tag for each item of luggage. He returned and found her to still be writing their names.

"You'd better hurry," he said.

"Well, I want them to be able to read the tags if our luggage gets lost," she told him.

After them, a hunter checked in a rifle and bow, and that caused a delay while additional forms were completed.

The agent behind the counter, a distinguished looking gray-haired woman in her late fifties or early sixties, wearing a long sleeve white shirt with a blue scarf, looked over her reading glasses at the line that was growing longer by the minute. I could sense her anxiety.

And mine. Now that I had a destination, I was anxious to get on with it and get on board. When I had advanced to second in line, there was yet another hold up with the very large man in front of me with gray thinning hair. The man had to weigh well over three hundred pounds, maybe three-fifty, and was talking quietly with the agent. He looked upset, even angry; she, stoic.

Although it wasn't my usual habit to eavesdrop, this time was an exception, and I stepped a little closer to hear.

"I'm sorry, sir," the agent said. "It's a new airline policy for certain customers... of size... that we charge for two seats."

"That's discrimination."

"I'm afraid it's perfectly legal, sir."

"Fat people are the only people you can get by discriminating against in this country. It's not right!"

"I don't make the policies. I just issue tickets and boarding passes. Do you still want to board?" There was no mistaking her authority.

"Let me get this straight, if I want to take this flight, I have to pay for two seats even though I'm only sitting in one."

"You have to pay for the one you sit in and the one next to it," she said, nodding.

"Look, I fly to Puerto Rico every month. I don't usually wait until the last minute to buy tickets, but this time something came up. No one said anything to me last month."

"Your travel agent should have told you."

"I book my own flights online. They should say something on the website. And now you're telling me I have to pay for two seats." He rubbed his chin. "Will you also sell the other seat and you get paid twice? Or will I have both seats?" He seemed defiant, yet still polite.

"We have the latitude to do either, but we usually don't sell the same seat twice. It'll remain empty. Sometimes if the flight isn't full, we can issue a refund for the extra seat. But, this flight is full, and the second fare isn't refundable." She motioned to the long line behind us. "I'm sorry, I will have to sell you both seats."

So, the flight was full. After going there on an inspired hunch, I couldn't take the chance of not getting on board. Thinking quickly, I edged part-way around the big guy. "Excuse me, I couldn't help but overhear." I was intruding, but this was a necessary intrusion. "Are you talking about Flight 5511 to San Juan?"

The big man leaned away on the counter and turned to train his eyes on me seriously. "Yep. That's where I'm headed." He was obviously annoyed at first, but his eyes flickered a bit when he looked at me, and his expression quickly softened.

"You said, that flight is full, right?" I asked the ticket agent.

"Sir, if you would just step back in line—"

"Hear me out, please. If it's okay with you," I looked first at the big man, then at the agent, "and if your company policy allows, I would like to buy the seat next to him." I leaned over the counter and whispered, "Even if it's a tight squeeze."

"It's not just that," she said quietly. "It's also about fuel costs for the . . . added weight."

"Oh." Then I thought about something. "But, look at me. I'm thin. Between the two of us, we'll average out." The big man pursed his lips, breathed noisily through his nose, and looked down at her. "If you don't mind sitting next to me," I said to him, "I would really like to have that seat. I've got to get to Puerto Rico. I'd be on the next flight to San Juan, and you'd only pay single fare. Win-win-win, right?" I looked back and forth between them waiting for their answers. The agent looked at the big man who had stopped talking. I knew that I didn't look very good and may not have smelled very good after last night and the previous couple of days. It was obvious I wasn't getting anywhere with her. "It's just that it's been real hectic lately. I've just got to get away. I'm a teacher. It's spring break. My house was broken into a couple of days ago, my stuff was scattered all over the place, I slept in my car last night—but, you don't want to hear my troubles. You've got your own. And I may be able to solve yours. At least one. What do you say?"

The big man turned to the ticket agent nodding. "That's okay with me, if it's okay with you."

She looked once more at the line and hesitated as if she were thinking about it, then gave a wan smile. "I think we have a solution." Quickly she issued the big guy's boarding pass.

After the big man moved on, I stepped up with my passport and photo ID and got my boarding pass and then went to security.

At the security station, the TSA officer gave me trouble over a battered and broken computer with loose wires hanging out of it. I hadn't thought about its appearance, but I suppose in this day and age, I should have.

"It still works," I said.

"What's this?" She had taken the xenocryst from its cradle with the dangling wires and held it up.

"It's an experimental material."

"Experimental?" She looked skeptical.

"Look. I'm a computer researcher. Here, let me show you." I waited for her to nod approval before reaching into my pocket to get my Finial U faculty ID which clearly showed that my departments were Computer Science and Applied Physics. She showed no reaction upon inspecting it. She turned her attention back to the xenocryst.

"It's glowing. And it's warm," she said, rolling the sphere around in her hand.

Again, I had to think quickly. "The glow is its natural iridescence—and it's reflecting the heat of your hand."

"The glow is moving."

"That's due to the changing angle of observation. It appears to move because of the change of colors as light waves are refracted. " It was hard to tell if she swallowed what I had just made up.

She ordered me to stand to the side for a minute, then summoned another TSA officer with her pointer finger. They talked in low tones. Then she made a short phone call. Minutes later, a dark-faced, bomb- or drug-sniffing Belgian Malinois they called "Lucy" was brought in and gave me and my bags a thorough olfactory scan. When Lucy walked away disinterested, two different officers patted me down, then one of them asked me to go through the body scanner a second time as the other one left.

"You're free to go. Thank you for your cooperation." They were curt and their appreciation didn't seem genuine.

"No problem."

Once I cleared the security station and was out of sight, I let out a sigh of relief. I had been terrified the whole time there that the crystal might be confiscated like an oversize can of deodorant under some national security law, and my plan to give it a proper burial would be foiled. And, even though there was plenty of time, I hurried down the concourse to put distance and people between me and TSA.

Chapter Thirty-eight

BEFORE LONG, I saw a beefy hand waving at me to come over. The big guy from the ticket line was sitting on a bench with his luggage parked in front of him. "Come over here and have a seat," he called to me. He was all smiles. I sat down. "Bradley's the name. Kent Joseph Bradley."

"Nice to meet you, officially, Kent."

"Just call me 'Bradley.' Everyone else does. My dad gave me three first names that are also three last names and, of course vice versa." He chuckled. "Like his dad did him and his dad before him. That was their sense of humor." He chuckled again. We shook hands and I told him my name.

"I want to thank you for saving me a wad of cash," Bradley said. "These flights aren't cheap anymore. Is there anything I can do to return the favor?"

"The only thing I need is a shower, a change of clothes, and to get to Puerto Rico." I knew I was the one who had gotten the favor. "You going there for spring break?"

"You mean so I can run around the beaches in a Speedo?" He laughed a little bit. "There's so much of me drooping, you'd never see the Speedo." This time, he really cracked up.

I shook my head. "Thanks for that image."

"Oh to be young and thin again— and have hair." He laughed and snorted at the same time. "How about you?"

"Yeah. This is my first time ever. I thought I'd go this year, especially after the break-in and all."

We talked about travelling and all of its inconveniences. About twenty minutes later, a lull came and I noticed Bradley regarding me closely enough to make me feel a bit uncomfortable until he revealed the reason for his staring.

"You remind me of my son. You've got the same color of hair and eyes, same smile, same build. If I hadn't been there when he was born, I'd say you were his lost twin."

"What's his name?"

"Thomas Eddy Bradley."

"Three first names, three last names."

"It's family tradition." Bradley smiled with signs of strain.

"What does he do?"

"He's in Arlington . . ." His expression fell.

"Texas?"

"Cemetery." His eyes suddenly saddened and reddened a little. "He was kill—he died in the war." His voice betrayed a bit of quiver.

"I'm sorry. Which one?"

"Isn't it a shame that you even have to ask?" He fidgeted while I felt awkward. "Hey—are you hungry?"

"Starved."

"Let's grab a bite."

Nearby was a sports bar and grill. We went inside for a quick meal. The walls were filled with mounted memorabilia like sports jerseys of famous players, football helmets, baseball gloves, hockey sticks, autographed photos, and so on. We ordered our sandwiches and fries and went to the nearest table. In front of us was a baseball bat autographed by the full roster of the 1956 New York Yankees.

Seeing the bat seemed to strike a chord with the big guy. He had a passion for baseball, and that was the one thing besides computers and physics that I could talk about extensively, especially World Series trivia.

"My boy was a catcher in college," Bradley said and paused for a moment. There was something about him that put me at more ease than I had felt in a long time, as if everything was going to be okay—at least for now. Maybe it was his kind expression or his easy laugh. Maybe it was simply something fatherly about him. "Just like I was. Can you imagine me squatting like that?" He laughed so hard I thought he'd choke. Then I realized I was laughing, too. "He wanted to go into the majors but couldn't quite make it. After he graduated college, he joined the army and became an infantry officer."

Thomas would have been better off going to the minors, but there was no need to voice that now. I was sure Bradley knew that, and I could feel that his pain was still fresh. For a fleeting moment, I thought of pulling out my machine and seeing if I could contact his Thomas. But, on second thought, I decided not to. There was no way of knowing how that might affect him.

"Who knows," I said. "He might have made it to the World Series one day."

"That was his dream. And to make a big game-winning play that goes down in the history books."

"Like the 1960 World Series between the Pittsburgh Pirates and the New York Yankees."

The big guy's eyes lit up. "Yeah, wasn't that sweet? Bill Mazeroski of the Pirates—"

"The Maz—"

"—hit the only Game Seven walk-off homer in World Series history. Cinched it up for the Pirates, and the Yankees had to walk off with their heads hung low."

"I used to be a pitcher," I said, "and I always daydreamed of pitching a perfect game. Just like Don Larsen, Game Five, 1956 World Series." I pointed to the autographed bat. "If only I could have pitched a game like that."

"How about 1977? Reggie Jackson hitting three home runs in three at-bats."

The Red Sox finally breaking the Curse of the Bambino in 2004, the injured Kirk Gibson hobbling around the bases for a home run in 1988; between the two of us, we could have written a World Series almanac.

We left the sports bar over two hours later, still talking baseball, and boarded the plane.

Hours into the long flight, our conversation dwindled and the big guy fell asleep, but I was wide awake. Before he drifted off, I had found out that Bradley really was a good man, a good father and grandfather. He worked for himself and had business interests in Puerto Rico where he flew once a month.

After the last economic downturn, crime in Puerto Rico, especially drug crimes, had shot up. Bradley had owned a small house in the municipality of Carolina where he'd stayed for a week out of every month. But crime had gotten so bad, and since he was gone three-fourths of the time, he'd had to move into a condo in the more upscale municipality of Dorado. "With an ocean view," he'd said with a smile, "If you look between the palm trees and squint—which is a lot better than the view through burglar bars." Nonetheless, the expense was a burden.

"Why not," I had asked him, "just stay in hotels?" He'd replied that staying in hotels never builds you any equity.

Now, with business down and expenses up, he feared the airlines' surcharges for his girth would eat into his shrinking profits, and though he knew he needed to shed a few pounds, that wouldn't happen any time soon. He was simply trying to make it to retirement and set up college funds for Thomas Eddy's children along the way.

In the quiet, with only the steady roar of the jet's engines in the background, I looked out the window beside me. From that altitude over the Atlantic Ocean, the sunset stretched from one end of the earth to the other, drawing an orange and pink pencil line of demarcation where earth and sky met. Above it, the pale blue of day had already given in to the blackness of night with sparkling stars, while the fireball at its center sank rapidly behind the horizon. It reminded me that ancient mariners feared dragons and demons they thought lay beyond the ocean's bounds and if the mariners had ventured too far, they would have fallen into the waiting mouths and arms of the monsters.

Still later, the Boeing 737 banked and began its descent to Luis Muñoz Marín International Airport, three miles southeast of San Juan. The seatbelt sign was on. The flight attendant had announced that all electronic devices should be stowed under the seat. I nudged Bradley with an elbow and told him it was time to wake up, we were landing. My ears began to pop.

Inside the terminal Bradley reached into his wallet and pulled out a business card with his address back home and his Puerto Rico address and gave it to me. "Keep in touch, Simon."

We shook hands. For a moment, I thought he was going to hug me. For a moment, I thought I was going to hug him. As Bradley went his way and I went mine, a crushing dark cloud of gloom returned. I knew what I had to do, but I didn't know how.

Chapter Thirty-nine

AFTER BRADLEY AND I PARTED, I wandered around the airport for a while, passing by convenience stores and shoe shine kiosks, looked through windows at souvenirs, and came across a barber shop that was closed for the evening. Duly reminded that I had been so preoccupied lately I hadn't shaved in a while, I stroked the lengthening whiskers on my face and moved on. I would need money—of that I was sure—so I looked for an ATM and drew out most of my remaining cash and left the building.

Outside, humid air tinged with car and jet exhaust swept past my face. I strode down to where a couple of taxis were lined up, hailed one, got into the van, and asked the driver to take me to the ocean.

"Here for spring break?" the driver asked.

"Yeah—Si."

"I know just where to take you."

The ride wasn't long. The driver chattered in Spanish on his cell phone the whole time, interrupted only by occasional pauses. I tuned him out. After so many hours on a plane, I was tired and my muscles needed to stretch; my head, my eyelids were heavy. I felt distant, dreamlike. It seemed we were going in slow motion past colored lights from a few bars and dance clubs and an Irish pub, of all things. I fought nodding off until chest thumping bass vibrated my eardrums and roused me.

"Here we are," the driver said, holding the phone away from his ear. "Playa Isla Verde."

"Is there some place else you could take me?"

"You here for spring break? This is where you wanna be."

"But, is there some other place — ?"

"I can't take you no other place. You're my last fare. My wife," he said raising the phone, "she expects me home soon. You'll be fine, have fun." He arched his eyebrows, smiled, and nodded.

I was too tired to argue. This would work as a starting point. He pointed to the posted fare. I calculated a tip, paid him, and set out toward the beach with my bag.

There were a number of hotels lining the beach, three within easy walking distance — major names, good places to stay, all full up.

I passed through palm trees, leaves fluttering in the breeze, towards the sand beach looking for a place to rest. My eyes and feet had conspired to rebel against going any further. Loud, drunken, crude people behaving badly were everywhere around me. Their music drowned out my labored thoughts. Guys in swim trunks, women in tiny bikinis, twerk danced, simulating mating. Just being there to see it made me uncomfortable. And, of course beer chugging contests were everywhere, too. Surely, the partygoers would call it quits soon. The music and dancing would stop. The siren's song of warm cozy beds would draw them in. At least I could hope.

After the partiers began to drift away leaving behind the die-hard hangers on, I claimed an empty beach chair to be my bed for the night. Nearby was a pile of abandoned dry hotel beach towels that I also claimed for my bedding.

Earlier at the airport, I had overheard a traveler warning other travelers about pickpockets at popular tourist sites, especially at the beaches. I decided to take no chances and tied the bag to my arm with one of the towels. I pulled the rest of the towels over me and stretched out with the bag resting across my thighs.

The laughter, the music, the gaiety. . . the voices. . . faded.

Not long into my slumber, I felt a tug on my arm. I opened my eyes and there were two dark haired young men, who looked to be in their mid- to late teens, trying to lift the bag off of me.

I rolled out of the chair onto the ground and sprang to my feet in one motion, grabbed a handful of sand, and pelted them with hundreds of granular fastballs right in their faces.

One guy wiped his face with the tail of his tee shirt that had the sleeves cut out while yelling something in Spanish I took to be cursing. The other wiped his eyes with his fingertips. I wound up another handful of sand, but they quickly departed, rattling off things I couldn't understand.

After that, I couldn't get back to sleep.

Chapter Forty

MORNING CAME. The night breeze stopped, the air got warmer, the sky got brighter. I threw off the pile of towels and sat up. While I had lain awake thinking, the next part of the plan had come to me, and I needed to act. I hurried across the sand back through the palm trees to the nearest hotel, stirring up seagulls along the way who voiced their grievance with piercing throaty squeaks. Wings fluttering, they launched into flight and circled overhead like floating M's.

Once I passed through the hotel's sliding glass doors and into the lobby, I found the business center for guests, a cramped space with Internet and a printer, vacant at that hour. Within minutes, I found and printed the coordinates for the Milwaukee Deep, the deepest point in the Atlantic Ocean, 19.583°N 66.500°W. At over twenty-eight thousand feet deep, it lay about seventy-five miles north of San Juan and a little west. I also looked up the address of the nearest dive shop.

By then, the hotel's restaurant had opened for breakfast, but the only other people there was a young couple who spent more time giggling and looking at each other than the menu. I wolfed down my breakfast of scrambled eggs and a short stack of pancakes with maple syrup and a dollop of butter, and sipped on a cup of coffee while I devised the rest of my plan. I would go to the dive shop and buy a weight carry bag, as many pouches of weight shot, the kind that divers put in their inflatable jackets, as I could fit in the bag, and a weight belt. I would put the machine in the weighted bag and tightly cinch the weight belt around it for added measure, then drop it into the Milwaukee Deep where it should sink to depths out of reach of all but the deepest diving, submersible remotely operated vehicles. A few weeks before, I had read that an expedition to map that part of the ocean floor had recently been completed. It stood to reason, then, that explorers wouldn't be back for a while. By the time future expeditions would arrive to do further mapping, if at all, the machine would have nestled deep into the thick silt on the ocean's floor.

And, at that location, earth's fractured crust lazily chewed and forced downward all that it ingested into the bowels of the earth, thus creating a hiding place clever enough to meet Plato's demand: a place where no one would ever find it. It would stay there waiting to be returned someday to the fires from which this knife was forged. Two-in-one. Problem solved.

All I needed now was to get to the Milwaukee Deep. Somewhere on the island, there had to be a charter boat that could take me out to open waters. I would find it.

Plan completed, I stirred my coffee pensively while watching the little eddies I made with the spoon. That snow globe feeling came back. When the waitress, an older woman, came to give me my check, I asked her for directions to the dive shop. She happily obliged me and told me that the owners sometimes ate at the restaurant and it was a little early, but I would know they were open if there were a diver down flag in the window.

I strode off to the dive shop and waited, looking, for the red flag with the white diagonal stripe to be hung in the window and told the sales lady the items I wanted to buy. She located them for me, then I asked her where I could charter a boat.

"If you don't already have one booked, good luck. You might start by looking over in San Juan Marina."

I set off towards the marina feeling a little detached from the surroundings.

The guard at the marina was friendly and wore a sharply pressed khaki colored uniform with epaulets. When I told him I was looking to book a tour, he eagerly let me in. The marina was packed with seafaring boats. It shouldn't have been hard to find a captain looking for a fare. The first captain I came upon was busy cleaning the deck and looked to be preparing for the day's excursions.

"Are you for hire?" I asked, looking up at the figure that towered over me.

"Two weeks from now, maybe. This is the busy season, with all of the college kids from the States wanting to go scuba diving and parasailing."

"Do you know where I might be able to charter a boat?"

"Sorry. I think you're too late." Without being rude, the captain returned to his work. "I've got a tight schedule," he called over his shoulder, his efforts now focused on arranging ropes and things that looked like parachutes. I thanked him and left.

Boat after boat, I talked to all the owners and captains I could find. Most of the boats were private pleasure craft. The ones that hired out for tours were already booked.

I asked one captain, "Any idea how I can get out to the Trench?"

"It's that way," he said, sweeping his arm in a long arc pointing to the horizon from left to right. "Seventy-five miles or so."

"Can you take me there?"

He shook his head. "Too far to go. There's more fun to be had closer in." He eyed the weight belt that I had wrapped around my waist for ease in carrying. "Not the best place for scuba diving either. Better things to see closer in."

"I'd really like to go to the Trench."

"Sorry. You'll have to find someone else."

"Do you know of anyone?"

"There's a marina close to Old San Juan. You could try there, but they're bound to be busy, too. You might try going to Fajardo. There's lots of boats there. But, that's on the east coast." It was also further away from Milwaukee Deep.

"What about someplace further west?"

He thought for a second holding his chin. "If you want to go west where it's not so busy, go toward Dorado, Barcaloneta, Manati, some place like that."

I shook his hand, thanked him, and left the marina.

The Iron Couch

I hadn't planned for this; but then again, I hadn't planned much lately. And what I had planned hadn't gone very well so far. It had become obvious I would need a car, so I went back to the airport, rented a Kia Rio, and scrunched myself into it. What a welcome relief it was to put the heavy bag onto the floorboard of the car. My shoulders ached and my hands had started to cramp.

I bypassed El Morro castle at Old San Juan and continued on west to Dorado and found no wharfs or marinas. At Barceloneta and Manati, it was the same. So, I kept going until I saw a name I recognized and pulled over: Arecibo.

Up in the lush green hills lay Mount Arecibo where the world's largest radio telescope was located. For a fleeting moment, I wondered why the great telescope hadn't picked up the signals my machine had detected. Or, perhaps it had and the results had not been made public. What could such a large telescope detect if it had an Emorite xenocryst programmed like mine? But, there was no time left for wondering. I needed to move on.

Not far away was a yacht club, but when I checked, it seemed that no boats would be leaving today. Discouraged, I left. As I pulled out to cross the highway, I spotted a wharf in the distance in the port east of the Arecibo Lighthouse. When I got closer, it appeared to be under construction, but some boats were already moored there. It was worth a shot. I pulled in, parked and made way to the first boat.

Beside it, a man slouched in a canvas chair on the dock, hat pulled over his eyes, a bottle of Medalla

Light sitting on top of a cooler with wheels and a handle.

"Are you the captain of this boat?" I asked.

He straightened up and pulled the hat off his eyes. "That I am and little else, but I am captain of the *Sea-Saw*. What can I do for you?"

I looked the boat over. From what I could tell, it looked seaworthy. It was clean, well painted and both sides were lined with large fishing rods and reels, nets, and oars.

"Are you for hire?" I asked.

"Could be." He eyed my weight bag. "But, I don't do scuba excursions. There's too much risk for me. And, I don't have any tanks or scuba gear. I just don't like it." The captain appeared to be in his mid- to late- forties, and his face told the tale of years of sun and salt spray. His hands appeared dry and calloused. He looked experienced and trustworthy. "We can go fishing, parasailing, sightseeing, whatever you want."

I set the bags down on the wooden planks with a thud and flipped my fingers a few times to pump blood back into them. Steel poles too new to be rusty held up the aluminum awning and squeaked with the rise and fall of each swell.

"Fishing is fine," I said, looking the boat up and down.

"This time of year, we can catch the end of the wahoo run. They're forty pounders and a lot of fun. Or we could find some black fin tuna. They're good eating. Forget mahi-mahi, though." He shook his head. "It's an acquired taste. Too strong a flavor for a lot of people." He wiped his brow with the back of his hand and said something that didn't register. I was busy looking around. "How many in your party, sir?"

"Just me."

No response from the captain.

"How much will it cost?"

"It depends. Do you want to go for half a day or a full day? If you want to go for a full day, it'll be next week before I can. But, I can do half a day today." He waited for an answer. My mission couldn't wait until next week, and half a day might cut it close. I could move on. When I didn't reply, he asked, "Are you sure you want to go alone? It's more fun in a group. Maybe I could get tomorrow's group to let you join them if you share costs."

"Half a day's fine." Decision made.

"I charge $750 for half a day." He paused for a moment, looking closely at me.

I turned around so that he couldn't watch and checked my pockets, then turned to face him. "I don't have that much on me."

"I take credit cards."

"I maxed it out to get here. Four hundred?"

"You're hurting my feelings now."

"That's every penny I've got."

"Barely covers my fuel costs. Five hundred."

"Thanks—Sorry I took your time." I fumbled around putting my wallet back in my pocket, turned, and walked away. Before I got to the parking lot, a tanned man wearing a white shirt, white shorts, and a captain's hat approached me.

"Excuse me, señor," he said. "You are looking for a boat to charter?"

"Yes."

"I heard you say you can pay $400?"

"Yes."

"U.S.? Not Canadian or Aussie?"

"Yes."

"Well, I'm your man. I am Captain Arturo Perez. See my boat over there? The *Puerto Pride*?" He pointed toward the boat at the wharf where I had just been talking to the other captain, whose name I hadn't caught.

"No, I don't."

"See? It's docked next to the one you just left. But mine's a little smaller, if that's not a problem. Perhaps that's why you can't see it. Come this way and you can see it better." The snow globe's glass walls still surrounded me. My vision had become blurred and outside noises were still muted. But, I heard him clearly and the longer he talked, the better his boat came into view. "Come back in three hours and I will take you out fishing. That will give me time to fuel up and get some provisions."

"Won't it be getting kind of late by then?" I asked.

"Certainly not. We can stay until dark. I know the way back. You will have a good time and lots of fish to eat."

"Will you take me out to the Trench?"

"I will take you wherever you pay me to go."

At the appointed time, I went back to the wharf and waited for Captain Arturo. By then, there was only one boat, and it didn't look familiar. And, I couldn't read the stained and weather battered name. The dock was in a no-wake area, but as I stood on it, swells moved it rhythmically beneath my feet up and down, enough to make me feel a bit nauseous, even though the swells weren't large.

It wasn't long until Captain Arturo popped up on the deck of the boat gesturing for me to come aboard.

The snow globe feeling stayed with me while I climbed aboard and settled into a passenger seat. For the moment I felt a little better. The sun warmed my face while I watched Captain Arturo make preparations to set sail. He checked the fishing gear, calling out each item. It must have been a routine of his. There were several poles with 130 pound line, several with 70 pound line, and a few with 20 pound line. He checked for large hooks and heavy lead weights, bait in the bucket, and a seine for catching more bait.

"You ready?" he called to me.

I nodded. "Here are the coordinates to the Milwaukee Deep where I want to go."

He took the paper, checked some instruments, punched a few keys on the marine GPS. The twin engines started with a powerful burble sound as the propellers churned the water. "Let's shove off." He took the helm and slowly backed out of the slip. After we cleared the no-wake area, we set off on a northeasterly course out to open sea.

I did some head math to double check my calculations on the pressures involved in water that deep, which were a thousand times greater than air pressure on land, and figured the bag was heavy enough to keep sinking all the way to the bottom where it should stay for the lifetime of planet Earth. To help out, the Milwaukee Deep has the strongest gravity pull of any place on earth because of its depth and the powerful forces pushing the earth's crust downward. The bag would definitely sink.

"Tell me when we're there," I yelled over the noisy engines, the wind in my face. "The Trench, that is."

The ride was long. The waves slapped the boat hard all the way out, sometimes splashing over the bow. I fought throwing up. When we arrived at our destination, Arturo looked down at the instrument panel and shut the engines down, coming to a complete stop. The boat bobbed in the water. The easterly trade winds were mild, and the seas had calmed but rolled enough to jostle the boat and keep me feeling wobbly.

"Welcome to the Puerto Rico Trench, Simon."

I didn't remember telling him my name.

We were all alone. After a couple of cruise ships had slid past the horizon a short time ago, no other watercraft were in sight. It was later than I had realized. The sun was hanging low in the sky, but it was still light.

Arturo opened the compartments on the port side where the tackle was stowed. "I'll help you gear up in a few minutes," he said and returned to the helm, turning his back on me.

Fishing could wait. I knew clearly now what I had to do. It was time to shut down the machine for the final time and bring it all to an end. The world wasn't ready for it. For that matter—I had finally come to grips with it—neither was I. The good thing was, nobody else knew about it. The world wouldn't miss it.

Nonetheless, a large part of me was sorry to see it go and with it the chance to talk to my father again, to form friendships with Plato and the others. But after all that had taken place, part of me was glad it would soon be over.

I unzipped the machine's burial shroud to have one last look and squeeze the air out before zipping it shut—not as if that would have made a difference. It was just that tending to detail made me feel better, and the more nervous I am, the more details I tend to. I took the weight belt off my waist and cinched it tightly around the bag and set it on the deck and crouched over it so that I could go through it one more time.

As I made the final inspection, I heard a low pitch power hum coming from the bow, crescendoing from barely noticeable to ear-shattering fortissimo that forced me to cover my ears.

I scooped up the bag and held onto it tightly and looked around to see what was going on. Arturo was still at the helm and began to pivot slowly toward the stern.

Except it wasn't Arturo. It was Philippes.

I stood there frozen, catatonic, bewildered. I must have been having a breakdown. Yeah, that was it. And why not? Everything that had happened to me in the last three months must have finally twisted my mind until it was all wrung out of shape.

"No, Simon. You're not imagining this. This is very real." Philippes, nemesis or friend—it was totally uncertain at this point which he was—stood in front of me, out of nowhere, expressionless, yet stern-looking.

"What's going on? Why are you—? How—? I don't get it."

"I warned you, Simon, your experiment was too dangerous and if you persisted you'd become a marked man. But, of course, you wouldn't listen to me."

"But, if you know all of that, you also know why I'm here. This will be the end of it." I gestured to the open water.

"I'm afraid it's too late. You've made contact with the most brilliant minds in human history and got them all excited. There are groups forming all over the place to plan what they can do to help proliferate your machine. They want to enlighten the world." He snarled when he said "enlighten," as though the word left a bad aftertaste. "You see, Simon, the domains of the universe of life where you live and the universes of the afterlife, or more accurately other states of life, are forever linked. But as long as there is mystery about them, the minds of humans can be manipulated. Knowledge is power. Power is advantage. Need I go on? Your machine changes all of that."

It was becoming clear that Philippes was no friend. "And where ever it is you're from, you manipulate in darkness, ignorance?"

"Exactly. It's so much easier that way."

"And after I've thrown the machine overboard, you'll take me back to shore?"

"No, Simon. It all ends here."

"What—?"

"You're going with it. To the bottom."

The wind picked up. The seas swelled again, pounding the boat. A wave, four feet, maybe six, crashed into the starboard side, spraying saltwater from stem to stern, and tossed me around. I tumbled head over heels, dropping everything in my hands. My pockets spilled out their contents. I hit the deck so hard it almost knocked the wind out of me. I must have hit my head, too, because suddenly I had a ferocious headache and felt woozy.

Philippes stood over me. "Stand up, Simon." I got to my feet. "Now, take that weight belt off of the bag and put it around your waist like you had it." I felt uncontrollably obedient, not like a small child obeying his parents, but like a trained animal who could do nothing different, and I wrapped the weight belt around my waist. "Now pick up the bag and clasp your hands around it." The bag was heavy. "Now jump overboard."

I knew in an instant why he wanted me dead. As long as I was alive, there was the risk I would reconstitute my work. Then there was the other thing, I reasoned on my own, or thought it was on my own, that I had penance to pay for my dead friends.

In one unhalting motion I stepped up on the boat's gunwale and then took another step. Splash. Water rushing up my nose. Feet finding nothing firm. Alarm. Panic. Sinking. Rapidly.

Snow globe feeling. Warm water. Stark silence. Calm. An eerie kind of freedom in all directions around me.

Below, the water went from greenish blue to dark blue to total blackness, and above, the silhouette of the boat rocked, its shape becoming smaller and darker, and the crush of the water pressed on my ribs, binding me like shrink wrap and the pull of gravity plunged me deeper into the swallowing mouth of the trench while the depletion of oxygen in my brain made me lightheaded, and I wondered how deep I was—

fifty, one hundred, two hundred feet—until I stopped caring and thought unconsciousness would surely overtake me soon, and I began to think that Philippes was right that I should die along with the machine, that it was my creation, and the deadly consequences were my fault, and if this was what it took to make it right and to deliver the xenocryst back to the depths from which it came, like Plato had suggested, then so be it, and everything around me became black and I was simply floating now, suspended somewhere that didn't feel like water—in fact, it didn't feel like anything—and I noticed I wasn't lightheaded anymore, my headache was gone, my sinuses didn't burn from the injection of saltwater, I no longer needed air, and the blackness all around me became red, bright red as far as I could see, and then the silence was broken when a voice said, "Look up, Simon," and when I raised my head I saw a large empty ante-room of some kind where the back wall was almost all windows looking into other rooms with tables and chairs, and I saw the ante-room was bright, and colors were vivid, but not glaring, and then my attention was drawn back to the voice that said, "Over here, Simon," and when I looked to my right I saw a small group of people coming toward me, and I wondered if I was really seeing people underwater, and then the thought hit me they had come to help me die.

"Dad," I said as the first one got closer. I hadn't seen him in person in so long, and this was better than anything the machine had to offer. "I've missed you. Am I—?"

"No time to talk now, Simon. There'll be plenty of time later. Go back."

From behind my father, another figure stepped out. It was Mom. I was wordless to express how good it was to see both of them again. But, Mom wasn't smiling. Neither was Dad. "Unhook the weight belt from your waist, Simon, and drop the bag. Hurry! This isn't your time."

Then, Hannah and Michael stepped forward, frantically waving me off, shouting, "Let go! Go back!" over and over.

Suddenly, brilliant white light surrounded me; a shockwave threw me around. I almost gasped a fatal gasp, but fought the urge with everything I had to give, while fading into the background, Dad was saying, "Hurry, Simon," Mom was saying, "Please, Simon, now!" I let go of the bag, clumsily unfastened the weight belt with fingers stupefied by oxygen starvation, and watched as they fell away below my dangling feet and got small and blurry. My ears hurt, my lungs ached—badly, but I knew I was still alive.

Then, I snapped out of it—whatever *it* was, the state I was in—looked upward, and began to kick and stroke. It was harder than anything I'd ever done. My muscles burned, my arms and legs felt like blocks of wood.

I wanted to live. Desperately.

I kicked and stroked as hard as I could. The barely discernible shadow of the boat got bigger. I stroked harder and faster toward it, fighting the involuntary urge to breathe. Faster still.

When I finally made it through the surface into open air, my mouth shot open, my lungs in a spasm. I gulped in hoarse gasps, wheezing, and coughing.

There I was, a stroke or two away from the boat, bobbing, gasping. With all the strength I had left, I swam forward and grabbed a rung of the stern ladder and held onto it with the crook of my elbow.

With Philippes still on board, I didn't know what I would face. Was he even real? Or was he imagined?

After regaining enough strength to scale the ladder on the back of the boat, I climbed to where my head was just above deck. Philippes was still there. He ran straight at me. This time I was determined to meet him head on. I took another step up the ladder. In an instant the same brilliant white light I had seen down below shot at Philippes like a cannon ball knocking him backward. The ladder instantly became too hot for me to hold onto and I fell back into the water while a fierce struggle took place on deck.

I tried again to climb the ladder but it was too hot to touch. Above me was a blinding light. I smelled gasoline. Certain the boat was about to explode, I leaned backwards in the water and pushed off of the hull with both feet as hard as I could, backstroking as fast as I could to put as much distance as I could between me and the boat before it had time to explode.

I got a good distance away, and it happened: the white light exploded — but not violently and not gently, either — and sprayed sparks all around that lightly touched down one at a time.

Then everything went black.

Chapter Forty-one

I'M IN MARGARET'S OFFICE NOW and it's going on one in the afternoon. It has taken me all morning to tell Margaret everything I remembered. I was sitting on the floor outside her office when she arrived this morning around seven-thirty. She looked at me with no surprise or alarm. Her keys jingled when she unlocked the door as they must do on any ordinary day. "You want to come in and talk, Simon?" she asked.

I certainly did; this was no ordinary day for me. I had a lot to tell her, everything about the last few months. Just the opposite of what I had anticipated for so long, there was no great joy or relief at having my memories restored. Margret listened without saying much and without taking notes, as before. Periodically through the morning she had to interrupt me so that she could cancel other appointments. Now that I'm finished telling her my story, I still can't make sense of it and hope she can, so I ask her straight out, "Am I schizophrenic?" My voice is so quiet, I can barely hear myself speak. "The voices. . . the apparitions."

"I don't see any reason for that diagnosis," she says almost as quietly, her voice full of compassion.

"But don't schizophrenics hear and see things that aren't really there?"

"Yes. Of course."

"But, I—"

"Who says what you heard and saw weren't really there?"

She seemed more sure than I. "But—"

"Simon, I know schizophrenia when I see it. Just as well as you know the insides of a computer or an atom."

"Then what—how much was real?"

"How much do you feel was real?"

"It all felt real then, but it doesn't now."

"That's typical until you become used to it." She scoots back from her desk with her cane in one hand and empty coffee cup in the other. "Spirit communications that is," she says as she gets to her feet. "I would worry about you if it felt too real at this point."

"Here," I say standing and reaching for her cup. "I'll get that for you. So, you're saying self-doubt is common when you're talking to dead people?" It takes a second, but the unintentional humor of my own dumb question sinks in, and I snicker. Margaret smiles.

"Yes, I would say that dialogues with the dead leave some room for doubt, at least initially."

The coffee pot is in the ante room of her office. I get us each a cup and return. It feels good to stand so we remain standing for a moment before resuming.

"Simon, you ventured very quickly into a domain new to you, an area of life that is simultaneously exciting, exhilarating, but fraught with dangers, both personally and on a larger level. When that venture is taken naturally, it usually requires a lot of spiritual preparation. Your machine, on the other hand, found a mechanical way that apparently anybody prepared or unprepared can use to gain access to that world. Even though I told you before that talking to spirits is as natural as talking to the living and anyone can do it, opening those channels can be like logging onto the Internet, and you can't always tell who's eavesdropping."

"And hackers and spyware could be watching."

"If proper precautions aren't taken."

"The séance sessions made it look so benign, even wholesome."

"I always start out with an invocation—"

"A prayer."

"Yes, if that's what you want to call it, asking for a blessing and protection from malevolent forces."

"You mean evil."

"Not only evil, but also the capricious, the busybodies, the bored. And that's what makes it benign and wholesome, beneficial, instructional, and allows us to receive so many other blessings."

"So your prayer acts like a firewall or an antivirus."

"In the mundane world, I suppose, that's a good analogy. I would like to think it's a little more spiritual than that. But, if that's what works for you, then okay."

That too familiar feeling I suppose everybody gets from time to time about living their lives over knowing what they know now came to me. If I could go back and re-do things, I would write those protections into the program, if I knew what to say. Or perhaps, getting proper instructions on how to use the machine to visit the spirit world would have avoided all the trouble. Maybe it was a mistake to have kept the machine a secret once I knew its capabilities. Maybe I should have discussed it with Geoff or Margaret before now. Maybe it was a mistake to sink the machine in the ocean.

I look out of the window beside Margaret's desk onto the granite bluffs across the canyon. For a moment, I wonder if the gorge below us is a good analogy for the separation between life and the afterlife and if that gap should even be bridged at all. At the same moment, I realize on the other side of the canyon lie clear running streams, meadows with purple, yellow, and blue wildflowers and wild life, songbirds, eagles, deer and elk and vistas of tree-topped peaks in distant places meeting the sky and above them floating white cushions. To not have bridged that gap would have denied access to the natural beauty that lies there.

My attention slowly returns to Margaret. She looks at me quietly, patiently. But, now I must ask the question I dread but have to have the answer to. "Are Michael and Hannah really dead?"

"Yes. I'm afraid so."

No other answer could be given. And the words, so generic, so bland, so simply delivered told the harsh truth with the harshest truth omitted. "It's my fault." What have I done? Michael and Hannah. Their lives cut short because of me. Whether it was because of the machine or because I didn't know how to protect the machine and its powers from abuse didn't matter. I was—I am at the center of it. What have I done to their families? Michael will never have the chance to work things out with his father, at least not in this life. And his father won't what I know, how much Michael really loved and admired him despite their differences. I could tell him. I have to tell him. And what about Hannah's parents? How does any parent withstand losing their child? I'll write them a letter and tell them about her work and how much I admired her. Maybe that will help. But, I know I can't do enough.

"No Simon." Margaret brings me back from my thoughts. "It isn't your fault."

"Yes it is."

"You need to know the truth."

"I know the truth. Whoever or whatever wanted me dead killed them."

"Simon, listen to me. Hannah was run down by her former professor and lover, Dr. Kendra Willoughby, who thought Hannah had turned hetero and had a thing going with you."

"I didn't have that kind of relationship with her." My secret wishes weren't acted on.

"I know. The police listed Willoughby as a person of interest, and she eventually turned herself in and told the whole story. It's in the paper. You can read it for yourself." Margaret reaches into her desk drawer and pulls out an old copy of the Glaser Falls Clarion that is already starting to yellow. I peruse the article and learn Willoughby had confronted Hannah about a suspected affair she thought Hannah was having with me as Hannah had done before with her. Willoughby thought I had converted Hannah and wanted to know what my secret was and why Hannah wouldn't go back to her. Hannah refused to talk to her. Later, Willoughby decided if she couldn't have Hannah, nobody could and ran her down while Hannah was jogging late one night.

I don't know what to say or whether to feel relief that Hannah's death wasn't really my fault. Yet, I was still remotely a part of it. I feel my fingers slowly crumpling the newspaper on Margaret's desk until it's wadded into a big ball and I fling it across the room.

Margaret just watches.

"I'm sorry, Margaret. I don't know what came over me."

"No harm done. Under the circumstances, I could have expected more than throwing a newspaper."

"Do you know what happened to Michael?"

"Are you ready to hear this?"

"I've got to know."

"After Michael's death, the sheriff opened an investigation which concluded there was no foul play. What they think happened is this: Michael had stayed behind while the other crew members went into town on furlough. He told them he had work to do. Tests showed his blood alcohol level was almost four times the legal limit for driving, but it appeared he tried to operate something called a spallation burner by himself. That's like a jet burner—"

"Yeah, I know. Michael told me about it."

"Well, it resulted in a fatal accident. That, too, is in the paper."

From what Michael described, it sounded as if spallation equipment takes a crew to operate, and he shouldn't have tried running it by himself. In the same thought, I can't help but feel that he had waited purposely until he was alone to prospect for more of the Emorite crystals. A foolish, drunken miscalculation.

Margaret starts to hand me the newspaper. I wave it off. My eyes sting and fill up. I lower my head and hold my breath with my jaw set hard to keep from weeping aloud. I hear Margaret scoot her chair back.

Soon she is sitting beside me and putting both of her hands on my arm. "I'm sorry for the loss of your friend." Her voice is calm and soothing, her hands are warm. "And your assistant. But you must understand you had nothing to do with either one's death. It was a coincidence that both happened on the same day."

"Coincidence? There aren't supposed to be coincidences. Everything is supposed to happen according to some grand plan."

"I know. It's hard to explain. It was no coincidence that Hannah was killed by a jealous ex-lover. It was no coincidence that Michael was killed in a drunken industrial accident. The concurrent timing can lead us to suspect there may have been a connection involving you. But, we must be careful to distinguish between truly connected events and independent events." Margaret puts one hand softly on the back of my head. My mother used to do that when I was small to calm me when she sensed I was going to have a meltdown. I haven't had a meltdown for many years, and I don't plan to start again now. Nonetheless, like my mother's hand, Margaret's feels reassuring. "In your case, Simon, I think forces worked on you to purposely lead you to wrong conclusions."

"What do you mean 'worked on me?'"

"I can't say for sure, but, I'll hazard a guess there were, maybe still are, forces—or influences—out to defeat you. Your work is important work. Knowledge is light. Ignorance is darkness. They didn't want the world to be illuminated, to know that the dead are not so dead, not so far away, to know things aren't exactly as have been taught for millennia, to see things through a different lens."

"And so they drove me to the point of attempting suicide?"

"They can do that, believe it or not. Ever since I started practicing psychiatry, from time to time I've seen good strong people who were defeated in their life's purpose for no apparent reason other than doubts and fears that seemed to come from within themselves. But, maybe it didn't really start there. I conjecture that a small slice of mental illness can't be attributed to neurological or environmental factors or chemical imbalances and therefore comes from outside the person, that is, evil malevolent influences whose purpose is to destroy human spirits. It works its way in. Sometimes that results in suicide."

"Am I one of those cases?"

"Not any more. My diagnosis is you had an isolated case of dissociation triggered by the stresses of the events you described, exacerbated by visitations from malicious influences. But now, I'm pronouncing you mentally *well*. And, you did fight a very tough spiritual battle."

"Did I win?"

"Did you?"

"It doesn't feel like it. Was Philippes an evil spirit?"

"Could be. Or, maybe he was who he said he was, devout in his convictions and simply afraid of the consequences of your discovery: that everything he had believed in in life would be reordered—"

"Don't they find out the truth, the real story when they arrive *over there*?"

"Not all at once, and not at the same pace for everybody. They have to learn, which means of course they first have to let go of what they knew or thought they knew here. This Philippes could have been kept in the dark and could have been himself deceitfully manipulated by dark influences. Or he could have been one of the dark entities."

"All of that is too confusing for me right now. I just can't wrap my head around it. But, I need to know something else. Why did this happen to me? If my spirit guardians knew about Philippes and what was going to happen to me, why didn't they tell me?"

"The answer isn't all that simple, yet it isn't all that complicated, either. We all have free will and we're supposed to use it to make our own choices. Spirit guides can offer a lot of help, but they can't and aren't supposed to live our lives for us, or even remove all of the peril. They don't know what choices we will make. Add to that, each choice sets off a chain reaction of consequences."

And more. My own work in quantum computing is based on every problem having a quantity of solutions and finding the best or highest probability solution. If the handle of a dinner fork illustrates a single decision or action and each tine were a possible result, and if each tine then becomes the handle of another fork, the probable consequences multiply wildly, and that's with just four tines per fork. The immensity becomes mind boggling when there are ten or twenty probable outcomes to a single action.

"It's a lot for a spirit guide to keep track of," Margaret says. "Spirit guides can often perceive the best actions for us to take, but they can't tell us outright which ones to make. Other times, they step right up and intervene, leaving us to puzzle out when and why they help us."

"Now you sound more like a philosopher than a psychiatrist."

She smiles. "Come with me for a walk, would you? I don't take many walks anymore and I could use a strong arm to hold onto."

We make our way to the elevator, out the door, onto the terrace and down to the grounds walking slowly toward an iron bench. I've never noticed it before, but it's exactly like the one in the thicket. We stop there. Everything looks different today. Greens are greener, yellows yellower; lines are sharper; the sky is unpolluted blue. I have a sense that nothing will ever be the same again.

"This old iron bench is more comfortable than it looks," she says while taking a seat. She looks towards the thicket and points with her cane. "There's a spot through those trees where I used to go for meditation and quiet reflection. I should have told you about it."

"I found it."

"I used to own that land and the house that sits there. I sold it many years ago to a family that owned a carnival." She looks at me with a knowing twinkle in her eye. "Andrea Siannas's family. You know, 'Drew the Seer.' I paid off the mortgage on the hospital with that money and some money I'd inherited from my father. That's what has allowed me to pursue my life's purpose here at Mount Liberty."

A long moment passes. "There's more that you should know, Simon, that you haven't mentioned. Do you remember anything else?"

"I told you everything I remember."

"I don't think there is any danger if I tell you now rather than waiting until the memories return on their own." She pauses. "Now that you have told me your story, I can piece together the missing parts." She puts her hand on my forearm as if to reassure me about something. "There was no explosion on the boat, it is still intact."

I'm caught off guard.

"You mentioned a Captain Arturo. I don't know of him. The boat you were on had been moored out of service for the week. All appearances are that you were alone and acted alone. I suspect this Captain Arturo was an invention this Philippes spirit used to deceive you."

"That would mean I stole the boat." I think about it a moment. "But, I paid him over four hundred dollars in cash. Where'd the money go?"

"I think you'll be getting it back soon."

"How—?"

She raises a finger to hold off my next question. "There's more. Based on the sequence and timing of events, you were really afloat for only three days, not thirteen. You were gone for five days in total."

"But, I counted thirteen sunrises."

"I think you were drifting in and out of consciousness, thirteen times or so. And, part of me thinks your perceptions were off, for instance about your pants catching on fire and you jumping into the water to put the fire out and the boat disintegrating in an explosion, because you just weren't ready to face all of the horrible truths. Our minds will sometimes protect us that way. I think your mind created a more acceptable story to go along with the deceptions put upon you by outside influences."

"Was the fight real—the one on the boat with Philippes?"

"I think it was. What do you think?"

"Yeah. It seemed real enough." A pair of walkers come close enough to hear, so I pause. When they're gone, I ask, "Margaret, did you know when you warned me that the 'someone' who would try to kill me was me?"

"No. I gave you the whole reading that I received."

"I still don't get it. Why did all of that happen?"

"The world you tapped into, as I suspect you already know, is where science, theology, and philosophy converge—"

"How do you figure that?"

She hesitates as one measuring her words. Then she speaks, "If science is about facts and knowledge, if religion is about truth, if philosophy is about seeking answers to the big questions, they must inevitably converge. They are all actually seeking the same thing."

"And they converge in some spirit world that I tapped into?"

"Could be a stepping stone along the way."

"And I got there because of the bizarre world of quantum effects?"

"I leave that up to you and to the future to decide. I'm merely saying, science, theology, and philosophy can, and I predict, someday will be reconciled. But, what will it take to get them there? And how long will it take? What happens in the meantime if the belief systems that are the glue that hold the world together morally, ethically are stripped bare? I will again hazard a guess that now wasn't its time."

Time goes by while I absorb all that has been said. The grounds are busy with people walking, standing, sitting, or simply keeping to themselves. In the weeks I've lived here, I haven't gotten to know any of them. I watch them, wondering who has hallucinations; who has delusions; who is dangerous to himself, herself, or others; who struggles with substance abuse; whose tortured screams I heard at night in the Cotton Ball. I wonder when their nightmares will be over and if mine ever will be. I wonder who among the patients are the ones Margaret talked about who suffer mental illness because of malevolent spirits and influences working to defeat them, the ones Margaret has been studying.

I'm slow to catch on, but it's me. I'm the one. But now I feel strong, clear-eyed, as one does when he's been driving all night and the sun comes up to light the road ahead.

Margaret looks at me and says, "Perhaps you should get some rest. You've been through a lot in a short time."

"I feel wide awake."

"Then perhaps I should leave you now and go back to my office and you can begin to pack your things. I can feel the work piling up from here."

Overhead a long white trail from an airplane flying so high it looks like a silver pinhead bisects the sky. I wonder if it's an airliner, and that triggers a thought. I touch Margaret's arm to keep her here a bit longer. I ask, "How did I get back here, Margaret? Back from Puerto Rico."

"I don't have that answer."
"I only had a one-way ticket."
Margaret goes on her way. I begin to remember.

Chapter Forty-two

WHEN I WASHED ASHORE, it wasn't exactly as I had told Margaret under hypnosis. There was no sun in my eyes as I'd thought I had remembered, no beautiful lifeguard resuscitating me, no crowd standing around cheering my recovery. It was dark. I awoke on my stomach, alone, coughing and vomiting salt water. I clawed my way up the beach and made it to all fours, my head hanging low. Eventually, I stood upright, had a look around, and recognized nothing. There were no hotels, no spring break revelers, nothing familiar to comfort me.

My head hurt so badly. Salt water must have filled my sinuses, too. I didn't know why I was there or where I had been. I even asked myself if I could have died and if this cold, damp darkness was what lay on the other side. I started walking along the beach parallel to the water. The wind was chilly, and I again feared hypothermia, but eventually my clothes began to dry out a little, and I adjusted.

An image came to mind — a face, the round face of a kind man. Bradley. He had given me a card with his number. I could call him. I checked my pockets. They were completely empty except for sand. I had no card, no wallet, no ID, no money. Nothing.

I closed my eyes to recall the image of his card. There it was. Kent Joseph Bradley. Yes. Three first names, three last names. There were two addresses, one local, one in San Juan. That's where I must have been, because there is no ocean near Glaser Falls. I couldn't quite make out a phone number but I saw the Puerto Rico address: Kent J. Bradley, 1 Cond Palm Breeze #145, Dorado, PR 00646.

By the time the sun came up, I had wandered aimlessly for a long time, holding the image of Bradley's address in mind. The sun brought with it a welcome warmth and the sight of a clear path to a street already starting to get busy. I made my way to a taxi cab.

"Bueno," the driver said, putting down the morning paper.

I told him the address. He said it wasn't far and took off as if he were in a race. Good fortune had deposited me on Dorado beach, east of Arecibo and southeast of Milwaukee Deep, the direction of the prevailing current. We passed by neighborhoods of square single story houses with flat or low-pitch roofs that all seemed to have masonry and wrought iron fences around their yards. It wasn't long before the taxi pulled onto a street with tall rectangular, flat-roofed buildings painted in tropical colors, sea foam green, teal, sage, yellow, with recessed balconies, columns, and lots of windows. The sign at the entrance had said Palm Breeze Condominiums. This was Bradley's place.

A panicky feeling hit me when I remembered I had no money and I couldn't pay the driver.

"Lo siento, señor." I know only a word or two of Spanish but hoped the attempt might soften him a little. "I don't have any money on me—"

"What? I should take you to the police station right now. Stealing a ride from me." The car lurched as he put it back in gear with his foot on the brake.

"I'm so sorry. I fell into the water and lost my wallet." I patted my pants' pockets to show him they were empty and still sloshy. "If you'll just stay right here, I'll go inside and get some money." I hoped Bradley was home and would front my cab fare.

"You think I'm stupid? You stinking American college kids think you can get by with tricks like this. You go into the building, I'll never seen you again."

"No really. I'm telling you the truth. Just give me a chance to go—"

"I'm going to start collecting up front from you college kids. Or no ride! This has happened to me before." He shook a fist at me.

"Just wait—"

"Go on. Get out before I change my mind and take you to the police. I'm not wasting any more time on you." I got out, and he sped off. But, before he did, I heard him yell, "You got my seat wet!"

I walked around looking for unit 145. It was a nice place, fairly new. There were carports filled with cars, and each ground floor entrance had an arched awning over it. Before knocking on Bradley's door, I closed my eyes again to envision the card to be sure I had the right address. With measured confidence, I knocked.

Bradley answered the door. Thank Goodness.

"What happened to you?" he asked. "You look like you've been for a swim already this morning."

"I don't know... I washed ashore. I don't remember much."

The big guy looked at me long and hard. "Your eyes are bloodshot. Been drinking?"

"No. I don't drink."

"Well, it's not as if I didn't toss back a few in my day and do some silly things. Come on in." He chuckled.

"Really. I don't drink. I don't know what happened. I was on the shore, the next thing, I was in the water, then back on shore. I almost drowned."

"You must have been swept out by a rip tide. They're nasty things. You don't even see them unless you know what you're looking for, and then they sweep you right out to sea. You're lucky you didn't drown." He stopped talking and looked at me again. "What were you doing in your street clothes?" Before I could tell him I didn't know, he waved his hand and said, "Oh, never mind."

Bradley motioned for me to follow him upstairs. "You can take a hot shower, and I've got some of my son's clothes you can try on. I'll lay them out on the bed in the back bedroom." He pointed down the hall. "That was... his room when he came to visit."

After the shower, I put on the clothes Bradley had laid out—a pair of jeans, a pullover shirt, and black high top Chuck Taylor shoes—and went to the living room.

"Do they fit?" he asked.

"Perfectly." And most importantly, they were warm and dry.

"Where are you staying?"

I couldn't remember checking into a hotel. "I don't have a room."

"You must've been staying on the beach. I don't blame you with all those girls in bikinis." He laughed a hearty laugh. "Like I said, to be young again. Well, you can stay here tonight. Say—aren't you due back on your job soon?"

"I suppose." I did have a teaching job to return to.

"When's your flight?"

"I don't know." What flight? If I'd had a flight, I must have missed it.

"It should say on your ticket receipt."

All I had was the wet clothes I had worn. "I lost everything in the water." That had to have been the truth.

"ID? Passport?"

"Everything."

The kindly face scrunched into a frown. Bradley regarded me long and intensely enough to make me wonder if he was going to throw me out the door. Then he spoke as if he were replying to an unseen voice. "Yes." He said it again, drawing it out, "Y-e-e-s. I'll do it." He left the room and came back with an attaché case that he laid flat on the couch and opened. From an inside pocket he pulled out a large manila envelope. From the envelope he pulled out some documents and handed them to me.

"Take a look at them," he said.

They were Thomas Eddy Bradley's passport and driver's license, still valid. He was right. I was a dead ringer for the big guy's son.

"Go shave off that growth and let's have another look."

I did as he suggested and returned to the living room.

"If I believed in resurrection, I'd say Thomas had come back to life." He held onto the passport and driver's license silently, then held them out to me. "Here. You take these to the airport. I'm sure they'll work just as well for you as they did for him." He seemed to think about it for a minute. "Nothing wrong with that, right? We're just getting you home the simplest way. Right?" Then, he reached into the envelope and pulled out something else. "This should get you there." He handed me an e-ticket printout to take to the airport for a boarding pass. "I got it to give to Thomas. . . before I got the news. It's been in my brief case—" His voice quivered a bit. "Never had the heart to do anything with it." He cleared his throat and coughed once. "There's still time. You may as well use it."

In the morning after a filling breakfast, Bradley drove me to the airport. He'd packed a carry-on bag with a change of clothes and sent it with me. When he let me out, he gave me some cash to cover the airline's change fee and to tide me over until I got home. I told him, "When I get back home, I'll pay you back for this—" I gestured with my head toward the money in my hand, "—and for the ticket."

"The ticket would have gone to waste. Don't worry about it or a few bucks. But the passport and driver's license. . . they're mementos. Can you get them back to me?"

I promised him I would. And I will.

Chapter Forty-three

I'M BACK NOW IN MARGARET'S OFFICE to get my release papers. There's no need to tell her everything. I don't want anybody but Bradley to know that I got back on a borrowed passport and identification, for his sake and mine. But, I do tell her that I wasn't, in truth, resuscitated by a beautiful lifeguard as I looked up into the sunny sky.

"I was under hypnosis, Margaret. Why didn't I remember it right?"

"Remember, too, that you dreamed some of your recovered memories. Hypnosis isn't perfect and dreams are even less so. Even at that, they were both apparently enough to get the process started. But, what makes you think you didn't get it right?"

"Because I really came to coughing up seawater alone on a dark beach."

"Alone?"

"Margaret, you're giving me that funny look." It was the look she gets before she gives a reading.

"Simon, you're quite rare." As if I didn't already know. "You had *two* near-death experiences. Yes. That's what I'm receiving: the first one underwater, the second on the beach. The beautiful lifeguard who resuscitated you was a spirit guardian. And, yes, you did stare into a sunny sky. It just wasn't in this everyday world."

A shiver crawls down my spine, and goosebumps erupt on my arms and legs.

A few minutes pass in utter silence while Margaret's words soak in. Then, I ask almost fearful to find out, "But, how did I get here at Liberty?"

"I sent Andrea to check on you." Margaret smiles.

The very mention of her name lifts my spirits. I see her face in my mind and feel exhilaration mixed with contentment and that sense of belonging I get whenever I'm with her. "I was worried for you after giving you the warning. No one had heard from you in days. From what she described, it sounded as if you were in a bad way, so she talked you into coming here and you checked yourself in."

There was still a question burning inside me, yet fearing disappointment I hesitated to ask. When I finally got it out, my voice was quiet. "Do I get to go home now?"

"As soon as I sign the release papers, you're free to go." She smiles and seems genuinely happy for me. "I've already made arrangements for Geoff to pick you up whenever you're ready. I'll give him a call while you go back to your room and pack." She reaches for a stack of papers already on her desk. "But first, let me tell you the rest of what you don't know." My heart sank as if there were one last "but" that threatened to change everything. "Your lost wallet and all of its contents, including four hundred dollars cash, was found on the deck of a boat named. . . let me find it." She searches through some papers. "The *Sea-Saw*, owned by a Captain Hector Luis Santiago Lopez." That revelation stunned me. "They tracked you down by your university ID. Police talked to university officials who put them in touch with Geoff. He knew you were here and told them so. They called but I wouldn't let them talk to you. Not without a warrant of some kind."

"Warrant!? For what?"

"There's more to the story. You see, it appears there weren't two boats at dock that day as you recalled to me."

"I saw two boats. I know that."

"Captain Hector told Puerto Rican police—"

"Police?"

"Hold on, Simon," she says holding up both hands. "He told the police that he had talked to a young man he thought was a college student on spring break. The young man inquired about chartering the boat but Captain Hector doesn't hire out. The boat is his personal pleasure boat. He sent the young college man away then Captain Hector left. A week later, he went back and his boat was gone."

"Now I'm as confused as ever," I say. "If there was only one boat, and if Captain Hector isn't for hire, then why did I think he was, why did I see two boats, and why did I think I had chartered the smaller one?"

"I wasn't there, I can't say for sure. But I'm willing to say that this Philippes or the influences he represented, the ones that made you want to destroy yourself and your work, simply played with your perceptions."

"Hallucinations?" I ask with a sick feeling in my stomach.

"Don't worry. You're not schizophrenic. But if they hadn't deceived you, which they are masters at, you wouldn't have stolen a boat, now would you?"

I sit back down. "So, are the police waiting to arrest me as soon as I get out of here?"

"No. You're not in trouble anymore."

"But, how—?"

"At first, the police wanted you back in Puerto Rico for questioning. In this day and age, missing boats and aircraft cause particular alarm. My attorney got some papers signed quickly by a judge, and based on my diagnosis and recommendation, and the court appointed him as your attorney. He did it *pro bono*—"

"I can pay him, Margaret. What's his name?"

She gave me his card. "I'll introduce you later. But for now, you'd better keep your money." I felt another bit of bad news coming. "You haven't heard this officially yet, but the rumor is that the university isn't going to keep you on." My insides feel as if a coil spring has been let loose. "I'm sorry, but I must tell you now so we can talk about it if you need to. I know it doesn't seem like it, but in the long run this will somehow work out for the best."

I'm absorbing the shock and I think she can tell because she waits before continuing. After a few moments, she goes on about the attorney. "He talked to authorities and told them that you were being treated for psychogenic amnesia and couldn't answer any questions. We agreed to keep you here until you could answer questions and to notify them before your release. That's all he would tell me."

Kicked again, I was deflated, sick. "So, I have to go back to Puerto Rico to answer questions?"

"No, Simon. All of the pending charges have been dropped." She signed some papers and handed them to me.

"Dropped?"

"You're free to go as of now." She smiles broadly. "Just go home and reconnect with your life. If you need me, you know where I'll be."

As badly as I have wanted to go home for so long, I can't leave just like that. "But, how did I get out of legal trouble?"

"In time, you will find out. The rest is not for me to say."

I get up to leave then ask one final question, "Was all of that legal trouble why I had to stay here this whole time?"

"That's part of it, and why you were in what you called the Cotton Ball a little longer than you really needed to be. Better there than in a jail cell awaiting trial. And, if I could help it, I wasn't going to let you go until matters were cleared up, including your memory. The other part is that there was too much danger that you could still harm yourself. I hadn't thought of this at the time, but as it turned out, if you had started talking to other people about your experiences and perceptions you surely would have been taken for schizophrenic and your reputation would surely be lost. Perhaps you could have been released sooner, but in my judgment this was a safer place for you—"She gets up with the help of her cane, comes over to me, and places her hand on my shoulder. The warmth of her hand is comforting. "—and the world."

I'm puzzled why Margaret went to such an extent to protect me when I had known her only casually before checking in here. But, I'm too grateful to ask. I thank her for all that she has done for me, then go to my room to pack.

Chapter Forty-four

GEOFF HAS FINALLY ARRIVED, and it's getting on toward evening. I set my duffel bag on the backseat of Geoff's car then get in front happy to be going home. On the way I ask Geoff if he knows how I got out of being in trouble with the Puerto Rican police. He doesn't answer right away.
"Geoff?"
"Well—I still have my rabat and Roman collar." His priest costume. I have seen photos of him as a young man wearing his clerical clothing, but have never seen him wear it in person. "Your escapade was a small infraction that could have been escalated by zealous prosecutors into something much bigger and more serious than it had to be. I just helped to deescalate it. Knowing that you wouldn't be at Mount Liberty and insulated from the police forever, I placed a video call to Captain Hector—I think you call it Skype—and asked for forgiveness on your behalf."
"Is that—"
"I have never done anything to betray my vows—except not show up for work. Besides, I was never defrocked . . . that I know of. And I never officially resigned. I just took a little license with Captain Hector, that's all." We pull up to the gate of Mount Liberty Residence, gravel crackling under the tires, and stop to wait for the gate to open remotely.

"Under the circumstances, don't you think a little forgiveness is called for?"

"Of course."

"Well, Captain Hector and I had a long talk about the vigor of youth and the foolish things we all did. Including priests. We swapped stories, and I think that gave him some insight that priests are ordinary people before they become priests. I convinced him your little jaunt was nothing more than a short joy ride and it would be a shame to mark someone for life because of youthful foolishness—"

"Under the circumstances, I didn't think it was foolish."

"Just go with it, Simon. It worked. Anyway, he actually said he had seen worse pranks throughout many spring breaks when the college kids had converged on San Juan—he'd just moved his boat from the San Juan Marina to the new wharf at Arecibo. He didn't have to think about it for long and was very gracious. He agreed not to press charges. Truth be told, I think he was angrier that the marina's security didn't catch you. Anyway, there wasn't any damage that seventy-five dollars' worth of marine paint wouldn't fix—some scorching that neither he nor I could explain. Some fuel costs. I offered to pay him, but he wouldn't hear of it and asked me for a blessing." Geoff must anticipate my thoughts. "Anyone can bless anyone, Simon," he says without looking at me.

"How did you know he was Catholic? That might not have worked otherwise."

"I took my chances. It was Puerto Rico, after all." Geoff smiles.

We travel awhile, neither of us saying anything. Then my thoughts congeal. "Margaret," I say abruptly.

Geoff keeps his eyes on the road. "What about her?"

"She was the psychic woman in confessional, the one you said who'd had the head injury, who came looking for absolution."

"I see your steel trap memory has indeed returned."

"The one who taught you how to talk to Fiona."

"If she were, I couldn't acknowledge that." But, I see him smiling big.

For me, that closes the circle. Geoff said he had known Margaret for a long time. She had to be the one. And her long term relationship with Geoff, and Geoff's with me, explains why she went so far to help me stay out of trouble.

We go a while in silence. Then something else hits me. "The car. What happened to the car?"

"What car?"

"I rented a car in San Juan to go to Arecibo."

"Did you turn it in?"

"I don't remember turning it in."

"You'd best check your credit card statement. You may have bought the ruddy thing by now."

"And—what about my mail—utilities, electricity, water, gas—I haven't been home for three months—"

"Relax, Simon. I took the liberty of taking care of a few things. It'll all be there when you get there. We'll sort it all out later."

How lucky I am to have such a friend. I suppose the things he did for me while I was away are the sorts of things a father would do, if mine were still here in this mundane world.

We travel the rest of the way in peaceful silence. When we get to my house, Geoff pulls over, puts the car in park, and lets me out. I sling the duffel bag over my shoulder and walk around the car to his window and extend my hand. "Thanks, Geoff."

"You're welcome, lad." He nods with a look of warm satisfaction.

We shake hands, and I hold on for a second or two. "I mean, really, thanks. For everything."

I wave at Geoff and watch him pull away.

Something in that wave, a gesture so common, usually an unspoken temporary good-bye, strikes me hard. I am alone now. Starkly totally alone. Death has robbed me again. And, my life's work lies at the bottom of the ocean, like so many other measures of meaning, out of reach. If I could retrieve it I would. What insanity to have thrown it away! And to have almost thrown away my life, too! What will fill my days now with no job and no work to do? What good will nights be? What am I to do? Nothing of my former life remains.

Nothing, except this house. I turn and look at it. It looks the same. White siding, black shutters that need to be painted, round pillars that hold up the porch roof.

Daylight is dwindling. Cicadas in neighboring trees trumpet their calls for a companion. Even insects know how not to be alone. Long fingers of shade stretch across my front porch. At the end of the driveway is the garage with my car that hasn't been started in three months. I notice now, my grass has been mowed. I owe someone for that, maybe Geoff, maybe the city. But, I'll deal with that later. Only one thing comes to mind now, one person I want to see, to talk to, to tell that I have recovered, to tell that I am back, I am whole.

What chance do I have with her? I who have never fit in anywhere except for a lab, an outsider always looking in, one who's always had to be complete within himself, whose spare time has always been taken up with machines, journals, and manuals. Do I have a chance? Whenever I was with Andrea, wherever it was, that was where it felt I was supposed to be. Whatever was good was better, whatever was bad was not as bad.

I think I'm in love. God, I am in love. I don't need an Italian tenor to sing about it, or crooners, or wailing guitars. A whisper of wind brushes my cheek, and I find myself wishing it were her breath on my face. I've got to go see her. Get my car started and go see her. I turn in the direction of the garage.

A step or two later, I notice there's something new in front of my porch, and I stop in my tracks. Flowers. Bright yellow and orange marigolds. Andrea told me once that French marigolds are easy to grow. I crouch to have a look and hold a delicate bloom in my hand afraid of hurting it. The sound of a car pulling into the driveway behind me draws my attention away.

It isn't a car; it's a red pickup, the one I had seen in Andrea's barn. I stand up in utter disbelief as she shuts the engine off, gets out, and holds the cab door open looking at me. Then, she runs toward me and I rush to her.

My heart pounds. A new and unusual feeling overtakes me. I smile—a big toothy smile. Then I laugh with a tear building in the corner of my eye. Before I know what I'm doing my arms are around her; I'm lifting her up, her head above mine, her hair dangling in my face. We twirl and twirl, laughing like school children on a merry-go-round, yet no words have been spoken.

Then, I just hold her for a moment, looking up into her eyes. Her body slides down. She stops when her lips touch mine. Such a feeling I've never had before, and I don't want it to stop. We hold onto each other.

And hold on.

Chapter Forty-five

WHEN WE FINALLY BREAK, we go inside holding hands. I take two cold sodas from the refrigerator and we sip on them while I tell her the whole of my story, holding back nothing. After a long while, I excuse myself to go to the upstairs bathroom. On the way back, I stop at the spare room where Michael stayed and open the door and look in. Visible from the door beside the dresser is the empty Blue Moon box I had earlier scooted out of the way. When I pick it up, I see it's been taped shut. What an odd thing for Michael to have done.

I take it downstairs and set it on the table. Andrea comes to my side.

"What is it?" she asks.

"It belonged to Michael."

I take a knife from the kitchen drawer and open the box. Inside is a handwritten note. Andrea puts her hand on my arm, lays her cheek on my shoulder as we read the note together.

> Simon, you always told me to back up everything. You're my backup on this.
> Michael

Beneath the note are thousands of perfectly spherical Emorite xenocrysts, light and warm, each one about the size of a grain of sand. I reach into the box and sift them then look at Andrea and smile.

"What?" Andrea asks, returning the smile.

"Nothing."

"There's something. What are you smiling about?"

"Cell phones."

Like *The Iron Couch* on Facebook, Daniel Ross Madsen

The author may be contacted at drmironcouch@cox.net.

Made in the USA
San Bernardino, CA
28 July 2017